THE
DIAMOND
ANCHOR

Jennifer Mills lives in Alice Springs. She was the 2008 winner of the Marian Eldridge Award for Young Emerging Women Writers. Her work has appeared in *Hecate, Overland, Heat,* the *Griffith Review,* and *Best Australian Stories 2007. The Diamond Anchor* is her first novel; she is currently working on her second. Visit www.jenjen.com.au

THE
DIAMOND
ANCHOR

Jennifer Mills

UQP

First published 2009 by University of Queensland Press
PO Box 6042, St Lucia, Queensland 4067 Australia

www.uqp.com.au

Typeset in 12.5/16pt Bembo by Post Pre-press Group, Brisbane
Printed in Australia by McPherson's Printing Group

This project has been assisted by the Commonwealth
Government through the Australia Council, its arts
funding and advisory body.

Cataloguing-in-Publication Data
National Library of Australia

Mills, Jennifer, 1977–.
The diamond anchor.
9780 7022 3695 2
A823.4

You walk in the door and catch your heel on the step. Everyone turns to watch you. They always turn at the unoiled door's gentle alarm, but for you they keep watching. They do this secretly, pretending to sip their beers or smoke or stare out at the sea.

You know you have an audience. I can tell from the way you move. As you lift your foot and reach behind to twist the heel back into place, your face contorts in sympathy. I imagine a dragonfly poised above the water, the stretch of a cormorant on a flagpole.

Your forehead furrows as the next tentative step is taken, then you throw the smile out for all: the wide grin that hints at imminent mischief.

You cross the floor towards me. I polish a glass. You come to me, sit at a stool, and lean your thin arms on the bar. You ask me to tell you a story, and I say, 'True or false?'

I raise my eyes with an expectant smile.

The bar is empty. You have vanished. I shake my head and wince, tricked like an old fool. I look up at the ceiling.

'Stop this,' I say. 'Stop it right this minute.'

The Danker creaks.

one

It strikes me as I carry the scraps down to Red and the girls: the warm ache of something missing. It's as familiar and physical as the other aches that come and go as they please. I can hardly feel them any more, just as I don't hear the ocean, though I know it's right here at my doorstep.

But who can complain of pain with the sunrise in their face? I blink in the shock of light and allow the aches to fall behind me. Let them walk with Mallee, my gentle shadow, and with his: the crouch and dart of Beth following at a nervous distance.

Red launches into crowing double-time when he knows his breakfast's up, and he scratches at the earth in anticipation. I shush him with a handful of yesterday's peelings before moving on to the girls.

'Morning, ladies,' I call. 'All present and accounted for? And how do you like your eggs?' They cluck and flutter from my groping hand. I pocket a few eggs from the warm straw. My eyes catch on the tortoiseshell camouflage of Beth a few metres away, slinking after something in the scrub. She's always been afraid of the hens.

It's back, right here in my knees as I stand and turn, cradling the delicate weight of eggs in my dressing gown pocket. The ache of your absence radiates with its own heat.

The world goes dark. It fades back slowly. It's the blood pressure, but I won't bore you with that. As my eyes clear, the Danker appears, bathed in a fresh, golden light that gives its battered face a certain charm. A few faded signs advertise long-extinct brews. The windows, warped by time, reflect a dozen sunrises. I can see myself in my gumboots and dressing gown, condensed into these small, bright repeats. Pink and yellow and a little worse for wear, we resemble each other, the Danker and I. My home is an indiscriminating mirror.

Mallee paws a circle at my feet and points his nose for home, so I follow. Up ahead Beth leaps along, scattering feral rabbits. We always return like this, in reverse order.

By the time I reach the kitchen, the glow has subsided. I drop the empty bucket beside the back door and kick off my boots. I set my socked feet on the mat one by one, balancing a little precariously despite years of practice. When I pull the door shut behind me, it squeals in protest, and my elbow answers. After these twin creaks there is silence. Closing my door on the ocean always feels like a kind of blasphemy.

'Off.' I evict Beth from the kitchen counter with a wave of my hand. She hops into Ted's chair and gives me a look I take to be murderous. 'Can't let this place fall apart now,' I explain.

It is though, slowly falling apart, protesting creak by creak. We're getting old, the Danker and me.

I fill the kettle, pop it on the gas, light the flame with a match, turn and lean on the cupboard to survey the room. This kitchen is the heart of the half-house I was born into. Beth and Mallee and the chooks and me, we're all that's left here of the family. We're too busy, though, to think of being lonely. At least, we were.

Sitting on the table in front of me is a white rectangle with my name on it. It has come into the room like an uninvited guest. It has made itself at home. It's outstaying its welcome, this letter from you. I've already read it several times. I would like to ignore it today, but I can't. I would like to set it alight and watch it turn to ashes. Instead, I keep returning to it.

I have held it down with a stone which has layers of history pressed into its body in lines of black, red and gold. The stone has been around. A doorstop for a while, it was promoted to a paperweight, then retired to a pot plant out the back. Some impulse must have made me bring it back inside after Ted died. Perhaps it was loneliness.

If it had stayed in the water it would have been worn to roundness by now, like the pieces of glass we used to find, blunted down to ovals by the ocean's repetition. I still pick them up. I still throw them back when they're not ready, like little fish.

My wandering mind is pulled back by the kettle's whistle and the phone ringing. I let the phone go. Tea wins. If it's important they'll ring back. I put your letter back in its place on the table. It has been here long enough to have a place. I am only as far as finding a clean mug when the phone starts in again.

'Diamond Anchor,' I answer. My throat is still clotted with sleep. I'm no good before the first cup, but Pat's voice comes flooding down the line like a drought breaker.

'Mum, it's me, did I wake you? I had to ring before work. I

got a new job on a charter boat. Weekends, cash in hand, boats! How good is that?'

'Mmm,' I reply. I am suspicious. 'Breakfast,' I remind him. Our regular Sundays – it used to be every week, now it's once a month – are important to me.

'Oh, Mum, I gotta be there at the crack and I'll be working all day but I'll be down soon I promise, you know I will, it's just that this is such a great opportunity and she's a real gem, thirty foot with the full setup.'

'Sounds like your cup of tea,' I say, remembering mine. I get the milk out while Pat lists the boat's specifications, which he is wont to do. He caught boats from Ted, of course, but rabbiting on is Pat's trick. He's the only member of my family who can. We're a quiet lot, most of us. Pat's halfway to running the whole business, clipper-ship and all, by the time I've ascertained the milk's okay.

'Great, Pat. Let me know how you go, eh?' I interrupt, stirring sugar into the cooling tea. 'And good luck.'

He needs it. Chances like this don't come so thick and fast these days, not when you're his age competing with a bunch of teenagers. My son is a late bloomer, I hope. It takes some people a long time to find their feet, though anyone could tell you he was always good in the kitchen.

I replace the handset and glare at it indulgently.

'Fine thanks, son,' I tell it. Lady Macbeth gives me an accusing look as I sit down opposite her, finally united with my cuppa.

'Well, it's no worse than talking to you, is it?' I counter. She blinks and looks out the window. If I followed her gaze I'd see that the yellow ball has intensified above the water, that the ocean is almost still enough to reflect it whole. I don't have to. I already know that this will be a warm, windless day.

★ ★ ★

I've had a lifetime of other people's stories. I couldn't count how many plans and deals and arguments, how many profound, absolute truths and bald-faced lies have been told over this bar. Every event in Coal has begun its telling in this pub, every myth has its seed here. They're all my stories. We're tied up in each other, and every line comes back to the Danker.

You don't work in a pub for fifty years without learning what a story is, its shape and feel, what it can do. You don't last as long as I have unless you see the connections between the tales. But seeing is not the same as telling. My da had the gift, but he passed it to his firstborn. Me, I don't talk much. I listen.

I am a good listener. They all love me for that, even the blowins. It's like people falling for their shrink, I guess. Any willing ear will do. Trapped behind the bar I'm a captive audience. I can do the job with my eyes closed, there's nothing to it. Pour and rinse and wash and polish, wipe and sweep and clear and pour. It's elementary, unless you count the listening. Listening is ninety per cent of the work, just like Da said. Some nights after closing, I have to stick my head in a sink full of cold water like a drunk, just to get their voices out.

When Ted was around, it never used to worry me. His unbreakable calm would soothe me. He was so quiet, he should have been a truckie. I miss those comfortable silences we had after closing, when the only sounds were the dying fire's spit and the tink of ice in Jameson's, the first and last drink of the night.

It helps to listen. It makes people trust you. I know there is a warmth there, born of my silence. This excuses me from the suspicion that I'm not being altogether generous. I've learned to keep my cards close. I've learned that it doesn't hurt to know more about people than they know about you. And thanks to you, I've learned to keep my secrets.

Before I open up for the afternoon, I do a little work in the garden. Retired people potter, but I insist on calling this work. It is work. I want to plant winter lettuces in time for them to sprout before the first chill winds, and I need greens for the bistro, though it's probably cheaper and more sensible just to buy them.

In the garden the chooks come and peck at the earth where I've pulled out the weeds. I yank at the old tomato vines, brown and fruitless now. The rocky soil flies away from the roots as soon as they're pulled. I throw the bigger stones overboard to make a tiny wall which will help keep the water in. It's been a dry summer and soon this will all be dust, but I've had some success in getting things to grow.

The girls make tiny clucking sounds and treat me warily. Unlike other animals, chickens never seem to get used to a human presence. I toss them some weeds and watch them discuss their options.

As I tug at the earth, I think about your letter, and I think about my future. Squatting in the dirt, I make a decision. Once I have made it I smile; there can't have been any other choice. There never was, with you.

I rise slowly this time. It's warmer now that the sun is nearing its height. The ache seems to have lessened a little.

In the kitchen, I dig out a pen and an old airmail pad that I've had in the back of a drawer for years. I set them down on the kitchen table and prop your letter against the fruit bowl. I set the paper square with the table and take up the pen.

I write the date in the top corner, then I scratch it out. I bite absently into the pen and feel it crunch between my teeth. I tear off the page, fold it, and put it to one side. I rearrange the fruit in the fruit bowl. A couple of the lemons are dried up and no good, so I throw them in the compost bin under the sink. While I'm up, I grab the broom and sweep the floor clean. By this time my tea has gone cold, so I put the kettle on.

I sit down to start again. The paper is too thin, the pen too heavy. I look up from the page. There is so much to do around this place. I set the pad square with the table again. I leave the pen on a casual angle. I will get to it afterwards, I think, though after what, I can't say. I get up to turn the kettle off, and impulsively, in a quick movement like a thief, I slip your envelope off the table. I turn it over in my hand before I open it again. The letter folds and unfolds without a preference now; you only have to breathe on it.

I swim back into it and try to find the thread of the story, to place the lines. To pick up the end of the rope that will pull you home.

two

*W*here to begin? It has been too long. This is my own fault, of course.

Perhaps by cutting to the heart of it: I need a favour.

I want you to tell me a story.

Once you said to me that we only breathe in our stories. I might have taken this too literally. My breathing is shallow; I doubt its efficacy, but I am still here. I always took things too literally, come to think of it. Even as a child growing up in that shack at the bottom of the cliff. Rocks fell now and then, gently reminding me to keep moving.

I remember my father's rough voice declaiming ardently on behalf of the workers, ranting about the perils of suffocation. I learned that men were trapped down the hole and choked on their own stale air. I closed my eyes in that still room and tried not to breathe. I wanted to see what it was like to die in a cave-in, but closing your eyes is nothing like dying.

I am sick now. I think I might have a kind of cancer. We've been fighting each other for this body for years. I'm afraid it's winning. Take this as literally as you want. You always had a great imagination.

Once, a man told me a story. It was in a teahouse in a desert country, where eucalypts stood so bold and strong and unapologetic that they frightened me. He said it was an old story. I don't know. It was short. I can retell it in a single sentence: A man seeking a long-lost diamond finds it was in his pocket all along. The teller made it longer, and funny. I burned my tongue on hot mint tea and felt like telling him, 'I am that man with the diamond, it's me, here,' and bringing it out of my jeans.

But my pockets were empty.

Discontinuity is the only thread that runs through my whole life. I can't begin with where I begin and end with where I am. I have to do everything the wrong way around; it's only fitting. Oh, I'm making excuses, I will shut the hell up and tell you.

A week ago, I was walking on the pebbles at Brighton which they laughingly call the beach, where I break from my day-life in London. I spend far more of my time in the breaks than the life, but when people ask me what I do, I tell them I run a small publishing company. Actually, I pay other people to run it, but I'm still proud of my little press (I almost put 'accomplishment', as if I were a dab hand at embroidery). It has saved many a writer from a fate worse than success.

I'm comfortable and uninvolved enough to travel at whim. I have friends, and I call them my surrogate family, though I try to keep most of my relationships work-related. I'm not too old yet for the odd fling, but I keep it uncomplicated and remain unattached to any of it.

Once, you told me poets and sailors were from the same stock. They both confuse loneliness with freedom and harbour a secret longing for death. You were fond of your father's adages. Never marry a sailor, they will leave you for the sea. They are constitutionally untied and not to be trusted.

But what if it's the untied ones who can be trusted? Anyway, I have no gift for poetry or sailing. There is too much navigation involved in both, and I get lost in my own flat.

I said I would shut up and tell you. I am not taking my own advice.

I fell over. It was cold, I wasn't thinking, and I was wearing the wrong shoes. They were not sensible enough for pebbles slick with the oily sea.

They have put me in a nice enough place. Seems it was just one of those things, a spell, a faint. They are keeping me under observation just in case. So they tell me.

They ask me if I heard voices or if I saw anything. Lights moving, that sort of thing. I tell them, 'of course, the bloody pier was flashing.' I won't give them the right answer. I am waiting to see what they will do.

But it all has to come out, of course. Why did I leave R if not for the drinking and the wearing down of his once affable persona? Was it his arrogance, our fights, my instinct to run? No. I was sick, or so they said. I bit him on the cheek and left a perfect red mark: twin dashed lines like a treasure map without an X. He provoked me, I can't remember how. I do remember the texture of his skin. It was unsalted, rubbery, almost tasteless — a little like squid. Then he put me away. I felt a silly kind of criminal, coddled in a high-class institute for ladies who made mistakes. They had awful floral patterns on everything. They did a lot of tests and gave me benzos. So this is not the first time.

It's not an illness. The only voice I hear is yours, calling my name in sodden rage. It is a desperate echo running down a wall of rock. A blind whisper at my window in the little shack. Or I wake in the night, feeling your heart syncopating mine, then realise I am alone.

Loss is something of a constant to the traveller. You learn to deal with its exigencies. When leaving things behind is your only continuity, you find comfort in the illusion of agency. In the familiarity of a world framed by the window of any train, anywhere, the shape's the same. The continuity of discontinuity, yes, but there's more to it. There must be, or else there is no more to me than a suitcase.

Here they are obsessed by childhood. 'Unlock the past,' they urge, but I keep my case shut under my bed, ready to go. The making of history is a naturally selective process, it has to be, our selves are too fragile. Pulling everything out of the back of the cupboard – skeletons and so on – endangers that careful construction.

So why have I picked up pen and paper? I am listening to their advice in spite of myself. I am trying to make peace with my past. I thought about it, and I made a list of all the things that I regret. It's here somewhere. Not finishing Finnegans Wake, *spending an entire winter in Paris, selling the little Picasso sketch R gave me, which was the first thing I did in London. Oh, and leaving you behind.*

I never gave you a forwarding address, not after you ignored that first plea for help. I understood that you needed your freedom from me. Don't think I couldn't see that I had placed you in bondage. I'm sure you know by now, you must have it figured out, you were the wise one. I was weak, I was afraid. Why else would I have tried to destroy you? Some days I can't bear myself. Other times, absolution floats up around me, unbeckoned and undeserved. That might be the Valium.

What is regret for? Pain has a physical reason, shame is a lesson, the psyche's little schoolteacher. Oh lord, grant me the serenity. A day on the lake without a care, none of the creeping bones that bite into my eyes. What do I care? I have done as I wish. No one may fault me, except of course myself.

I'm not very good at taking stock of myself. I'm too busy moving and seeing. It's arrogant, this: to move through life as though it was all one big backdrop, a series of tableaux for my entertainment. Even the souls I meet are characters, charming or grotesque.

I was recently in a Catholic church in Siena. I went in to look at the frescos, and the little light above the booth was on. Just for a laugh, I went in to confess. I couldn't think what to say. Where to begin. I mumbled an apology in broken Latin. The priest gave me Hail Marys anyway, which I never learned how to say, even in English. I knelt before a row of candles on the cold damp stone and said your name.

There is a schizophrenic girl here who sees the sign of the cross everywhere: in the flight of a butterfly or the motion of cars crossing intersections. The universe is forever telling her something. There are signs.

I'm not mad like her. I don't think they are signs from God. I think they are messages from you.

I could accuse you of telling me lies. But you also told me stories, stories that made the world seem bright and vital. Without them I would never have left Coal. Maybe I'd have been content in a small town, married some local boy and spent my life near enough to you. Who broke whom, who pushed whom away, who cast the first stone, who can say what split our path into two distinct forks like the tongue of a snake?

I let the letter fall back into place on my kitchen table. I know the rest; I've read it before. As to who's responsible for that forked track, I think you are already well aware of the answer.

Confession. I might not be as educated as you, but ironies do not escape me, Grace. And all you can do is mumble the right words.

I'll tell you the only story I know. It's the one you starred in, the one where I learned how to breathe.

I take the pen in my hand and let it hover over that empty space. I could almost allow it to fall at random. Wherever I begin, your outline is already there, a designated space waiting to be filled. Perhaps your absence was always there, and the form of you only temporary.

Either way, I have to start as I am now: without you.

three

The Danker has to begin it. When this place came into my family's possession, I hadn't yet been born. You know me and I know myself only as a part of it. My first steps learned its floor, my eyes adjusted to its light. How I sleep, eat, and dream are moulded to its demands. There's no image of my life without the Danker in it. And yet I've never felt stuck here, I've only ever felt grounded. Thick roots bind me to my piece of country.

Da claimed he woke up with the deed in his hand and a hangover so violent he couldn't read the words on the paper. I'm sure he knew what he was doing the whole time, but it's a better story his way. I guess you know where I got this tendency to weave history into the shape of a tale. I can't match his gift, but you asked me for a story, and I'll tell it as true as I can.

The Danker begins it, but the Danker has a beginning too, and roots of its own.

★ ★ ★

This bit of country is a stretch of coast that runs between Sydney and Wollongong. It was all bush, once: a strip of wet forest pushing up between the cliffs and the ocean. I can still see it as it was sometimes, when I blink out the developments. There were wetlands down around the bottom of the cliff, cabbage-tree palms along the creeks, eucalypts all the way up the rock, and some old figs holding it all together between thick roots. People lived here then, another people who knew the land without having to excavate its secrets. There were stories that made this place before there were people. They talked this country into being. I guess they have a birthright. I envy them this.

Me, I come from people who say they believe they were made by God. We don't mean it, we've just been pretending for too long to remember any different. This country laughs at us. It's too old for tricks. It sees right through our game.

We have other stories, older ones, but none of them belong here. We have learned that we have only what we can make, and even that is no worthy answer to this country's ancient laughter. It leans back and studies us and says to itself, these people won't last.

That laugh is audible in the crash and crack of water beating against rock. The conversation between land and sea is at once affectionate and brutal, like two old friends meeting for a drink. What better spot for a pub? But I'm getting ahead of myself.

The British found coal here almost as soon as they arrived. They spotted the seams when they first mapped the coast. They could see the lines in the cliffs from their ships. Black diamonds, that's what they called it. That's what drew new people here and kept them, beckoned them down into those dark pits. That's what made them stake their claim.

The people that already lived here were mostly shot or driven away. It was early days. No one knew any better, or that's what we like to say. Makes us feel better about making our livings out of other people's grief.

They started to dig in little patches at first, making holes in the escarpment like mice do in a pile of sacks, purposefully but without pattern. They were making sure of the black diamonds, and soon made their livelihoods fast with land grants and promises of work.

Later, the railway came. Steel lines weaved through and over the rocky coast like a serpent, bringing machines to dig out room for more machines, bringing empty cars to pile high with the black diamonds they took from the earth. It brought jobs and hope and a bright industrial future to the proud women and men who stood to watch it grow. The women stood in their homespun wool, a kid under one arm, and watched as their men left their patches of earth to plough diamonds from the rock. With wonder and fear they watched the light of the train emerge from the tunnel.

The trains changed the scale of things. Larger claims bought out smaller leases. The pits began to eat out great sections of the cliffs. The people pulled out trees and rocks and then great chunks of coal, high heaps in the carts that tipped into the freight trains. Sometimes they pulled out men: men whose lives had been snuffed along with their gas lamps, men who had been crushed when the rock protested, when inadequate struts snapped under the weight of the cliff. The crushed men and the gassed men left behind widows.

Then the first war came and it seemed like all that was left was widows. Widows, and children that couldn't grow fast enough to fill the pits and feed the gaping mouth of the army. The bright industrial future had taken the men away, to dig other dangerous holes in other places and to die in them.

When the war finally ended, the men who had stayed at the coalface felt that they had fought it. Like soldiers, they had been told their lives belonged to Britain. They had struggled hard and seen too many of their mates die, but they weren't heroes. There weren't any parades to remember the ones who suffocated in a dark shaft. Instead, there were speeches from the bosses about lean times to come. There were closures, now that the army's furnaces didn't need to be fed. The men who were left, who had listened eagerly to the promise of a bright future, watched the last carriages pull away into the tunnel, laden with coal. They stood above ground, stunned and lost. Black diamonds had cut lines in their faces and holes in their lungs.

The women, of course, adapted. They wouldn't let their men feel sorry for themselves. 'We have to fight against the closures,' they said. Because the women always fought, and no one ever said they deserved a parade.

They sent their men back down the pits to strike. The men locked themselves underground, shuffling their worn-out boots through the dark towards lamplit meetings. They talked, and the women talked, and the men stayed down the hole until their terms were met. They fought their way uphill again and as the mines re-opened they came out with decent lamps and the right to build the struts that held the rocks at bay. They won boot allowances and breaks and decent wages for a time. Even the eight-hour day. And it looked as if everything would be all right. One more fight, they said, one more strike, one more meeting at the sly grog shop and we'll take our bodies back to the coalface and work strong, and we'll see the back of all this widowing.

★ ★ ★

Over the next ten years, a small town grew around one of the mines, and the railway named it Coal. The rough dwellings strewn along the bottom of the escarpment were made fast. Weatherboard shacks grew brick walls, holes in the earth grew into dunnies. Once their homes looked more permanent, the people built a church, a school, and a hall for dances. The sly grog shop that had perched on the tip of the headland for as long as anyone could remember was bought by a speculator named Parson, who got a real licence and built a real hotel. Rich guests came down from Sydney and stayed there, and Coal shone.

They built a steelworks down the coast only an hour by bicycle, less by horse if the horse wasn't tired. So you could take your pick of work for a change. Coal boomed and blossomed. Women grew town-proud and formed committees. They fixed the roads, got a hospital, planted a public garden with roses. There were talking pictures at the hall.

Then someone in a bank somewhere made a mistake. That's how they explained it when the mine closed, initially for three months. 'No problem,' said the women, 'you can go down the steelworks for a bit, or you can wait. Things will improve.'

Everyone waited for things to improve. They got worse. But they were getting worse elsewhere, too, and staying to wait was no real choice. People took what they could get. Hundreds came from other places with less, travelling up on the freight or simply walking here with their swags and expectations. Soon a small shanty town grew up on the hill above the park, between the boss's place and the church.

The dwellings crowded into the bush on the north side of Coal. They gathered like tideline debris, forming a cluster between the escarpment and the sea. The shacks were built from whatever was handy: old railway sleepers, tarps and string, hay bales and hessian bags. As time passed the occupants would add a brick here, a bit of two-by-four there, until they ended up with a sort of house on the land they cleared themselves. Squatters, like the old days, but without a licence from the government.

Three months became a year and the hundreds became thousands. The mine was still closed more often than not. The briefly proud town hung its rose-covered head and strained under the weight. The shanty town was filled with hungry men, women and children who all had to fight each other for bread.

One of those men was Sean McCabe, my father.

My father came to Australia on a leaky boat, fleeing a past in Dublin. The country he left behind was at war, and many young men had expressed their loyalties with explosives and ended up on the run. I like to think he was one of them, but I never knew. He brought nothing with him from Ireland except the clothes on his back, the old tunes, and a taste for the triple distilled.

He didn't stay in Sydney. He travelled New South Wales getting work on sheep stations, making little more than what he could drink and living 'the free life', as he put it. After several years, he found himself working in the fields in Nowra for a stocky farmer with seven sons. When they held a dance in the town, he stood among the other itinerant workers and watched as all seven of the boss's sons took turns dancing with the girls. But one girl stood with her arms folded and refused them all.

Annie Bailey was sixteen, with dark, sparkling eyes and a serious expression. Her hair was as black and shining as wet coal. She was an only child, daughter of tenant farmers who had come out from Ireland with hopes of a new life. Like most only children she was independent of mind and sure of her place in the world. She only liked the look of one man in that room. She ignored the boss's sons, strode straight across the room and boldly asked him to dance.

When Da told this story, he used to sing, 'And her eyes they shone like diamonds.'

They married right away, despite the fact that neither of them had any money or real prospects. At the time it was thought that anyone could make their way in Australia. If they worked hard, they would surely find a place of their own in no time.

'I tricked her into marrying me,' he'd say, winking at us from the head of the table. 'I promised her diamonds. Me, just another landless bastard wandering this godless earth in hunt of work of any kind, and her with a little patch of her own down by the Shoalhaven. I wasn't rich enough to buy as much as a tin ring. Still, I had plenty of ideas. It was a boom time for people with ideas. I'd be in bonds or insurance or farming depending on the weather and the day of the week.'

Mam stayed in her family's little farm in the Shoalhaven while Da went off to find work. He heard there were jobs in the mines up the coast, so he jumped on a train and joined the queue. This was in 1926. There were jobs to be had for the taking in Coal, offering real wages and security. As much as he missed my mam, Da considered it his responsibility to provide. He'd go down on the train to visit his wife on Sundays. She was always refreshed by the morning at church and ready to smile and flash her eyes at him.

He built a little shack on the hill beside the other men who worked down the pit, and tried to be frugal. When he got his envelope at the end of the fortnight he'd put it aside, less a little for his tea and a pay-day visit to the public house. It was still

Parson's Inn in those days, a bright, sprawling holiday place for the rich Sydney folks who came to take the air and promenade along the white beach. The publican was a clean-cut fellow, always dressed in a white shirt to show which side he was on, and he'd curl his lip at the miners in their dusty work gear.

Mr Parson was a lot more democratic when his wealthy customers weren't looking. He loved a game of cards, and the miners would often oblige him. Most of them ended up in some debt to the tidy publican, and many of them swore off when they realised he would happily take their money from the table, but he'd never give them a single schooner on tick.

When Da would go and get his ration of two pints a fortnight he'd end up being begged for a game. My da had gambled plenty and lost plenty in his wandering days, but never with a family behind him. He restrained himself. He had responsibilities now, he'd remind himself, thinking of my mam, now with one little boy and a new baby. There was just work enough to keep them.

When the crash came, it didn't hit hard at first. There were enough jobs for those who lived here. The steel mill was still running and it was thought that the closure would be short-term. Da waited around the coalmine, hoping for work.

As more men came they built the growing shanty town. In the mornings the mine boss, a stern man named Thorne (who everyone called Thornbag behind his back), would come to the gate and point at whoever looked likely. It would have been hard to look big and strong without any breakfast in your belly. Some were worse off than others. Many had families with them and no bread to share. Da was glad his growing family were down at the farm, because the kids in Coal were dropping dead of typhus and starvation.

The paychecks were no longer regular, and Da had to survive on a few days of work here and there. He'd seen hard times before and weathered them, but always been able to move on to where the work was. This time, it was hard everywhere. Da would grow wistful for his 'free life' – nights spent sleeping under the stars, being bitten by bugs through the holes in his boots. As a third son was born and the money continued to dwindle, his promise to his wife seemed more and more foolish. He couldn't bring himself to admit that he'd somehow failed. It didn't make any sense. The land of opportunity was just another rort.

One night, the wind was so wild that Da's hessian walls billowed out like sails. He remembered the leaky boat and his dreams of a new life. He was tired. Tired of being covered in coal dust. Tired of hunger and failure. He was at the end of his rope, but he still knew a few tricks with a deck of cards. He gathered up his last few coins and carried them to the public house.

Parson was pleased to see him. There were no rich visitors from Sydney any more, no groups of idle ladies down to take the air and give away their money. He welcomed my da with a bright, white smile. Da pulled up a barstool, tossed down his tiny pile of coins and rubbed his hands together for luck.

The last thing he remembered, so he told it, was the bottle of good whiskey coming down off the top shelf. He woke up the proud owner of Coal's only public house and a roaring headache.

When he returned to the shack in the morning to collect his few belongings, he found that it had blown away. The hessian walls were halfway up a gum tree. He stood on the exposed dirt floor and laughed until a crowd gathered. He turned to face his puzzled neighbours.

'I'll trade a week's free beer with anyone who's got a pen and paper,' he announced, and sat down in the dirt to write to his wife, telling her to come at once.

Da always laughed aloud at this point in the story. I imagined him standing in something like our chook pen, a younger, more jubilant version of himself. I imagined his laughter sounded like a song.

'It was the second luckiest day of my life,' he'd say, and look at Mam with meaning in his eye. Us kids knew where we stood: third, fourth, fifth and sixth respectively.

Mam came up on the train with Patrick, Callum, the baby Brendan, and a few chooks in a basket. The other passengers were mostly men in search of work. They eyed her basket hungrily, and she held it close.

Da met his wife at the station and she handed him the baby. It was only the second time he'd seen his youngest son. He would have preferred to be holding Annie, but she was busy with a basket full of squawking birds. Loaded down in this way, they walked slowly to their new home.

'I told you I'd find you a diamond,' he said. 'Just you wait and see it.'

She smiled when she saw the place, not in the best nick but at least the sign was shiny and new-painted: The Diamond Anchor. The diamond in question was marked more black than white. Da had chosen the name with care, adding an anchor because it was a good fishing spot, and because he hoped they'd stay.

The building itself was formed from two shoddy-looking storeys of brick, and seemed to have been dropped on the headland whole. The lower level had a jutting porch, the upper a balcony wrapped around it like a moth-eaten scarf. Above that, there were hints at a shallow attic. A couple of broken windows collected the sunshine. The roof iron made a dismal noise in welcome.

'It's all ours,' Da said. 'I won it at cards.'

The smile left my mother's face. She put down her basket, turned to her husband, and slapped him hard across the cheek.

'You're never to gamble again!' she shouted.

But the smile hadn't gone far, and she put the chooks down, took the baby up, and climbed into his arms so he could carry her and Brendan over the threshold, with Patrick and Callum in tow.

'I believe you were conceived that very night,' he'd tell me, putting one thick hand to Mam's waist.

And Parson? The man left town with his bright clean shirt tail tucked between his legs, glad to have passed the place on.

When the Danker came into our hands it wasn't worth the patch of dirt it stood on. Parson had left it in debt to all his suppliers and several angry investors. A cutaway bit of scrub on a rocky hill that stuck out to sea, the land was no good for planting either. There were no more rich visitors from Sydney. Instead there were queues of people at the back door every morning asking to chop wood for a shilling.

They had been married for ten years by the time they moved in here, but my parents had never lived in the same house. Those first years were a time of negotiation – with each other and with the locals. Mam's stubborn will and her ability to listen were what got them through, but even she would sometimes admit that she couldn't have done it without Da's warmth. His open charm and fireside conversation transformed the impersonal Parson's

Inn into a local pub. They knew they had won the affection of Coal when people stopped calling the place Parson's and began to refer to it, with typical foreshortening, as the Danker.

Few of the old families that started here were left. There were the Cullens, who owned the adjacent piece of coastal land to the north and tried hard to feed their growing population of sons with their own produce. Thorne hung on to his mining lease, not suffering the same privations as the rest. One of the original widows still lived in an old stone cottage up the hill, surviving on her pension and charity. Her garden grew wild with dandelions. The bulk of the town was dirt poor, and while the mine was starting to pick up again it was five more years before the long string of debts seemed to have an end. Those years were hard, but there was enough trouble around to keep things interesting.

The chooks my mother brought up from the farm never seemed to lay here. Da tried all sorts of things to get them settled, perches and feed changes and even singing to them. Mam used to laugh at him. I can see her eyes flash, imagine them before they had crow's feet and shadows.

My parents were lucky, but most were not. The shanty town was still full of hungry, gaunt men, sad-faced women and children with distended bellies. Da couldn't forget that life so easily, but the Danker couldn't offer much beyond the odd free schooner.

He and Tom Cullen would talk this problem over in the bar. Tom already shared all that he could spare from his garden, but something more had to be done. One night, the two men hatched a plan.

During the Depression, when the freight train came down

from Sydney to collect the coal, the long line of empty carriages was used to carry supplies for the shops further south. When it emerged from the tunnel, the train had to slow down to take the corner. That corner also hid the engine and its driver from view. Tom had watched it come through the tunnel and figured you could step right on it if you were careful. He proposed to my da that they take advantage of this opportunity, and one night the two men took out their bicycles.

They rode up the track in the dark and hid their bikes behind a tree. They crossed the tracks, leaned against the wall at the tunnel's mouth and waited, rolling cigarettes they didn't dare to light. When they heard the rumble of the train and the squeal of its brakes, they stood ready. Sure enough, it slowed, and the two men leapt onto a coupling and hung on as the machine began to accelerate.

Cautiously, they clambered up the steel rungs at the end of the carriage and unhooked the canvas cover. Four eyes peered into the dark. As they adjusted, they saw a fantastic bounty: huge sacks of oats, boxes of tea and sugar, and bags of flour and rice. The two men roared with joy. Tom climbed in and passed the goods to Da, who threw the heavy sacks out into the bush, blinking in the rush of dust. As the train passed through Coal, they ducked down to avoid being seen. When they'd passed the lights they popped up again, Tom clambered out, and they threw themselves from the speeding freight.

Realising they would never be able to carry all the goods down the hill alone, my da and Tom recruited a group of their most trusted friends, at least the ones who had their own bicycles, and a gang was formed.

The day after a raid, the bicycle gang would come down to the shanty town and distribute the food. Tom and Da came up with all sorts of excuses for their excursions, from helping mend a fence to union meetings, and this seemed to work for weeks – though knowing Mam she was probably only pretending to be fooled.

One rainy night, Tom missed the coupling and launched himself onto the side of a carriage. Da went to follow, but the rain had made the steel slick. He missed his footing, panicked and threw himself off the train before it could pull him under. His mate, struggling to hold on himself, took a while to notice Da was missing. He found him back near the tunnel, lying in the bush with half his knee scraped off, biting his wrist so he wouldn't cry out with the pain and give himself away.

Da came home limping, his leg bandaged up in a sleeve of his shirt. Mam nearly killed him, despite being heavily pregnant with me.

'You can't be taking those kinds of risks,' she said, washing the gravel from his skin. 'You're a damned stupid fool of a man, and this is the only shirt you have left.' She soaked the rag in a bucket and wrung it out.

'I can't let them all go hungry. They're dying down there,' he said. 'We just thought we could help.' He winced at the pain in his knee.

'I know, Sean.' Mam smiled. 'There's something I haven't told you, but I might as well mention it now.' She paused and put a hand to her belly. 'The chooks have been laying all this time. I've been sneaking the eggs down to the women.'

'So that's what's wrong with them!' Da laughed.

It was clear they were better off working together. Da promised he would help to distribute the eggs and Mam said she would give him all her spare sacks to split up the grain, oats and rice. All was forgiven, for a while at least.

A little later in the evening, while sorting out the sacks, he had a sudden thought and turned to her.

'I suppose Cullen's goats haven't been eating all my shirts either,' he said.

Mam stuffed a corner of a sack in her mouth and made as if to munch.

There was a storm the night I was born. Rain beat down on the roof and poured off it again in streams. A wild wind leaned into the Danker and it creaked, shook, and began to spring leaks. Mam lay in her bed upstairs, alternating between moments of serenity and biting down on wet rags like an animal. The hospital was an hour's bumpy ride up the dirt track and Mam had insisted I wasn't going to come into the world on the back of a bicycle in the pouring rain. Da paced and pleaded with her, but to no avail. Mam, like most of the town's inhabitants, firmly believed that hospitals were for dying in.

Finally, she sent him to get Mrs Green, the war widow who lived up the hill. She had attended every birth in Coal for as long as anyone could remember. Da's knee was still giving him trouble and his nerves were worse. The combination got the better of him. He made it as far as the bar, where he proceeded to make a dent in the whiskey.

Fortunately, Da had the presence of mind to send my brother Patrick up the hill in his stead. Patrick was a clever ten-year-old by then, and proud to be trusted with such a mission. The widow came straight down, tutted her way past my inebriated father, strode up the back stairs and took charge. With her help, Mam let me out without a fuss. When they called him upstairs my da was so relieved, or so happy to have a daughter, or perhaps just so far into the turps, that he cried fat tears to match the rain, and Mam had to tell him to pull himself together.

Me, I screamed loud enough to shake the drops of water coming into the room, to match the racket of bangs and rattles made by the Danker.

As I settled down, the wind calmed and the storm passed. The violence of the night had all but vanished. No one could find the leaks in the roof afterwards. They must have closed themselves.

The name they wrote on the certificate was Mary, but that was too hard to get my tongue around when I was a kid. I called myself May, and it stuck. Mam never minded. I guess she needed to distinguish me from the Blessed Virgin.

Now that I am in the world to tell it, my story changes shape. It ceases to be built on what I have heard, and begins to rely on my memory. I start to feel my way.

Perhaps it's a sign of my da's gift that I trust his ability more than my own. But it's also because my story will always be an addition to his, like a modern extension on an antique house. My existence supplements the family myth.

My earliest memory is a rope. One end of the rope is knotted above my head, and the other is attached to my father. He is pulling me up the headland in a basket, hand over hand. I can hear my mother's anxious voice below me. I can just make out Da's face looking over the precipice above, and beyond him, the towering shape of the Danker.

The basket was full of pumpkins which Mam had brought up from her parents' place. She'd taken me down to visit my grandparents, which I don't remember. I know we stayed a night down there, and I know there was another storm while we were gone. When Mam and I returned, Da came and met us at the station with a long length of rope.

'Trees down everywhere,' he explained. 'We'll never get all this up the track.'

I was a toddler and still wanted to be carried, but Mam was heavily pregnant with the one who was meant to come after me, and she needed help to climb. The track up to the Danker was strewn with fallen trees. It was impossible even for Da to clamber over all those trunks with a child in his arms.

Mam walked out onto the rocks under the headland, carrying me in the basket. Da climbed nimbly up the track and lowered the rope. My mother kissed my head and told me to keep still. 'Heave away, then,' she yelled to the little figure of a man on the crest of the rock, and she lifted the basket full of me and pumpkins over her head.

I watched the rope shorten. The knot in the top of my basket was solid as a man's fist. The sky rocked, I rose, and Da's face grew close above me. He said my name. Behind him, the Danker rose up like a storybook giant. Da picked me up in his arms and took me inside. I was home.

He ran down to help Mam up the track, but it was too late for caution. That same week, the one who was supposed to come after me was born. She was dead before she ever breathed. They buried her in the churchyard, under a cross without a name. There were no more after that. I had no more chance of a sister.

I was the last in line. I got second-hand jumpers and third-hand slippers and fourth-hand blankets. I learned early on that if anything in my family was going to be passed on, it would end up with me.

★ ★ ★

After their first joy at having a home, Mam and Da had to work out how to make it pay. With a tick list as long as the bar, they managed to keep everyone watered despite the continuing shortage of work. Each time the mine re-opened, the Danker filled with noisy celebration. My parents welcomed the people of Coal regardless of their ability to pay. While Mam had her doubts about keeping the whole town in debt, she settled them by joining all the committees, taking the eggs down to the camp, and spending her evenings listening. Each time the mine closed again, a steady stream of troubles lined up at the bar.

With all those leftover debts to pay and hardly any money coming in, they fought just as hard as any other family to survive the last years of the Depression. Not everyone was convinced of this, however. There was always someone who resented their property or their luck. When I was four, a brick was thrown through the front window in an anonymous attack. But magically, nothing was ever stolen except the odd chook. Come to think of it, it had more to do with my mother's approach than with magic.

Mam was furious about that brick. She displayed it on the bar for a week. She regularly announced that the window cost a fortune and if anyone owned the brick, they should come and claim it. One busy night, the brick disappeared off the bar when her back was turned. In its place was a new pound note.

When the second war came, the people of Coal had cause to celebrate. They were grateful for the return of a hungry army. Wars need steel and coal, and the mines ran regular hours again. Between miners and soldiers, the camps were quickly emptied of their stock of idle men. As I grew, the demand for workers began to outgrow the labour force. Coal began to bloom again, albeit a little less boldly this time.

We put ads in the city papers to encourage visitors: 'Drop in When Passing and Try our Cool Beer, Fresh Air and Country Hospitality.' We fixed as best we could the sprawling building, two storeys of 1920s glamour that the sea and the wind and the lean times had aged beyond its years. We fitted our lives in behind the bar.

The dark wooden bar forms a strong dividing line between the house and the pub. Stainless steel fridges line up behind it like an elderly hall of mirrors, and high glass shelves catch the light. Back then a scent of mustiness seemed innate to the place. Behind that bar, to my child's eyes, everything seemed to be made of glass and dust.

The pub takes up most of the ground floor. The dining room – a few tables and a servery – was arranged in a back quarter, where the bistro is now. Through a swing door which connects it with the bar, the kitchen takes up the other corner. We slept upstairs but we lived in that kitchen, in earshot of potential customers.

Da fenced a yard behind the kitchen and planted vegetables, which always suffered and usually perished in the salty, rocky soil. At the northern edge of our yard, which borders Cullen's place, there was a young flowering gum tree and a convenient hole in the fence.

Squeezed in with the kitchen are the back stairs, which lead up to our bedrooms. Mam set up a little laundry at the base of them. We lived in two rooms upstairs, divided from the guest rooms by an ominous wooden door.

There is a separate, grander stairwell that runs up from the bar, so hotel guests don't have to mingle with us. But the wooden balcony, with its rail of wrought iron in flaking arabesques, circles the upper floor, so us kids could get out of our bedroom door and come in again anywhere we liked.

The Pacific Ocean is so close that the Danker practically stands in it. I'm sometimes surprised I don't get my feet wet, even if we are elevated high on the edge of this rocky headland. I still fear that one day the Danker will have a tantrum and throw itself into the sea. In the meantime, it complains.

It's a noisy building. It talks, and it always has. My brothers and I, the four of us lying in a row of beds in the one room, used to stay awake at first, afraid of the noise, but we got used to it. After a time, the erratic creaks and howls came to sound like music.

My father's music inhabits this building too.

Da had sea-blue eyes that were rimmed with yellows instead of whites. They flashed when he sang. He had a fiddle, an old, worn thing he'd picked up in his travels, but he rarely played it. It was cracked down the middle with age, and it sounded rough and cranky. I liked the fiddle; to me, it blended in with the Danker's conversational creaks. I loved it when he sang the old songs from his travelling days, or maudlin lyrics about lost love.

It was the piano that I hated. ·

The piano was a folly of Da's that he acquired from a customer's house in the next town. I was about five when that family had to move up to Sydney after the husband was killed in the war. Da always knew where to look for a bargain. He sent the mailman down to get it with the promise of a night's free beer.

We had to winch the thing up onto the balcony to get it upstairs. It wouldn't fit in the kitchen and Da said it'd be a waste putting it down in the pub where no one would play it. That was more to avoid being asked, I think, because everyone loved to beg Da for a song when they were drunk and sometimes the Irish would come out in him and he'd oblige. He had a beautiful voice, aged to a fine timbre by whiskey and pipe tobacco. The fiddle came out for special occasions, but the piano would have been asking for trouble, so up on the balcony it went.

And there it stayed until the week he died. We couldn't get it in the door to my parents' room. The old instrument had rotting teeth, more than a few of which were missing, and a gash in its front where you could see through to the strings inside. I was terrified of it. When my brothers played the thing, it sounded salty and sinister. The sea air was terrible for it, but Da would insist we learn, and in my turn I found myself up on the balcony practising my out-of-tune scales at the sea. Da would pop his head out of the balcony door and sing along, his lopsided grin matching the piano's.

He picked up tunes from the customers, traded them along with the drinks. But Da never managed to teach any of us enough that it would stick. Some days now, listening to the building talk, I think I hear snatches of a melody. But it's always gone before I can catch hold of it.

Though he sang, played, and poured their drinks, the customers never called my father a musician or a publican; he was always a storyteller. Coal wasn't big enough to have any other entertainments. The Danker had to provide it all.

'He's got the gift,' more superstitious types would murmur, crossing themselves or tapping the wooden bar to avoid contamination from the devils which must have made a contract with my da.

This would cause Mam to roll her eyes and laugh.

'Oh, he's a storyteller all right,' she would smile, 'otherwise known as a liar.' But she never stopped him from telling us tales.

Some nights Da wouldn't have time for a story. Some nights he'd drink too much and pass out in the bar, splayed in a chair by the fire with an empty glass balanced in his hand.

I used to stand in the doorway and listen to him snoring in his chair. I thought he might stop breathing if I stopped listening. But he moved around a lot in his sleep. My brothers and I would sneak up on him, hide behind the chair, and try to wake him with a shout. When we succeeded, he would grab us by the scruffs of our necks and we would beg him until he let us sit down at his feet.

Sometimes he would tell us true stories about his life here, like the ones I have just told you. Sometimes he shamelessly fabricated tales of childhood daring, and other times he dug up old myths which he adapted to our landscape. He never talked about what his life was really like before he came to Australia, and we learned not to ask. Instead, he told us about the sea people who came onto shore to steal young men away from their families; about the little people who caused small and great disasters to those who did not respect their space; about the howl of the banshee that meant someone in the house was going to die. This last story terrified me. I was convinced the screech of the freight trains as they passed in the night was that very howl.

My oldest brother Patrick would watch my da patiently, hiding his big, dark brown eyes under a flop of hair. Afterwards, when Da had finished his story and we were all up in our room together, Patrick would squat down in the moonlight by the balcony door and retell it, start to finish.

I was the littlest, and I learned to listen. I learned it from Mam, but I have never matched her ability to hear, which verged on the psychic. She always knew what was about to happen in Coal.

One afternoon she called to me through the swing door. 'May, get your feet off that chair and run and ask the Cullens for some milk for tomorrow's breakfast, your da will be up at the crack of dawn with the strikers,' she said, without turning her head.

Moving my feet from the chair under the table, I answered her. 'They're not on the chair and there's no strike is there and I don't see why one of the boys can't go.'

'They've got schoolwork is why. Now go.'

I went reluctantly, and sure enough a strike was announced the following day. Somehow my mother saw right past that formica table and into the future.

Later, after I became a parent myself, I asked her how she did this.

'I did nothing,' she said. 'It was the pub telling me. I always knew there'd be a strike from the way the shutters sounded in the wind.'

By then, I already knew what she meant.

By the time the Forties came along, we'd had the Danker for long enough to know its character. The upstairs has always been a warren of a place, and its darkened, dusty hallways were nothing but inviting to our young eyes. My team of brothers and I learned its every cranny. We crawled into the attic, disdaining spiders. We crept along the balcony, tracing the walls with our hands. We tried to pinpoint which stairs were the creaking ones (which was most of them). We tried every door of every cupboard in every room of the hotel. Sometimes one of us found a glove or a hatpin, pirate treasure from the time before, and we'd fight over who had earned it. I never had a chance at these trophies, of course. I was too busy trying to keep up without injuring myself. There was dust all over every surface and potential dangers lurked everywhere: loose boards, or thick rusted nails sticking out of the floor. As a young child on unsteady legs following three boys around, I learned to step over such perils.

While technically we weren't allowed in the bar, Mam had nowhere else to put us most of the time. When it got dark and we weren't allowed to play on the beach or on the headland we would come inside. My brothers and I would make up elaborate contests that involved various landmarks in the pub. We'd race to the bar, play hide and seek between the tables, jump out at people from behind the door, and generally run amok until we got sent upstairs to our beds.

The customers had started to include American soldiers down for a Sunday with their girls. The tourist trade was beginning again, despite the rationing and the shortages, and the pub seemed to be riding a bright Pacific wave to prosperity.

The Danker was a giant, unpredictable playground, and growing up here charged my curiosity – but didn't satisfy it. I was impatient to go to the school my brothers attended. At fourteen, Patrick was already about to finish. Brendan was seven, and could read to me at night.

I stood on the balcony in the intricate shadow of the iron rail, imagining I could read a language in those flaking curves. Through them, I would watch the sea, its horizon a smudged, permeable border between my life and the unknown. I was tempted by the possibilities of another country, another place equally teeming with life. In that place, everything here would have its mirror and its match.

four

You walk in the door and catch your heel on the step. As usual, you demand attention. But I have been warned today, and I refuse to be fooled.

I was warned by the noise that woke me this morning: a crash of glass breaking like a small wave. When I could find no cause for it, I knew the Danker was up to something. All day I have been working under the pressure of this portent, not knowing what form it would take. When I see you, I am almost relieved.

I stand behind my bar and I refuse. I restock, polish, and sweep. I scrub the Danker hard, like a mother trying to get the stains of crime off her child's skin. I work until you have passed across the room, out through the wall, danced over the cluster of houses and disappeared into the bush beyond. Only then do I raise my head, put a hand on the bar, and breathe even.

This bar is my barometer and my fortress as well as my occupation. From behind it I can gauge any mood, defend myself against any incursion, and divert myself with any number of distractions. I've perfected the art of looking busy but relaxed. If your ghost could see, you'd know it takes a long time to learn this. I used to be restless, but boredom is a young person's disease. I used to pour myself lemonades, polish glasses like a maniac, find things to rearrange (which Da always provided piles of, in his day). I've slowed my pace now, but I remain occupied. There is enough to do just keeping the disorder at bay.

I stack glasses in a tray and watch Louie sink in the corner of my eye. He's playing with change, waiting for his wife to come in. Giving her another five minutes before he slides off the stool to slink into the corner and use the blue phone, tell her he's still here. Where else would he be? She often arrives before he makes it to the payphone and orders him out of here. I make silent bets with myself on who will win this endless race.

Louie's real name is Edmond but I doubt even he remembers that much. He can't have kept it long in this town. He used to hang around the men when he was a kid, try and follow them down the mine. They named him after a fly because he bothered them, but in doing so they may have planned his whole life for him, because he has spent most of it on one of my barstools.

He still thinks of himself as a young man. He is young, just over fifty, but something about him reeks of being finished. I can see it in the way he slides the empty schooner over for a refill before the foam's even had a chance to settle off the sides. Or maybe it's the way he tells me his endless business plans. Today he has a new scheme, something about hair removal, and I nod noncommittally as he enthuses.

'For men too busy to shave,' he says, and I think this is the epitomy of laziness, but I don't tell him my opinions. I just listen, like I have for years.

'I want to do something different,' he says for the fourteenth time tonight. 'I'm bored here. Maybe . . .' It takes me a moment to realise he is not saying my name.

I glance over my shoulder at the clock. Still another two hours to go before eleven. 'You know what Lou,' I say. 'Why don't you go away somewhere for a bit? Just for the weekend or something. She'd love that.'

'You trying to get rid of me, May?'

'Nah. Just thought you might like a holiday.'

'Holiday from what?' He gestures at the beach, the bar, the moonlit night, and smiles. 'Got it all right here,' he says, and I can only agree.

I finish stacking the tray with glasses and slide it into the fridge. I grab a rag, flip up the trapdoor and walk out from behind the bar to clear the tables. I could leave them dirty; there are so many initials carved and burned into the old pine that I doubt anyone could identify a spill among them. But I will not let things slide.

I hold an empty schooner glass in one hand while I wipe a table down. As I lean to reach the far end, the glass slips out of my hand and falls to the ground. It shatters, and the pieces shoot across the floor. The sound hits me like the breaking of a wave.

There are rain clouds hanging around off the point tonight, big billowing things, fat and grey. They have come up all of a sudden. Winter is on its way, and with it the winds and the long, freezing nights. I'm not looking forward to it. I don't like it when I can't leave the Danker at night; I get sick of the smell of stale beer and cigarettes, though most of the time I don't even notice it. Winter brings quiet, though. No tourists, and often it's only myself and the fire which make the place look alive.

Lisa and the Rat were down yesterday, and perhaps that's why I'm a little distracted. I caught him knocking for termites in the door frame.

'That's been here longer than I have,' I said as I poured their drinks: white wine for Lisa, squash for the driver. 'Where's Ernie?' I was disappointed they didn't bring my only grandchild with them.

'He's with David's sister,' Lisa said, tugging at her red-blonde ponytail. I have met this sister a couple of times. She's a teacher of some sort, an unfazeable woman, as different from the Rat as you could get. This gives me hope. Perhaps greed is a recessive gene that won't be passed on.

Eventually, of course, we had to have the conversation we always have about when I am going to retire and sell the place.

'Are you kidding?' I tried to react calmly. 'I love the Danker.' Lisa didn't pull the usual trick of telling me she's worried about me living on my own in this enormous liability of a building, while the Rat looks at the ceiling for signs of decay and tells me how much work it will take to fix it. No, this time I got the hard sell.

'Do you know how much you could get right now for the block alone?' He smiled encouragingly, used to speaking a universal language of money. Lisa played with her glass and let him give me the talk.

'It's a perfect time, the only time you'll get what this place is really worth. Realistically,' he added. He emphasised this word, as though by not doing what I am told I am being unrealistic, a naughty child. 'Realistically, you won't get another chance like this for fifteen, twenty years, and who knows? By then . . .' He lifts his eyes to the ceiling and shrugs. The man has a knack for stopping short at the limit of my tolerance.

What I would like to do is tell him what I really think of him, or at the very least raise my middle finger and politely request that he fucks off. I have thought about telling them my plan for when I am really too old to work here, which is a long way off. I want to sell the business but keep the building. I'll leave it to little Ernest, who is four, and put in a clause that he can't sell it for fifty years. You can do that, I've checked. I know what would happen if Pat and Lisa were to split it. Straight down the middle and out the door as the Rat collects the cheque from his developer buddies.

Between my place and Joe Cullen's next door, we're holding out. This headland is the last bit of undeveloped coast left, unless you count the almost vertical rock of the escarpment, which they can't build on. The point is an ugly reminder of what would happen to the Danker if it was sold. I'd sooner let them amputate my arms and legs.

I smiled, poured them more drinks, and told them I would think about it. There's nothing they can do, short of having me declared insane, and even the Rat wouldn't sink that low.

I can feel the rain about to hit. The weight of it makes me sleepy. I'm a broken record tonight, dwelling on the possibility of loss. I know that eventually – maybe not for another ten years, but eventually – my daughter and her Rat will be right.

Look at the rest of this town. There's a new café on the beach now, with a menu full of stuff we'd never heard of a few years ago. It has made a dent in the bistro's trade, so I only do summer weekends now. The point is covered in a mass of cement-rendered townhouses. We lost that fight, despite our best efforts. The next headland is disappearing under the weight of big glass houses that belong to half-arsed Sydney sea changers who still commute to jobs in the city, a foot in either camp.

The gentrification of Coal has an impression of inevitability about it.

My presence here, the Danker's presence, is a symbol. I can't maintain a locals-only stance, never have; that would be suicidal. But I know that our existence provides a link, a kind of continuity. People need continuity. They need to see something not change. Every time I have to replace the carpet or fix up the furniture I try and keep it as much like it was before as I possibly can. I hope the place still has that old feeling about it. I would like to think of it as homely. I might be striving for authenticity. I might be trying to defy the onset of irrelevance.

I simply can't leave. If I did, the walls would fall down. They think I am ridiculous working behind a bar at my age, but I'm barely seventy. Anyway, I'm happy. I like my little patch of earth. That's the great irony of being accused of being unrealistic. If there's one thing I'm good at it's having my feet on the ground.

All this must have made me drop that schooner glass. Most nights I move automatically, but tonight I was thinking too much. The sound embarrassed me, even if it was only Louie in the bar to hear it. I wonder if the shattered glass was proof I'm past the age that you can honourably retire, before you begin to be accused of a lack of reality.

After closing, I sit in the kitchen and stare at your letter. I trace its familiar texture with a finger, testing my answer. My feet are so firm on the ground these days that they have roots. If I tear them up the soil will go to dust. But it wasn't always like this.

five

Your stories held me, May. I let myself live in them, resting my head on your lap in the grass, your hands in my hair. I miss that. What else have I done with my life but try to restore it? Even the press is an attempt to atone. I am a caretaker for other people's pretty lies.

It's almost certainly too late to salvage some common understanding, some trivial acknowledgment, from the wreck of what might have been a great knowing. I didn't just let go of you. I let go of a whole self I have never recovered. I fell from Grace.

I am tired. You don't belong in the false-bottom pocket of my suitcase with a dozen spent tickets and all those maps of cities that may as well have ceased to exist. Memory suffocates. Better to invent the ways one might have lived. This is one of the secret joys of travelling alone: a mastery over stories. There is no one to corroborate or deny.

Except that you have been my other eyes. Every temple, palace, mountain, sea, I pull at your sleeve. 'See this?' I say. 'Look, it's beautiful.' It's a habit, talking to you.

Love never relents. It's a perpetual voice, lodged in the part of the brain that automates breath. What is that? The medulla something? I will ask the nurse. Maybe that's the part that's broken.

An invisible cancer of the mind. It's quite a comparison. A little dramatic, but then, I always was.

I would have to go and faint in public like that. When I came to on the beach, a couple of young women were standing over me. One bent to see if I was all right, the other brandished her mobile phone. They conferred over me as if I wasn't there: 'Should I ring the ambulance?' 'Yeah, better.'

The black and grey spots of pebbles were enormous in my face. Between two stones there was a peek of something round and green: a hunk of glass polished smooth by the sea. I pocketed it without thinking.

I pull apart paper flowers today. They gave me some fake ones. I dismantle them very slowly. Someone comes in while I do this.

'Oh, Grace,' she says. 'All the hard work that went into them.' Somehow, by pulling them apart, I have taken all the hard work out of them. Where did it go?

You can have breakfast for as long as you like here. Sometimes it takes up most of the day. Then I read the newspapers, the reviews, and the only book I have brought with me, an old hardbound volume of Proust which is so depressing I'm surprised they haven't confiscated it.

I press the paper flowers in my book, even though they are already dead. Dead wood pressed into paper, shaped into the form of a plant. The book is dead wood too. Artifice upon artifice. I press them in secret. They are in a progression from budded to wide open. I have to tear them.

I try to explain this to the nurse. I tell her that everything tears everything else. To let this happen is not the same as being a victim of circumstance. To let this happen is the ultimate act of courage. Surrender is a leap of faith. Relinquishing the will is an act of overcoming. I try to draw meaningful conclusions from what is basically misbehaviour. She sees through me, but she doesn't take my book away.

I will check myself out soon. I should appreciate the comfort but I have had enough. They treat me too much like a child. I can't explain to them that as a child I was treated as an adult. My father used to shake my hand and call me comrade. Being a communist is a harmless eccentricity now that we have transferred our terror to the terrorists.

They let me out, of course. It is not one of those involuntary places. Sometimes I go for walks in the town. It is a young town, full of students making efforts to be colourful.

I see you everywhere, in every age, in every body. Sometimes I follow them. I give them your face, as I remember it. But they turn, and they wield the faces of strangers.

If I unsteel myself to memory, unsteal the faces of you, I can't quite breathe. I refuse to give the strangers back their masks.

If I unsteel myself. To love you is like that. You are a stranger.

I am tired; my ups and downs come too rapidly. Love is for strangers. I should know. Oh, they might charm me, and then I remember that's all there ever was to love: an outstretched hand, a moment's entertainment. Clothing spread out across the floor like an exhibit. Everything after you, that is.

There is no age at which one suffers less. Only now that I am older, it no longer has the advantage of surprise.

The doctors gave me a personality test. They haven't told me yet if it came back positive. My favourite question: 'Do you pretend to be a better person than you really are?'

'You know,' I said, 'occasionally I catch myself pretending to be worse.'

I thought they would enjoy that, but they didn't react at all. I imagine all my answers to be banal to them. I wonder if the doctors do anything to make the exercise more interesting. Lay bets with each other, perhaps, or play a guessing game. They write everything down. The thought of my answers floating on pages like that, autonomous, frightens me. I should be used to it. Anyway it is better they do not leave the pages blank.

I reserve the best observations for you. Not that I have anywhere else to put them. The greatest writers I have known, and I count R reluctantly among them, write the tersest letters. He hardly wrote to me, he abbreviated. He even contracted his affection to a cross (which I bore, ha ha). I asked him once why he used full sentences in notes to the maid but always wrote to me in shorthand. 'She can't be relied upon to grasp subtext,' he said. I was left with the space between the lines.

I wrote you blank cards with a precedent.

Although I had money and a maid and enough wives of his friends to keep me company, and it should have been easy without children to care for, I never made a very good wife. I wanted to at first, when I still had marriage confused with freedom. My ticket out of the backwoods. When I had the arrogance to believe it was me he wanted and not the credit for who I was. Never having had to struggle himself, I suppose he thought it was his duty to carry me up a class. If he couldn't be a self-made man like so many of his peers, he'd make himself a woman.

I told him once that I thought it was fortunate that our generation was too young for the war, forgetting as I often did that he was old enough to fight. He might have died somewhere, like your brother. Liberating Germany, or getting syphilis in a Dutch whorehouse. He was drunk for three days after that conversation.

I was never one to placate egos, to smooth things over. I considered it a waste of my intelligence to be polite and careful. And yet I've made my business the promotion and care of other people's talent. But my writers *don't expect too much from me. If they are fragile they eventually end up elsewhere.*

My partnership in the business is becoming more and more silent. I did try to set it up as a feminist collective, but the others resented my divorce money, while openly delighting in my little triumph. I now have a staff that I respect enough to stay my hand. I am invisible. This means I don't have to live in London ever again, if I don't want to. I keep the flat as a place to stay between countries. London is not itself anywhere except London. Though it would take an Australian of my generation to call it neutral territory.

Do you remember why I didn't want children? I didn't want to become one of those women who only has one topic of conversation. I didn't want to commit to anything for twenty years. I didn't want responsibility, or to have to stay in relationships that didn't work for the sake of a third party. Well, I've done all that anyway, for the sake of the press. And now I've put it behind me like an empty-nester, and am wondering suddenly, as though on waking, where I am and what I'm doing with my life. Now I'm free again; free to fill myself with doubt and become lost.

But I was always lost. An image looms at me of you in that dingy little room I had with the Greek woman in Sydney, the sun coming in the window and the smell of honeysuckle and fried eggs. You sleeping or feigning sleep as I pretended to read beside you. Wanting to wake you so that we could make love again.

I can read no further. My eyes are watering. It is the strain of reading in the half-light, in the small hours.

I have to polish my glasses again. Feels like I'm always

polishing glass even when I'm not behind the bar. The contact lenses they gave me were bloody annoying so I turfed them down the sink. My eyes are all right, the glasses are just for reading and writing.

These things happen gradually, without my noticing. A gentle fade. Sometimes, though, things fall apart suddenly, without any provocation. The Danker is living proof of this. I go to sleep thinking every inch of it is solid and in the morning a post will have leaned, a door will have sunk on its hinges, a rusted sign will have shucked off its weathered nails and be hanging by a corner.

I do the repairs myself, mostly because I can't afford to get tradies here every time something breaks. I've always fixed everything myself, with the help of the odd customer since Ted went. It's called responsibility.

We have grown together in this way, the Danker and I. It is part of our conspiracy that we keep each other afloat. The place still rattles and snaps at me, makes the odd joke, keeps me on my toes, but I know it feels looked after. It might be stubborn of me, it might be unrealistic, but this is my home. Neither of us is going anywhere.

It's a perfect morning. Even the Pacific resembles its name for a change. One black speck of a surfer is out there, a punctuation mark at the end of a wave. He or she must be learning, because it's flat as a tack out there. I hear Ted's voice as I think this, young and calm and ponderous. *Flat as a tack*, it's his phrase. Beth jumps out of Ted's chair, the chair he used to splay himself in at this hour, stirring three sugars into his tea. He'd drink half of it in a gulp before announcing that he might go and see if anything's biting, as if this wasn't something he did every morning. Beth's out the door before I can apologise, frightened of ghosts as always. She resents sharing her space with so many of my memories.

I wash my mug under the tap and pick up a book to wait out the morning. It's not always like this. Sometimes I have lots of work to do, but I've been letting things slide a little. I've been thinking too much.

It's Friday today and it's likely we'll be empty till five or six anyway, unless Louie pops down early, or some off-season tourists come through. By six there'll be a 'crowd' – a dozen locals on their way to the RSL where the drinks are cheaper but you need a few under your belt to handle the atmosphere. Some of them like to wait here until after the minute's silence. That's the kind of place we are now: a quiet one on the way somewhere else.

I abandon the book. It's a bland historical novel that Lisa gave me for Christmas. I don't have time for the Renaissance. I suspect she lets the Rat's secretary do her shopping. One of these days I'll slip and call him that to his face.

In one of those maternal coincidences, the phone rings and it's my daughter, battering me with details and efficiency. She still sounds like a self-important thirteen-year-old on the phone. She's not coming down for breakfast on Sunday either. Ernie's got a cold.

'Make sure he drinks plenty of liquids,' I say, and get an exasperated noise from the line.

'I know, Mum.'

My daughter and I exasperate each other frequently. It's probably petty, but she started it. As a teenager she was always frustrated by my version of order. 'You're the only mother in

51

the world who makes a mess of her kids' rooms,' she'd complain. She treated me as if I was a younger child who needed instructing. All my advice was outdated, my mothering hopelessly inadequate.

I respect her, of course. She has her grandmother's spine. We are just playing a game. I think we both derive too much entertainment from the dynamic of mutual exasperation to abandon it. I know she doesn't really resent me, because I've heard her on the phone to the Rat when she's visited without him.

'Yes, everything is fine,' she says. 'Mum's great,' and there's no strain in her voice.

Of course, she could know that I'm listening.

My friend Clare thinks Lisa is rebelling against growing up in a pub. I told her I grew up here and I haven't rebelled.

'Not yet, you mean,' she replied.

Clare's our latest eccentric. It was a month ago, maybe two, when she first appeared in the bar. She turned a slow circle, taking the place in, and then slid herself onto a stool in front of me. She's only young, in her late twenties, with spiked black hair and black eyes. She was wearing a stringy jumper which was more hole than wool. I don't usually bother with the blow-ins, but I sort of took to her.

'What can I get you?' She ordered a black beer. I should have picked it from the black everything else.

'You look tired,' I said as I passed her drink over. 'Travelling through?'

'Been moving house all day.'

'Where to?'

She said the name of the street, the house up the top. I still think of it as the dandelion woman's house, but it has since been colonised by generations of young people, all piled in together. The yard is clean and mown now, and a newish place stands straight and tall in the front by the street, but the old stone building still leans against a tree at the back.

'In the old house?' I asked, and she nodded.

'My new studio.'

'You paint?' She nodded again, took a sip of her beer and watched me over it with alert eyes.

'Oh, you an artist?' Louie joined in. 'I'm an artist meself.'

'Bullshit artist,' I corrected him.

He leaned towards Clare, tilting his stool at a dangerous angle. 'You should come around and see me etchings.' He cackled like a cockatoo.

'This is Louie. You can trust him with your life but don't believe a word he says.' I took his empty glass away and wiped the bar.

Unmiffed as ever, Louie took one of Clare's cigarettes out of the pack in front of her. She shrugged and drained her glass.

'Another?'

She shifted her eyes, which I took to mean that she had work to do.

'I'll have another,' Louie said hopefully.

'Course you will, Lou. Course you will.'

The story came out soon enough. Clare is mending her heartbreak up there with paint and canvas. She's retreated to avoid being left behind; the ex-partner took off to India on a spiritual mission.

'She wants to become a *nun*,' Clare frowned.

I was surprised when this made me blush.

★ ★ ★

53

I take the piece of polished glass from my pocket. It is not quite a diamond. I look through it at the light bulb. I see a blur. The last I saw of you, walking to the station in ill-fitting tweed, my eyes were blurred like this, matted by the light, the champagne, the thrill of an adventure, and by shame. Did this piece of glass cross two oceans to remind me what I threw back into the waves at Coal? They pound and pound. The very earth will dissolve.

I leave it up to you. We can write, at least. Live out the rest of our lives in the company of words. I give you this address, they will forward things to London if and when I get out, once I have recovered from my little fit.

They are very good here, really. I will entrust this to the young male nurse who changes the flowers in my vase as if they were real. Perhaps I will ask him to bring me some real ones. White lilies, as there are no red-bristled bottlebrushes here. White lilies will do.

I offer you the choice, May. No, I challenge you. My hand stretches ten thousand miles across the ocean. If you're still there, I want you to take this hand and tug it like a rope, pull me ashore. There is something there, there must be. I can still see you in the glittering palace of a pub that once bewitched me. In the mustiness of every hotel mattress, I can smell your body. Beyond the rumble of this sleepy sea I hear the roar and howl of our Pacific. In every story, I hear an echo of your voice.

Tell me a story now, and make it true. True south is what I need. I cannot navigate blind.

There's only one story I know that can turn a compass, Grace, and that's yours. Stop me if you've heard it before. I know you were there. But if you're in that place now, if you don't trust your memories, then you mustn't see yourself as I do. As the heart of it. Of course there was something there.

six

You were born in a tiny house, one in a row of terraces which were only distinguishable by their varying states of decay. It was in the slums of Sydney, back when the inner city had slums. There was no food in your kitchen, no electricity to light your parents' nights. There was nothing but the fire and a belief in a better world to keep Jack and Faith Harper warm at night.

They were revolutionaries, fighters of fascists, dreamers. They were card-carrying communists, and they were about to bring their first child into a world that cried out for change. Faith didn't stop attending meetings, even when she had to walk with a hand in the small of her back.

She loved the story of your birth. I've heard it so often it's like I was there. If you listen to them hard enough, if you retell them to yourself, other people's memories can almost become your own.

Your mother was alone in the house when her waters broke one afternoon. She yelled through the thin walls for her neighbour to get the doctor, who lived a few blocks away. Your father was on his way home from a miners' meeting, where he'd been trying to negotiate conditions. He came in waving *Common Cause*, the union paper. He was so excited, he forgot to remove his cap.

'Listen to this, Faith,' he said. 'Events in Spain leave us breathless!'

She was breathless enough already. 'Shut up, Jack, and boil some bloody water!'

He looked up and jumped when he saw the doctor bent over his wife's splayed legs. Jack tipped his cap to the man and fumbled his way to the small kero stove in the corner to put the kettle on. Once he had the thing lit, he stepped back, but not knowing where else to put his eyes or his voice, he continued to read aloud. 'The heroic masses of Spain are fighting a terrific battle against the forces of Fascism and reaction: a fight fraught with grave danger to the peace of Europe and the world, a fight in which all those who are opposed to fascism should be interested . . . What do I do with the water?'

'Stick your arse in it and see how I feel!'

'There now,' the doctor murmured. 'Breathe.'

'I'm breathing, for fuck's –'

'That's it,' he said calmly, and Jack continued.

'It says here, the Spanish people are fighting the fight for the people of the democratic world; they are fighting so that another country shall not fall into the foul hands of fascist reaction . . . the forces of reaction in this city are applauding the advance of fascism in Spain as an antidote to the menace of communism . . . Menace!'

The doctor, who was not a communist, mopped his brow with a handkerchief and kept his head down.

When Jack got to the part about Britain sending planes to Franco, your head crowned.

'There's a ban,' your mother exclaimed between clenched teeth. 'Reactionary –' and screamed you out along with a profanity.

'It's a travesty!' Jack declared. 'A betrayal!'

'It's a girl,' the doctor muttered.

'Grace,' your mother declared, and passed out.

The Harpers saw no conflict between child-rearing and the struggle. Faith saw no reason why she should become housebound. They handed you back and forth between them as they each rushed off to their committees, disputes, party meetings and rallies. Faith took you with her when she went to work in the textile factory. Jack took you along to union meetings. At marches, they carried you down the street between them wrapped in a red rag, and you loved the bright colours, the whistles and trumpets, and the singing.

Your parents were good, strong fighters and they made a formidable team. Jack was the showman, the man of the grand gesture, the man of ideals. Faith was a genius at what they now call networking, which we used to call the art of getting other people to do things for you. But none of it was easy on them; it was no settled life.

You moved around a lot when you were small. Your father was constantly running from the fights he got into: dockyard disputes, busted night raids, bar brawls that sprung out of political disagreements. The unions might have been strong then but there was always someone who had to be paid off, bought out, argued with, or blackmailed. Certain people were unhappy with your father's ideas. Jack was forced to flee Sydney before he ended up at the bottom of the harbour with rocks in his pockets.

With no sign of the war in Europe abating, the potential withholding of coal was an important weapon for workers everywhere. Jack's experience with both dockworkers and miners made him perfect for the role of negotiator, and the union decided to move him down to Coal. The promotion meant that Faith could stop working at the factory and focus on the struggle. You were old enough to go to school, and Faith was ready for a quieter life – one without so many threats to her safety. They packed their flags and pamphlets in the bottom of the pram and climbed onto the train.

When I first met you, you had a blue-tongue in your apron pocket. The lizard lay still against your warmth. It made no attempt to escape. A thick length, a grey weight the size of your arm: some stories have a shape.

You stood at the edge of the scrub that led up to the Danker. Your bright blue eyes watched the waves in wonder. A few fishermen stood out on the rocks in rubber boots. The sight was as still and lively as a painting.

'Hello,' you said, turning to face me. I was standing a foot below you, trailing a toe in the warm sand. We stared, each sizing up the other, for a full minute.

You were thin, with the sickly skin of the city dweller. You had damp yellow hair and your exposed arms were cool and shining; you had just come out of the sea. Eventually I remembered to speak.

'I live there,' I said, pointing up to the Danker. 'Where do you live?'

Your brow furrowed and your hands felt for the pleats in your apron. 'I don't know,' you said.

'You have to live somewhere,' I said, wondering if you had really come from the sea like the people in my da's stories. If you had come to steal somebody away.

The bleak look faded from your face and your smile came out like the sun. 'I have a lizard,' you said. 'Look,' and you opened your pocket.

I leaned forward to find out if what you said was real or some mermaid's trick. I could see the scaly thing, its legs tucked beneath its body, and see the shiver in it. The creature, at least, was solid.

'You have to put it back,' I said. I knew the right thing to do with lizards. 'Give it,' I attempted gently. I put out my hand.

You strode off up the track, so I followed you. I was worried you would keep the lizard in your pocket until it died, but you knelt beside a big flat rock and lifted up your apron. You let its long, fat body roll out. It lay quietly on the stone, submissive for a moment, readying itself for another smash and grab, but your little hands left it alone. The lizard glared at you and stuck out its tongue.

'Look, it's blue,' you said. Your finger hovered dangerously close to its mouth.

'Don't scare it, it'll bite you.'

You shoved your hand in your pocket.

'Go on,' I said softly. I could talk to things then. The creature blinked at me and ran under the stone. When it had gone, we both stood up. You turned and climbed the track towards the Danker, and I followed.

'There,' you said, and pointed. We were standing at the top of the track. I could see all the houses on the north side of

Coal, where it narrows, nuzzling against the sandstone. We still called that place shanty town, even though only a few of the houses remained, on cleared blocks. They were still hardly more than shacks. Your finger pointed to a small wooden house with a veranda that stood on the other side of Cullen's place. 'That's where I live.'

Having vindicated yourself, you turned to face me. 'I'm Grace,' you said. 'What's your name?'

'May. Or Mary.'

'How come you have two?'

This I didn't know how to explain. The grand façade of the Danker stood glittering before us on the headland like a fairytale palace. Lacework hung on the balconies and sunlight shimmered on the iron roof. Bright advertising signs shone from its face, urging the cockatoos hanging upside down in the branches of nearby trees to try a number of refreshing beers.

'The Danker has two names,' I explained. 'One's short.'

'What's the Danker?'

'That,' I said proudly, and pointed at the bright mess of my home.

'Oh.' You stared at it, mesmerised. 'It's beautiful.'

Someone called your name from the beach below, and the smile went behind a cloud. Without another word, you turned and ran back down to the sand, back to where you came from. It was so bright that the sun's reflection almost blinded me; I couldn't see whether the waves had swallowed you.

When I reached the kitchen door, I looked back down at the beach. I could see your figure trailing behind two other, certainly human forms. You hadn't vanished after all.

★ ★ ★

60

Later that week, you came up to the pub at teatime, on an official visit. Your parents came looking for a feed and a bit of company, drawn to the warm light and the cold beer. After you'd eaten, Mam invited Faith into the kitchen. We sat on the floor beneath their feet, immediately drawn into our own little world. I don't remember what we talked about, if we spoke at all, but I can still see your face, narrow and intelligent in the shadow of the kitchen table and I retain the sense of a secret conversation beginning.

While our mothers watched us, our fathers leaned on the bar and had a yarn. I could hear their voices through the swing door. My da was laughing. He had started laughing at Jack from the moment he explained his position, and he barely stopped to interrupt.

'So, you've been sent here to teach us how to organise, have you?'

'Well.' I heard Jack fidget with something and cough. 'It can't hurt, can it. Bit of help.'

Da grew serious. 'It's all very well saying you're here to help, but don't tell us we need you. We've done quite well on our own. All this time we've been asking for support from the union, and now that there's enough jobs to go around, we finally get it.'

'I'm an expert,' Jack said, 'I know how to get things out of the bosses. I'm not saying you need me. But I'm only here to do my best and make sure everyone gets the pay and conditions we deserve.'

'What we deserve,' Da muttered, 'depends on what we expect.'

Jack took a pouch from his trouser pocket and rolled himself a cigarette. 'We should all expect to be equal,' he said. 'That's the basic premise. The bosses are ripping us off. This land, this earth, is the birthright of the working class.'

'No it's not,' said Da, refusing a cigarette with a wave of his hand. 'Another country was mine, and that was taken away. I left all that behind. Birthright doesn't mean a thing to me. Not here.'

I could tell from the way her feet tapped under the table that Mam was listening to several conversations at once. Above us, Faith was enthusiastically telling her about the house.

'It's bigger and brighter than anything I've ever seen,' she said. 'I don't know why we never left Sydney until now, only we get so caught up in the struggles. It's so peaceful here. I hope I can adjust.'

'We always do,' Mam replied.

Meanwhile, Jack was trying another tack. 'You worked all over for a pittance before. Don't you realise you've been exploited?'

'Who by? Look, mate, maybe you were born into a family that expected something, some kind of reward for being alive. Maybe you grew up thinking you deserved a stinking wage and a mortgage and to die with enough in the bank for a decent burial. I didn't. Everything I have is due to my luck. I have the Danker by pure chance and another man's bankruptcy to thank for it. And I know that's all it is, dumb luck. Which most of the people around here haven't had much of. Nor did we ever expect to. When you live in sacks, six to a room . . . well, you can't be angry at something taken away if you never had it.'

'But if we organise, we can have it. There's enough to go around if we only take it.'

Da smirked at this and cleared the glasses off the bar. He touched the place on his knee where the scar rose like a hill, his reminder of the bicycle gang.

'The worst is already over,' he said. 'There's the war now, and jobs enough. You're late. Anyway, we weren't all sitting around waiting for you to come and save us.'

Jack looked sheepish, but he persevered. 'Don't you believe in the struggle?'

'I believe in nothing,' said Da. 'Just the hand in front of my face.'

I knew he was lying. He was the one who filled my head with tales about banshees and mermaids.

'I want a better world,' said Jack. 'That's all I want.' He emptied his glass. 'I might not know this town from a bar of Sunshine, but I mind what happens to it. To all of us.'

'That's more than anyone's asked of you,' Da said, and took the glass away to fill it. He returned and held it out with ceremony.

'Well, you've got my welcome,' he said. 'Good luck with the rest of 'em. They're not an easy bunch, but when you get to know 'em, you'll see.'

Jack set to work trying to organise the little cluster of miners into a force to be reckoned with. In turn, they set to work convincing him that a hard day's labour wouldn't kill him, and they were quite organised enough, thanks very much. Union or no union, the resistance to a bloke from the city coming down to tell them how to run things was inevitable.

On one of the first nights he spent in the new shack, Jack awoke to a rustling sound. He got up and peered out the window. There were figures outside, barely visible in the moonless night. Tom Cullen and his eldest Tim, Greg Barrett, and young Victor Gowan were marching into his yard as silently as drunk men could. Tom, the leader of the group, was carrying a pick. The second man was carrying a dead rabbit, wrapped in a red rag and sporting a pin that one of them had lifted from Jack's coat, an emblem of allegiance to the Soviet Union.

Jack waited until he heard the men approaching the porch. He knew where the board creaked, and timed his response. He pulled open the door to the sight of Tim holding up the rabbit while Tom prepared to stick it to his front door with the pick.

They looked at one another, embarrassed. Jack held out a hand which none of them dared shake.

'Thanks for the welcome,' he grinned. 'Hope you brought some rosemary. Can't abide rabbit without a bit of rosemary.'

'Um,' said Tim, letting the rabbit dangle and looking to his father.

Tom merely shrugged. 'We was just having a laugh,' he said.

'Fair enough,' Jack replied. 'I don't know about you, but hunting rabbits makes me thirsty. I've got some Scotch in the cupboard. Come in for a drop?'

The drink quickly killed their embarrassment. After a few tumblers there were five men laughing at your kitchen table, and Jack had been accepted.

Meanwhile, I was trying to work out a way I could forge my own allegiance with you. I got my chance when I had to go up the hill to steal from the dandelion woman.

In spring, when dandelions are in flower, you can only eat the bright green leaves; the rest is poisonous. Before they flower, though, you can pull the plants out by the stalk, roots and all. There was nothing dangerous about the dandelions, but I still refused to gather them alone. They were far too fiercely guarded.

To me, the dandelion woman was a terrifying old witch who

64

lived in the rotting stone cottage halfway up the escarpment. Back then, it was surrounded by the bush. If she caught us in her yard, she would uproot herself from her porch and give chase, her hair and ragged dresses flying. We were all petrified of her, but Mam needed the medicine. She brewed a thick bitter tea from the roasted roots and fed it to Da for his liver, an antidote to the whiskey of which he was deeply fond. Usually, she sent at least two of us, but this time she asked only me.

'Oh, Mam, can't you send one of the boys to come with me?'

'The boys are helping your da with the deliveries.'

'Please!'

'Now, May,' she frowned, and I could hear in those two words the hint of the shouting down I'd get if I resisted her. I decided to change tack.

'Can I go and get Grace then?'

'Well, I don't see why not. Yes, that would be good of you.'

The mission to the dandelion woman's house was suddenly more exciting than terrifying. I tumbled out the door and ran across the grass until I reached the flowering gum tree. I ducked through the hole in the fence and bolted across Cullen's place to your house, quick as a rabbit. A backyard was a whole paddock to those small feet. This impression was aided by Cullen's cow, who eyed me sleepily as I rushed past her. Their old, three-legged dog raised an ear to suggest it would join in the fun if it was not otherwise occupied with its afternoon nap.

I landed on your back porch and stood to catch my breath. I knocked gently on the open door, hoping no one would hear me. I only knocked out of a habitual respect for thresholds; I didn't really want to give warning. There were sounds and smells in your house I wanted to appreciate while I stood in that doorway. The murmur of Harpers mixed with the notes of a gramophone record. I smelled eggs and a hint of printer's ink. The life inside had a strong suggestion of the exotic.

Before I had gathered enough of these details to satisfy my curiosity, Faith spotted me. 'May, what can I do for you? Have you come to borrow something for your mother?'

'No thank you, Mrs Harper, I've come to borrow Grace if I can,' I replied in my best polite voice.

'Call me Faith, child,' she said, and called out for you.

You came running down the hallway. Your bare feet made no sound on the raw boards. Unused to people my own age, I had difficulty speaking. Should I be polite? Direct? An odd sort of doubt began to grow in the centre of my chest, and I folded my hands into the pleats of my dress. We stood facing each other until your lips took on a quizzical twist.

'Dandelions,' I said. I swallowed and pointed up the hill. I grabbed your hand and tugged you away. We ran together as far as the road, then I let go of your hand and explained what I meant.

'Collecting dandelions for Mam, you want to help?' Which was a bit superfluous, because apparently you'd already agreed to come on this adventure blind. You merely nodded and I led the way into the bush. I crashed through the scrub and caught all the spider webs and scratches along the overgrown track. We stopped at the dandelion woman's fence and squatted, pressed against the wire, trying to catch our breath. We watched the little stone house for signs of fright. It was silent.

'She's not there,' I whispered. 'It's okay.'

'Who's not there?' you whispered back.

'The dandelion woman. She comes out and chases you and if she catches you . . .' I swallowed. 'We'll be quiet,' I said, aloud and brave. 'Follow me.'

We crept under the fence on our hands and knees and crawled through the grass at the edge of her property to the place where the best wild dandelions grew. They were weeds, used to a drier climate. In her yard, they had taken over. Huge bulbous buds grew two feet tall, the leaves rising up in circles around them like cabbages.

I believed it was a sign of witchcraft that the dandelions grew so high. The fact that we were gathering medicinal herbs for my mother never crossed my mind. As far as I knew from stories, witches didn't make medicine, they ate children.

With being eaten such a strong possibility, we were careful, but at that age we were not the most subtle of thieves. As we gathered the plants, I filled you in on the woman's mad dresses and dirty slippers, on her wild hair and monstrous cries. She was only old and poor, but to me she was a creature of mythic proportions, and worthy of awe.

You laughed at my descriptions, and the more warts I gave her, the more noise we made. Eventually we were both rolling around giggling.

It was then that I heard the creaking of her door. I lay flat in the long grass, but you couldn't resist raising your head to see the monster.

The dandelion woman spotted us and called out. To me she seemed to shriek like a galah. She slammed her door and shambled towards us. I stood and saw that one of her slippers had fallen off on the porch, a pink shape against the rotting wood. Like a hag Cinderella. At the bottom step, she stopped to kick the other one off. I grabbed hold of your arm and backed away.

We made it to the fence and ducked under it as quickly as we could without necking ourselves on the wires. The dandelion woman yelled something after us, but we didn't stay to figure out what it was. We ran for our lives, holding our skirts against our stomachs to carry the dandelions. I could hear that shriek following us down. the track. We kept running, ignoring the scratches of branches and leaping the fences of neighbours, until we arrived, hot and breathless, at my kitchen door.

'Mam, she chased us, I was almost eaten!' I panted.

'Oh, May, you and your imagination. She's only a harmless old woman.'

'If she's harmless, why don't you just ask her for these,' I asked, tipping the plants out of my skirt onto a wooden chair and prodding you to do the same. You gave a bright little curtsey as you presented your haul.

'Well,' Mam said, 'Mrs Green . . . she isn't well, is all. Now go and get out from under my feet.' She shook a sadness from her face.

Dismissed and at liberty, I took your hand in mine, and we set off together.

The two of us quickly carved a track across the back of Cullen's place where the hole in the fence let us reach each other faster. We made marks on this headland with our bare feet. And whenever we could, we ran out into the wild country to explore.

I can remember my childhood as a series of smells. The sea seemed fresher then, and much closer to our noses. There were different eucalyptus smells depending on the time of year: bushfire, decay, new growth after rain. Lantana smelt of bitter, musky flowers and a high probability of spiders. Coal was also saturated with the black dust that flew up from the processing plant and smelled like old pennies. It made sense that black diamonds, which saved us all when the mines were open, smelled like riches. This was before we knew anything about pollution, of course.

We knew about the dust though. It settled on every surface, and Mam said you needed the vigilance of a saint to keep it off. I took you to the railway line to steal the chunks of coal that fell from the train. Later we would come home covered in it, and Mam would shake her head and say we looked like wild beasts.

Wildness applied to everything, even the man-made structures that pulled coal out of the rock. No machine, however noisy, could intimidate us. We explored our world without much respect for borders or for laws. The only taboo places were the railway tunnel and the parts of the escarpment that were excavated into instability. I took you into the bush to skirt the edges of these abandoned shafts, holes in the earth with unknown depths of muddy water in the bottom. I showed you my favourite trees and told you the names of birds. I taught you the tracks I knew.

By some peculiarity of our parents' generation, you and I were the only girls in Coal of our age group, apart from Mercy Thorne. It must have been something to do with the mines, or something in the water, but all anyone had was boys. It's little wonder we forged such an immediate bond.

Mercy wasn't very strong competition for your friendship. As the daughter of old Thornbag, she was the only child representative of the ruling class in Coal. She lived in a brick house which wasn't falling apart. Her mother ordered her things from Sydney instead of going to the next town like everybody else. She was frequently ill and kept indoors. She smelled like proper soap. We all knew Mercy would come to a bad end.

She was a whole year younger than us, anyway. We were climbing trees in the schoolyard while she was still wetting her pants in front of the class. Tomboy that I was, I had little patience for her tears. My opinion was learned, of course. Mam and Da didn't always agree, but they were fiercely united against the coddling of children.

'Spoiled girl,' Da would say, every time the matter of Mercy was discussed at our table.

'Poor thing needs some fresh air and exercise,' Mam would add. 'Nothing like a bit of hard work to put colour in your cheeks.'

As she always judged health by the colour of our cheeks, my brothers and I thought we could get away with any number of lies. No guilty flush would put us in danger. That and Patrick's brilliant ability to tell a credible story would keep us safe, we thought, but we rarely succeeded in fooling her for long.

School was fantastic. To me, the tiny portable classroom that sweated in summer and cracked with cold in winter was a gateway to the rest of the world. What child doesn't get excited by the prospect of books, with their waiting possibilities? I was desperately impatient to learn, and in particular to read like my brothers could. Patrick had bought himself an atlas with his own money, and I wished I could decipher the names he read to me.

We were pressed behind wooden desks and given slates to make our letters on. It was slow and difficult to sit still, but there were days when our teacher, Mrs Gowan, a short, strong young woman with a long braid of brown hair, would take us out to the yard to look at leaves and insects, or down to the beach to examine the rocks for creatures. There were days when the world was so full of wonder that I was stunned. Back then, the sun was so bright you could have cut yourself on your own shadow.

There was a strip of bush behind the mine where a mountain of lantana grew, sticky-sweet but excellent cover. It was a good place to escape from adults. Most of the kids spent time there, you could tell from the lolly wrappers and the initials carved in the thick stem. Of all our explorations, I saved this place for last.

Hiding in the lantana that day, I watched your eyes run lightly over it all. I'd followed my brothers into every corner of the bush, but this was different. I was in charge.

'You got no brothers or sisters,' I said.

You rolled your head back to stare at the roof of leaves and sighed. 'Just me.'

'I was going to have a sister, but she died,' I offered.

'Faith says she can't have any more children because the world is too crowded,' you told the roof in a matter-of-fact voice. I felt a sudden stab of sympathy. I couldn't imagine what life would be like without the company of a gang of brothers.

'You can be my sister, if you want,' I proposed. I picked a branch off the lantana and pulled off the leaves.

You nodded slowly, but did not take your eyes off the canopy. 'It's like a house,' you said.

'Like a house,' I agreed. 'Imagine if we lived here.'

You lowered your eyes to mine. Their blue was strangely lit in the mottled shadow of the towering weed.

'Let's pretend,' you said.

★ ★ ★

71

I started with my father's tales, of course, as they were what I knew. But it wasn't the fantasy creatures of childhood that really drew me; it was our bush, here. I don't know why, but I started at the top of the escarpment.

The swaggie was a local legend. An occupant of the shanty town, a stranger who never told anyone his name or where he was from. He only spoke to say what work he could do. He lived in a solitary shack further up the escarpment than the rest. They called him 'the hermit' or 'that mad bugger up the hill'. He didn't get a lot of work but never complained of the hunger; he'd go bush now and then and live off the odd possum or rabbit, which he shared with whoever came to his canvas flap of a door.

As time went by, the hermit shared his tucker and his time less and less with the expanding population of the shanty town. He disappeared into the bush for days at a time. Eventually he stopped appearing in town.

It was said he never left the escarpment, unless he came down to fish off the point, or sneak round our houses at night. When socks went missing off the line or we misplaced something in the pantry Da used to joke. 'That's the hermit,' we were told as children. 'Watch out he doesn't come for you next time.'

This could even be his country. That would explain the possums, the reticence about telling his neighbours where he was from. The necessity of isolating himself from a growing crowd of white men fighting for their bread. After a long time – way beyond a reasonable lifespan – the hermit became a part of Coal's folklore. Children would warn each other that the old man on the cliff would catch and eat you. We rarely ventured up there after dark.

It was only much later, when I met Aunt Betty, that I learned there were real spirits on that escarpment. Bright and green in the mornings, by afternoon there is something sinister about the place. When the sun sinks behind the cliff at three or four o'clock, the bush drops its veneer of colour. In the darkness beneath, it fills with the shrill cries of cockatoos and the chatter of trees battered by offshore winds. There are other sounds that have no obvious cause, voices that seem to belong to the shadows themselves.

There are shapes up there I recognise. In the sandstone at the top of the cliff, if the light is right, you can make out a human figure, its thin, bent arms raised in threat or warning. The stones seem so heavy and precarious, they should have fallen long ago. But they stay there, as if biding their time.

We fitted into each other's lives so quickly, I might have invented you. Perhaps I'd been waiting for something exactly your shape and size to arrive. I had dreamed up my match from the other side of the horizon. I was growing out of believing my father's stories, but I never lost the impression of your having wandered out of the sea.

You took to the water as if it was your natural element. When the waves were gentle, we splashed around in the shallows without a care in the world but to amuse our mothers on the shore or to catch up with my gang of brothers. When the waves were rough, we jumped them together, daring them to pull us under.

Often, it was only Faith on the beach watching us. Our mothers had formed a quiet alliance, but they soon saw that while their heads were both strong and set, their differences were absolute. Where Faith had her shining socialist future, Mam had Heaven and its angels. Where the Harpers had a poster of Lenin on their wall, my mother had a cracked plaster statue of the Virgin propped on the kitchen windowsill. Still, they tolerated each other's differences. And Mam was probably delighted that I was being kept busy.

Even if Coal's tiny size – the war had reduced the population substantially – hadn't made our socialising inevitable, it would have been impossible for anyone to tell me to stay away from you. I was dazzled. You were a charmer, Grace, even at that age. You were able to play at whoever the other wanted you to be, with a natural generosity that didn't embarrass anyone.

Besides which, you looked up to me. Not as an idol, but as a trusted source. I knew the answers to your questions about Coal, I knew how this piece of country worked. And what I didn't know, I could invent.

My da was the authority when it came to explanations. If I had a question, Mam would tell me the right answer straight off, but Da would tell me the prettiest one he could think of.

I remember asking my parents what was on the other side of the ocean. Mam frowned and said 'New Zealand', but Da launched into pirates, islands, treasure, and lost cities, and Mam muttered about filling our heads with foolishness. She was right, of course. Like all good storytellers, he sowed dangerous seeds in our minds.

At school, we had an ancient, dog-eared copy of Hans Christian Andersen. It was so decayed that the spine was coming apart. Mrs Gowan would only let us read from it if we sat right beside her and she turned all the pages. I always begged to be the one to read aloud, but I couldn't manage without running a finger along the lines to keep track of the words. Usually she would lose patience and read to us herself.

You and I were sitting on the floor at Mrs Gowan's feet when she read us *Thumbelina*. The rain was so loud on the iron roof that I could hardly hear the words. Those pictures, though, are still etched into my brain.

When Thumbelina came across a dead bird, I sat up straight. This kind of thing happened to us all the time. I'd seen plenty of them lying motionless in the gutter, their eyes full of ants, their wings akimbo. Dead birds were something I knew about.

This bird was several times bigger than Thumbelina. Its size didn't seem to worry her, but its suffering did. The tiny miracle girl pulled a leaf over its body for a blanket. At this point, the bird came back to life.

My eyes went wide. I'd seen my share of dead things – chooks, rabbits, bugs and so on – and none of them ever did that. I thought once you were dead you stayed dead. What if I was wrong? Someone should have explained to us that it was just frozen, but to a bunch of beach kids in a hot tin classroom, that was impossible. None of us had ever seen snow. Being young and used to learning new and surprising rules about life, I trusted Mr Andersen's judgement more than my own.

Later that week, I woke in the night. It was after closing, and the Danker had been left to its own devices. A strong offshore wind made it squeak and cry; the noise must have woken me. I checked that my brothers were asleep, slipped out of bed, and tiptoed down to the kitchen for an illicit drink of milk. I prised the foil lid off one of the unopened bottles and took a lick at the cream. As I replaced the foil, I heard a strange groaning noise coming from the pub.

The swing door between the house and the Danker was

never locked. I pushed it slowly open and slipped through into the dark hollow behind the bar. I was just getting tall enough to see over it, if I stood on my toes.

The place had a kind of mystery when deserted. It smelled different, of night air and dead fire as well as the usual pungency of tobacco and stale beer. There was only a sliver of moon hovering over the water. You could see the stars through the windows, millions of them, and the little silvery pieces of moonlight grabbed down by the sea. There was no sign of anything that might have groaned, and I was just about to give it up as the wind when I saw a boot on the floor.

The boot was sticking out in the space under the trapdoor, in the gap that separated the bar from the pub. I slipped under this and saw that the boot was not alone. It, and its twin, were attached to the legs of my da, who was lying prone on the carpet with his head under a stool.

Da had been in a bad patch that week, ending his evenings with too much drink, and Mam had taken to leaving him wherever he passed out. I crawled around to his head and carefully moved the stool away.

'Psst,' I said in his ear. 'Wake up.' He did not react. I pinched his nose; nothing. My da usually rolled around in his sleep, but this time he was motionless. I put a hand on his chest. I couldn't feel a heartbeat through the layers of his clothes.

'Da,' I said, closer to his ear this time, 'are you dead?' The Danker gave a menacing creak, but my da didn't budge.

The carpet came up easily, as it had been rolled out in small sections. I tugged at a corner of it and pulled it over his still body. I patted him gently, then sat back on my heels to watch him. Eventually, Da snorted in a great quantity of air and sighed it out again. Satisfied, I crept back up to bed.

When I came down to breakfast the next morning, Da was already at the table, tucking into several eggs and gulping his tea. Mam slid a plate in front of me. I snapped off a corner of toast and stirred my egg with it, not taking my eyes off Da.

'Don't play with it, May, eat it.'

Callum glanced at me from across the table. Patrick had already left for the day, off down the mine before dawn. Brendan had his nose in a book. I gave Callum a look I hoped was innocent, and he raised an eyebrow but turned his attention back to his plate. We ate in silence until Da finished, clattered his cutlery down and sighed.

'So,' said Da, wiping his mouth on his sleeve, 'which one of you jokers decided to roll your poor father up like a swaggie?'

I hid my guilty face in a mouthful of eggs and looked from Brendan to Callum and back.

'I've heard of sweeping it under the rug, but Jesus,' my da continued.

'Don't hold us responsible for the works of Mr Jameson,' my mother said, taking his plate with a frown. 'It's your own fault if you can't take your drink.' This kind of remark always made him sit up.

'Now I may have had a nightcap or two,' ('Or seven,' Mam uttered under her breath), 'and I may have decided to kip down on the floor so as not to disturb you, my love, and to take a little rest in my own establishment. But I would never roll myself up in the carpet like a damn caterpillar! Imagine. What do you think I would be doing in a cocoon? Turning into a bloody butterfly?'

Me and the boys laughed uncontrollably at the thought.

'Shush, the lot of you. Time you went off to school,' Mam intoned, her morning litany. We pushed our chairs back and gathered our satchels.

'Either way I'm shaking that rug out today. My beard was dusty as a dead man's this morning!'

I gulped and backed away, beating my brothers to the door. I ran across the yard to the edge of Cullen's place, where you were waiting for me under the flowering tree that had become our meeting spot.

'I did it,' I said. 'Thumbelina!'

As we walked to school, I told you all about my da lying prone on the floor, my midnight rescue. In the tale I was guiltless, ministering heroically to a blinking Lazarus of a father. I took your hand and swung it mercilessly.

Your face had a flicker of doubt but you let it go. I wanted to glue myself to that little leap of faith.

'You have to promise not to tell anyone,' I insisted, squeezing your hand.

'I promise,' you said, and we stepped through the gate and into the schoolyard.

It was a normal school day. We must have learned something, but it wasn't distracting enough to take my mind off my achievement. By afternoon I couldn't wait to get out of the place.

On the way home, you spied a dead bird on the side of the road.

'Look,' you said and nudged me.

I paused. Here was a test. We squatted to conduct an experiment.

I pulled a leaf over it, then another, muttering an incantation I invented. I felt your eyes on me as I did this, and tried to appear vaguely competent.

'Watch this,' I instructed hopefully. We watched and waited

for the corpse to move. Its feathers were splayed out in the mud and the dead leaves didn't disguise the smell. A fly came along, picked at its gaping eye, then went away. Finally I lost patience and pulled the leaves back off the body. The bird was still quite dead. I poked it with a finger.

'I think it's been dead for too long,' I said, feeling helpless. 'Its soul must have gone to Heaven already.'

'There isn't any Heaven,' you said.

'What do you mean?' This was tantamount to saying there was no bird, no school, no me.

'Faith says it's only a story, and religion is the . . . the pea the masses ate.'

'What pea? Anyway, even if it is a story, it's got to be true.'

But we had no time to finish our theological discussion. The Cullen boys were coming down the street in a bundle, Tim the eldest in the centre, then Daniel, Alfie, and little Joe stumbling behind. Taking final glances at the bird and each other, we went our separate ways home.

As I crossed the road to the headland, I glanced at the beach below. I stood for a moment and listened to the waves crash and draw back, crash and draw back. When the ocean was laboured like that I felt its sadness. I wasn't sure that I was right, but I thought there had to be a Heaven. Mam had told me that was where we were headed, and I couldn't imagine myself going anywhere without you.

seven

Little Joe remembers that dead bird with me. He tried to pick it up after we were gone, but his brothers dragged him off it. He says he was only interested in it because we were.

Joe is still around. He was up this morning for a cup of tea after his swim in the lap pool. I tried to get him to stick around to meet Clare so they could talk about painting, but he just dismissed the idea.

'Oh, she doesn't want to talk to me, I'm only a dabbler,' he said. Joe paints for himself, never selling much. It's his form of domesticated problem-solving, he says.

I glance up from the page and I start. In the corner of one window, something has moved. In that warped old glass the outside light has made the shape of a face. I've been awake for too long, the corners of my eyes are starting to spook me. When I go up to the pane and peer through it, I just see outside: the fence, the headland, the light of a cargo ship waiting on the horizon. The familiar.

It's no wonder I used to set my ghost stories up on the

escarpment, in the less predictable bushland that towers over us. I'm sure that old swaggie really lived up there once, his story simply carved into the rock.

I want to go back to that simplicity. Childhood belongs to the invented and the unreal, not the static facts of history. Though history invaded our lives.

Maybe we tried to avoid reality because of the war. But even in peacetime it would have made sense to pretend together. We were connected to each other by some powerful kinship that didn't work in blood lines. An imagined belonging, so fragile, yet so hard to dislodge.

Was it all a relation of mind? Is that why you're losing yours and I'm forgetting mine?

eight

We learned what war was on a wall map so stuck with tacks it was tearing in places. Our boys were brave in punctured cork and ragged paper. Mrs Gowan taught us who the King of England was, and where England was, and (somewhat reluctantly) who ruled the waves. How Australia was discovered by Captain Cook in 1770 (and that was the beginning of the story). There was a neat order in belonging to a far-off country, imaginary and at the same time more real than this one.

We also learned what to do in an emergency. Emergencies generally involved a bomb being dropped on us. We were quite used to explosives going off, and thought it was all great fun, but many of the adults had begun to jump and look at the sky when the mine blasts echoed up the cliff.

In our second year at school, we practised what to do if there was an attack. It was supposed to be very serious, but seriousness was a hard thing to accept. Bombs might have hit Darwin, but most of us only vaguely believed in the existence of such a place. As the drills involved a lot of urgent running from one side of the yard to the other, they were very much like the rest of the games we played, except that we had to line up afterwards and be counted.

In autumn, Japanese submarines materialised in Sydney Harbour. This was a far more credible threat. We had all met people who had been to Sydney, if not visited the place ourselves. The entire school, a dozen or so children of varying ages, walked down to the water that afternoon and watched the waves. We squinted at the horizon and mistook dolphins for periscopes until hunger sent us home. We found no submarines, but the war found me. It did come out of the sea, in its own way.

My brother Patrick came home from the mine that afternoon with an announcement. Patrick was almost one of the adults to me. He was sixteen and had already been working down the pit for two years. He was tall, as tall as Da, and strong enough to carry me around on his shoulders. He could even have beers with the men. Still, sometimes he played hide and seek with the rest of us, or helped us build cubbies in the bush out of sticks and bark.

Patrick told Brendan and I to play outside, so we stood below the kitchen window and listened in. He had gathered Mam, Da, and Callum to the kitchen table. He asked them to sit down, and placed his grown-up's hands on the formica.

'I'm joining up,' he said. I gasped, and Brendan pinched me to keep me quiet.

'What?' Mam was rarely shocked. Her voice sounded strange, like it had jumped out of her throat.

'The navy, if I can. I don't want to be down the mine when I could be doing something.'

'You are doing something, Paddy,' Da said, calling him by his childhood name. 'They need coal just as much as fighters. Don't waste yourself.'

But my brother was restless, called by the sea. You could hear it in the tone of his voice. It was the same way he sounded when he told stories about faraway places that he dreamed he might visit. In the yard under the window, Brendan gave me a look. He held a hand to his lips and stood on his toes to see inside. Pushed out of the way, I drifted towards the door.

'I have to go,' Patrick was saying. 'I feel useless here. You don't need me.'

'Wait a while,' Da said. 'Just wait a while and see. Who knows, the war might be over tomorrow!' His voice was jolly, but forced; you could hear he wasn't convincing himself. Mam coughed, and I peeked in at the kitchen door. Callum was silent, staring at his hands in his lap. None of them were even looking at each other.

I marched inside and stomped over to Patrick. We were supposed to be proud of 'our boys', but I wanted mine around. I stared at his neck. A line of coal dust met his collar where he'd missed a spot with the washcloth. 'You can't go,' I said, 'who's going to tell us stories?'

'May, go outside.' Mam had finally noticed me.

'No!' I must have started to cry, because Patrick put a hand on my shoulder.

'You tell them, May,' he said. 'You know how.'

For a short while after that conversation, nothing changed except that I was relieved of most of my household jobs. Every time Mam found something that needed doing, she'd ask Patrick. She installed him behind the bar as soon as he got home from the mine, and if she was working alongside him she'd always be asking him to get things off the top shelves for her, though she'd never needed help before. More often, she would disappear upstairs to 'make the rooms', which meant she was having time to herself. Let off the hook, myself, Callum and Brendan would follow Patrick around and tease him mercilessly.

'Can you do my homework tonight, Patrick?'

'Mam wants *you* to wash the dishes Patrick.' He took it all in his stride, but he was still dreaming. In the evenings I was first in bed, but I often woke when Patrick turned in. He switched on a light by his bed and pored over his atlas, whispering the names of places to himself: 'Cairo . . . Thessaloniki . . . Tokyo . . .' To me, they sounded like incantations.

Despite Mam's best efforts, his spells proved stronger than her strategy. He passed the exams for the navy and prepared to leave us. I became terribly excited, not because he was leaving, but because we were all going to Sydney to see him off.

My first trip to the city! Apart from a few weekends to visit my grandparents' farm down near Nowra, it would be the first time I had left Coal. Newborn lambs were one thing, but this was a real adventure.

'Can Grace come?' I asked Mam the day before Patrick was due to sail. She'd just come down from 'making the rooms', and I thought it was a good time for favours. Unfortunately I had cornered her in the dark place at the bottom of the stairs, and noticed too late that her eyes were red.

'May, for once will you get out from under my bloody feet!' she growled. I didn't dare to press the issue, but it didn't matter. I would tell you all about it and, in the telling, who knows how grand an adventure it would become?

★ ★ ★

It was a grey day when we saw Patrick off at the Quay. The rain was so soft that it was barely more than a mist.

'This is Irish rain,' Da declared as we emerged from the train station. Callum strode ahead to where numerous boys in sailor's uniforms mingled with every kind of person imaginable. Sailors kissed girls openly in the street and mothers pressed handkerchiefs into sons' hands. Brendan and I hid behind Da and pretended to salute each other while Mam and Callum went looking for Patrick.

We waited a long time. Brendan and Da leaned on each other like two sulking horses. Da sang himself a quiet, sad song made up entirely of toora-looras. I marvelled at the sights and smells of the crowd, made an inventory of observations to share with you.

'Here he is!' Callum's voice strode out of the crowd, followed by Callum, who was dragging Patrick by one sleeve of his uniform. Mam was nowhere to be seen, and there was no time to wait. No one mentioned her absence. We said our goodbyes, hugged each other, and waved as Patrick climbed the gangplank.

Mam rejoined us then, clutching a small card in her hands. She stood near us to wave at the ship, and we all kept waving long after it disappeared into the mist. My brother was bound for the world across the sea, for pirate islands and mermaid songs, for the magic names he had conjured from his maps. I would sooner convince myself of this than believe in the great, dark shapes of enemy submarines, those potent new monsters of the deep.

On the train, Mam showed us the photograph. She had waited for the man to develop it instead of saying goodbye, traded a moment for an image. A false image, at that. Posed stiffly in a sailor's uniform, one hand on the harbour rail, my dear, dreaming brother already looked like a stranger. When we got home, Mam found a frame for the picture and placed it gingerly on the kitchen windowsill, next to the Virgin. She still hadn't shed a single tear for him.

I told you the story, of course, and you listened unquestioningly. I didn't lie to you, though I may have stretched my descriptions a little. Even now, it's hard to separate my memory from what was told. Once something is spoken aloud, it can acquire a weight that equals the truth.

We were sitting on the front porch of the Danker one evening, looking across the lawn to the scrub opposite. We weren't supposed to sit on the porch where people drank, but we managed to position ourselves right on the edge beside the railing so we could jump off if we were seen. We were fairly safe. Our fathers were deep in discussion about whether Russia was going to save the world from the fascists, and the bar was full enough to keep Mam busy.

After my brother went to sea, the war was close to me. I'd been touched by it, and I felt special. But fascism was a fairly nebulous threat to an eight-year-old. I was more interested in local enemies, like the rabbit.

There were always dozens of rabbits on this headland. That night, we watched them forage in the dusk. Their small, grey-brown shapes moved gently across the darkening slope. We were occupying our hands at the same time by breaking sticks into smaller pieces and throwing them at the trunk of the pine tree on the edge of the car park. My stick missed and landed beyond its target, startling a rabbit out of the scrub. The animal hopped out onto the grass and sat still as if it was waiting. I stared and stared. The rabbit was pitch black.

'That can't be a rabbit,' I said.

'It looks like a rabbit,' you replied.

'It looks like a rabbit-shaped hole in the ground.'

'It has eyes,' you pointed out.

'So? Even the devil has eyes.' I shifted uncomfortably on the concrete. 'It has to be a ghost,' I said.

Your eyes regarded me, wide and indigo in the half-dark. 'A ghost?' You whispered the word. I tried to look serious.

'I'll tell you the story,' I said. I picked another stick up off the ground and toyed with it while I began to improvise.

'A long time ago, there was a woman who was in a terrible despair,' I said. *Despair* was a new acquisition. 'She was in a terrible despair because her husband had died in the war. Not this one, the one before.' I knew there had been a war already before this one, a long time ago. But the women I knew without husbands were not in a great deal of despair. Perhaps they were too busy.

'One night, a night like this . . .' I paused for effect, enjoying myself. I looked around at the warm, cloudless sky, at the stars appearing gently against a blanket the colour of work overalls, the blue of our kitchen tablecloth, and changed my mind.

'A night like this,' I said, 'except darker, and with a cold wind howling. And a big storm coming up.' I pointed south, which was where storms came from. In the distance you could see the flaming tower of the smelter, the factory skyline lit up against the dusk.

'The woman climbed up here all alone. She walked to the edge of the cliff, and then . . .' I waved my stick, then held it still in the air like a wand. I leaned towards you. I pursed my lips, dropped the stick, and whistled a slow descent.

'Splat,' I concluded.

You gulped. 'She jumped?'

I nodded. 'The storm was so bad that no one could go out on the rocks to look for her. They never found her body. And when you see the black rabbit . . .' I paused to gather my story into a conclusion that would frighten you.

You gazed over at the scrub. The feral bunny reared its paws and folded back an ear before falling softly onto its feed of grass. Your face had gone blank. You stared slackly into the darkened scrub. I felt your body shiver slightly beside mine, a tremble perhaps. I flattered myself, for you pulled your cardigan around your shoulders.

'When you see the black rabbit,' I repeated, 'you know it's her, warning you. It means someone's going to die.'

'Who?' you asked, in the reverent voice of an owl. Your face was a half-moon in the gentle light from the pub. I glanced out at the dark water, and felt suddenly nervous. My brother was out there somewhere, battling submarines that could pull a whole ship down, crew and all, like giant squid.

I kicked at the stick where it sat in the dirt. 'It's just a story,' I said flatly.

The door behind us opened, and my heart skipped a beat. I turned my head. Mam had spotted us. She said nothing, merely stood with her arms folded and tapped her foot as we trailed in like two delinquent sheep. She sent me straight to bed.

I climbed the stairs to my room, but went outside to watch you from the balcony. You walked close beside your mother, holding her hand against the dark. As I watched, you looked over your shoulder at the scrub, gazed up at the Danker, and scanned the wrought iron for my face. I hid myself in the curling shadows and smiled with secret triumph.

★ ★ ★

After that, I grew bolder. I looked around for new victims, and (to my present shame) selected the most vulnerable.

The dandelion woman's status as a witch was an established fact, handed down to me by my brothers like one of their old jumpers that stretched to my knees. But I could do better. I soon decided that the eating of children wasn't frightening enough, especially when we could outrun her so easily. Instead, I devised new forms of evil.

I told you she only pretended cannibalism. In reality, she captured the children and conducted vile experiments on them. If she couldn't get a child she'd use family pets. When Cullen's three-legged dog disappeared, it was the witch, at least until the old animal was found curled up dead under their porch. When Mercy's mother had a deformed baby that died, I told you the dandelion woman was responsible. She brought about these strange occurrences by vague methods involving what I knew of science, knowledge I mainly gleaned from Brendan's toy chemistry set and the advertisements in the back pages of his comics. I imagined her up there in some kind of medieval laboratory, no childish witch with pointy hat, gingerbread and apples, but a scientist with glass contraptions, distilling souls above her fireplace.

We were terrified of her anyway, and these inventions made things a little more manageable. I still had to go up there and get the thick dandelion roots for my da's liver, and it helped if I could scare you on the way. I never thought of the cruelty of my actions, not even when the witch tried to end her torment.

I was loitering in the bar when a railway worker strode in, threw down his hat, wiped the sweat from his face and called for brandy. The man had mud on his shaking hands and a red cut across his cheek. Through chattering teeth he explained that the dandelion woman had been found in the tunnel, waiting for a train. The worker had seen her and pulled the emergency brake in time. He had carried her back to her little stone house, her ragged clothes soaked with rain. It was she who had scratched him on the cheek so hard that it bled.

We knew the place, of course. No one stole directly from the freight trains anymore, but us kids went near there for our pocket money. A bag of spilled coal collected from along the railway line would earn a coin or two, enough for ice-cream or fizzy drink from Charlie's shop across from the beach. The tunnel was off-limits to us. That rule was almost unique in being respected.

After they found the dandelion woman there, the rule was reinforced, but the respect ceased. The tunnel had become magnetic. Kids would dare each other to run past the point where the daylight reached, into the dark. I never did, too aware of the danger from my da's story about his knee, but you were always the first to risk it.

It was during the winter I was nine that you and I saw the last of the dandelion woman. The weeds had all but died off. We had no reason to linger at her back gate, except that we were idle, curious children with only each other for company and only Coal and its inhabitants to entertain us.

It was easy to imagine her dissecting frogs up there in her shack, especially after the railway incident, which had pushed her over some invisible edge. Mam said the doctor gave her something to calm her down, but she still looked wild to us. She stepped out onto her porch in her dressing gown and slippers and stared at us from under her bird's nest hair. We stayed where we were. She had nothing on us. Our hands were empty.

We watched her standing there for a long time, and she didn't chase us. She just stood with glazed eyes, holding onto the rotting porch with one claw-like hand, and coughed. A little smile played on her lips, and when she opened them we braced ourselves, ready for that galah cry. But instead of a scream we heard something even more terrifying. It was a high wail. A song, though it only had the bare bones of a tune. 'And did those feet . . .' she began. I watched her pink slippers.

We edged away slowly, reluctant to turn our backs on the frightening sound. Her wail followed us down the hill: '. . . and was Jerusalem builded here, amongst these dark Satanic mills.'

Later we sat on your back porch and you tried to get the knots out of my hair, which was always full of burrs. Neither of us had recognised the Protestant hymn.

'Satanic mills,' I said. 'Ow. Maybe it's a witch song.'

'If she catches pets,' you murmured aloud, 'what would happen if she caught the black rabbit?' We pondered this for a while, feet hanging down into the grass. Beneath us we had buried treasure a long time ago, but we now disdained our pirate finds of pennies and pretty shells, which was fortunate as we were also too big to crawl under the step.

'She'd die,' I said. 'No one can catch the black rabbit and live. Not even a witch.'

You stopped pulling at my hair and rested your hand against the back of my head.

'You shouldn't say that,' you murmured. But your voice wasn't scolding, it was spellbound.

The old woman never recovered from the soaking she got the night of the train. Pneumonia developed, compounding her existing madness with delirium. A week after we last saw her, she was dead. But she was only Mrs Green in the paper, widowed and benign. Mam said we were cruel to stalk the woman.

'Her with her nerves. And how would you feel in her shoes?'

'She never had any shoes,' I replied. 'Only those old pink slippers.' My imagination was adventurous, but my empathy was not yet sufficient for other people's footwear.

When her funeral was held on the following Sunday, all the adults went. I supposed this was from pity, because no one had had much to do with her when she was alive. It was only afterwards that I realised she was the woman who attended the births of each of their children, before those same children learned to tease her. She was the woman who delivered me into the world, and I had just about killed her.

While the adults were away at the funeral, you and I went looking for the black rabbit. We crouched as quietly as we could in the scrub, but could see no sign of the animal. We clambered down the headland and walked around on the rocks. The tide was a long way out, and the pools were full of interest. Sea slugs, anemones, periwinkles, starfish, the snaking fingers of some bright, crimson weed. We were soon distracted by the proliferation of life.

I could read the newspaper and I knew a few things about the war, but in my mind Patrick was fighting it by himself. I was always surprised the paper didn't mention him by name. We had a few letters from him and I read those too, but they were disappointingly factual, the stilted prose was out of character. I wanted adventures, not an itinerary.

In my stories, for which you were the only audience, my

brother was shipwrecked on a tropical island, rescued by mermaids, joined a band of pirates, and sailed the world. He went to all the places on his map and quite a few that I had only heard of in stories. I finally let him settle down in Africa, where he married a tribal queen and lived in a palace made entirely of gold teeth.

I knew you didn't believe me, but I kept talking anyway. The idea of Patrick walking around in stories made sense to me. They had always been his element. Besides, in the tales I made, the deep-sea creatures never pulled him under. He chopped at their tentacles with a sword, and they always sank back defeated.

On some winter nights, it was so cold that we were allowed to sit in the pub by the fire. You asked me for a story, either true or false. I looked around. Mam was safely out of earshot.

I conjured my brother from the fire, crowned him chief of the village. Because I had begun to forget his real-life face, he was a perfect likeness of his photograph. In uniform, in sepia, identical in all ways except for the crown made of bones.

A hand landed on my shoulder, and he vanished.

'Don't you make up lies about your brother, May. You pray for him.' Mam shook her head at me sadly and returned to her work. I watched her reinstate herself behind the bar and share a joke with one of the miners.

Prayer? Mam had her way, I had mine. I stayed by the fire with you and talked quietly until the coals were almost out. I knew that if I made it all true, I could really pull my brother out of the fire and bring him home.

A few months later, I saw the black rabbit again. It was spring, but there was still a chill in the air. The creature looked more cute than sinister, nibbling long grass in the afternoon sun. I wanted to run and tell you, but you were away with your parents at a party conference in the city.

'Ah, it's a silly made-up story anyway,' I thought. 'I'm almost ten, too old for it now.' I went up to the Danker instead, and pushed at the door to the pub. It was locked.

I walked around the back to the kitchen door. Mam and Da were sitting at the table, Callum was getting the tea, and Brendan was hanging onto Mam like a much younger boy. Mam was staring out the window, her gaze stretching beyond the Virgin and out to sea. Da was watching her with red eyes.

'What's happened?' I asked as I stepped inside. 'Why are we closed?'

Da coughed and said nothing. He looked at Mam, but she wouldn't meet his eyes. He picked up a piece of paper from the table and showed it to me. The telegram was from the navy. It said that Seaman Patrick Sean McCabe was lost at sea. I read the words myself: *lost at sea*, and the date, in undeniable print.

How could they have lost him? He was big, bright, healthy, and not prone to wandering off. I looked up at my family. Mam sat strangely still, my two remaining brothers scratched themselves reverently, and no one spoke. Finally Da stood up, scraped his chair back, walked into the bar, and poured himself two inches of whiskey.

Mam reacted to this by hitting the table with her fist. She still hadn't even glanced at me. She stood up and went to the window, took down the photograph, and looked at it angrily. She put it back face down, and sighed.

'My boys,' she said. She took Callum's shoulder in one of her hands and rested the other on Brendan's bowed head. I crept into the bar and leaned against my da's leg until he noticed I was there and pushed me away.

I couldn't run to you, so I ran upstairs to my room and sank to my knees. Mam was right about me. I should never have told stories about Patrick. If I had only prayed for him, he would have come home.

After a little while I realised that my knees were sore and that I didn't know how to begin. I must have had a concept of God, but I had no idea what the rules were for arguing with him. I stayed kneeling despite the soreness, and bit at my nails until I realised it was late. Too late. No one had called me down to dinner, but I wasn't hungry anyway. I crawled into Patrick's bed and fell fast asleep.

nine

Early this afternoon, not exactly peak hour, the place was deserted. I was standing behind the bar, facing the wall of postcards. Cairo, Thessaloniki and Tokyo are up there, but the names have lost their powers. I wonder if they left with Patrick, or years later, with you.

When I heard the door swing open, I jumped a little; but when I saw it was Clare, I was glad to be interrupted.

'How's the painting?' I asked as I set her schooner down in front of her.

'Oh, abysmal. The usual. The light here is so . . .'

'Unforgiving,' I offered.

'Frank,' she said. We smiled at each other. The trade in adjectives could just as easily have described her gaze. I swallowed, and was absurdly reminded of the tiny medical cameras I've seen on TV. The ones they push down your throat to get a look inside. She knows, I thought, though what she knew I couldn't have put into words.

I looked down, found that my hands were straightening a

small pile of cardboard coasters, and willed them to be still. When I could meet her eye again, Clare was leaning on the bar with an unlit cigarette in one hand, the other curled around her beer.

'Tell me a story,' she said.

I felt myself blushing. I turned my back and pretended to be engaged with the till for a minute. I cursed the Danker under my breath. I arranged some stray coins into their rightful places. The smell of old change made my stomach turn. How is it that people appear like this, to remind us of our unfinished business?

I slid the drawer closed and composed myself. I knew there was only one answer to that request. It was always an order, poorly disguised. I might as well obey, I thought, though it's been a long time. Most of a lifetime. I turned to face her.

'True or false?' I asked.

'Oh, either one. Both if you like.' She sipped at her schooner with a casualness that was so obvious, it might have been an act.

So I told her about the day I learned to breathe.

Mam hummed a lonely sort of tune as she pinned my hem. The dress was made out of a white lace curtain she had taken out of one of the rooms, and it was heavy and awkward. I had to shift my weight to counteract my cold legs, the scratchy lace around my armpits, the tingle in my fingers from holding my hands above my head.

'Don't fidget,' she said through a mouthful of pins. 'Stand up straight.'

I stretched to the ceiling. I didn't complain, because I knew this was important. It wasn't the dress that made me aware that some rite of passage was imminent. It was the fact that a law of nature had broken, in that I was being allowed to stand on the kitchen table. The highest things in the room were my raised hands and the lightbulb. I wanted to turn and examine the bulb up close, but I was forbidden to move my head.

When freed, I stood listening as the pub noise wafted up the stairwell to my room. I had my own room by this point. Well, technically it was the same room. Mam and Da had decided I needed a space of my own as I was growing, and I was sad but proud when they partitioned off a section of the big room I shared with the boys and put in another door. In the process, Patrick's bed was removed without comment.

We never spoke of my brother at home. I had almost started to feel that he was another invention of mine. Mam had taken the photograph of him in his uniform down off the kitchen windowsill. She'd stuffed it in her dresser drawer with her other mysteries. Sometimes when she was occupied in the bar, I would creep into my parents' room and take it out, just to reassure myself that he had once existed.

My room was a little space, and the new wall was so thin that if I put my ear to it I could still hear the boys breathing and roll-ing around in their sleep. I could hear my parents too, if I rolled across the bed and put my ear against the other wall. The bed was jammed between them, and the closeness was comforting.

When I got out of the dress at last and into bed, I put my ear against the wall, but the boys were sleeping silently. I knew Mam was downstairs as I could hear the Singer going. I lay there and thought about the ceremony. I'd never tasted wine before, only a sip at my brothers' shandies when they weren't looking. That would be something. And maybe once the Catholic Church let me in on its secrets I could have a talk with this God about what he thought he was doing with my brother.

I must have fallen asleep trying to work out my argument. When I woke up it was light, and there was an angel in front of me, all in white, with no arms or legs and no head. Mam was holding it up.

'Get into this now May, we'll be late,' she said.

When it started, we were lined up like at school, except that everyone was dressed up and pretending to be solemn. It was cold in the church and the statues were all staring at something that wasn't there, like Da when he'd had too many whiskies.

Before we got to eat and drink Jesus, we had to go to confession. The little church didn't have a booth. Father Bryant had set up a partition along the side made of an old hospital curtain. When I went in, he sniffed at me, but I wasn't daunted. Mam had made me practise.

'Bless me Father for I have sinned,' I recited carefully.

'Yes,' he said disinterestedly. I could only see him from the lap down, separated as we were by the olive green curtain. I was glad he couldn't see me. He smelled mothbally, though that might have been the curtain. I waited for a while, pondering my argument, until I realised I couldn't find the words. I coughed, but the priest was silent, his hands folded in his lap. I thought he might have fallen asleep.

'I murdered my brother,' I confessed. 'I killed the dandelion woman too.'

'Oh, child,' Father Bryant said, and he sighed impatiently. 'You did no such thing. God takes His children away when He wants them in Heaven.'

'What did he want all those soldiers for? Is there a war on in Heaven as well?'

The priest clicked his tongue. I saw his hands smooth the vestments over his knees, almost ladylike. 'Do you have anything to confess, May?'

I paused, thinking of something to offer the man. Since he'd worked out who I was, I made an attempt to explain myself.

'I've been telling lies,' I began. 'Stories, I mean. About my brother, and the dandelion woman. And they're both dead. The rabbit —'

The priest sighed impatiently and pulled the curtain back to bless me. 'Say three Hail Marys, obey your mother and father, and never, ever tell lies again. In the name of the Father, send the next one in, would you.'

I went out to line up in the row with all the other Micks and tried to look penitent and hopeful, but I was ashamed. When I took the host, it stuck in my throat. The wine wasn't enough to wash it out, and the rotten-tasting mixture stayed in the back of my mouth for the rest of the service.

After an age, it was finished, and the priest, who had changed into a white dress too, but without the lace, waved us out with his silver ball of incense on a chain. I didn't feel blessed at all, just angry, faintly embarrassed, and very hungry. They hadn't let us have any breakfast, but there was cordial and cake on the lawn outside. We all walked slowly and I didn't swing my arms, though not because Mam had told me to walk properly, just because the lace was tight there and it hurt if I did.

You were standing outside on the lawn, come to watch the tiny parade of white. You were wearing red overalls, and your blonde hair was bright in the sun; the combination made you look like a parrot. Your father was there with you. He took off his oily cap as we filed past, bent his mouth in mockery, and did a little bow. I burst out laughing. I couldn't help it.

Francine Barrett presided over the cake table with her daughter. Her two children went through the ceremony in previous years, but she was always involved in church activities. I didn't drink my cordial because Mam told me not to run with it in my hand, and running won. Despite our parents' protests at the likely ruining of our clothes, a game of hide and seek was instated with quick consensus. Francine frowned at the game, but didn't comment when Ted, her son, was selected as It.

You and I conferred in whispers. It was your idea to hide in the church, but I quickly agreed it was the perfect place. We thought no one saw us enter, thought we were the cleverest kids in Coal. I closed the door behind us and it clicked shut easily.

The church, emptied of people, seemed unnaturally dark. White, red, and purple candles still burned on the altar, shining a weird light on the wall behind. You stepped boldly past the altar and stood on the box under the crucifix to look out the small, high window.

'I can see the sea from here,' you said.

'Grace, get down. You're not allowed up there.'

'Says who?'

'Says God. That's the tabernacle.' The box was just a tea chest covered in white material, but sacred was sacred.

I approached you cautiously, wondering at what point my feet would offend God. Was it at the altar or beyond that the boundary lay? I suddenly realised I'd forgotten all about my Hail Marys.

You stood on your toes to get a better view. 'What did the priest say?'

I stopped where I imagined the invisible line to be. 'He said I didn't kill my brother. God did.'

You laughed. The sound rang around the small church like a

bell, returning harsh and flat. 'Don't you know anything? There isn't one.' You turned your eyes towards the sea in irritation. 'Religion is only there to trick people into obeying stupid rules.'

I looked down at the ground to hide my annoyance, and realised there was a simple test. If there was no God, there was no line. If there was no line, then I could step across. I put one foot forward, closed my eyes, placed it on the ground, shifted my weight onto it. I opened my eyes. Nothing happened.

'Then it was me that killed him,' I muttered.

At that moment, a thunderclap sounded. Ice ran down my spine. It was the ground opening in rage at our trespass. A hole in the earth gaped behind me. I was a killer, I had nowhere to go but down. As a bright light entered the building I dared a look over my shoulder. The priest was striding towards us, a black silhouette growing against the blinding sunlight.

You jumped off the box, but it was too late. Father Bryant was already upon us and yelling in a hoarse voice. 'Out! Get the bloody hell out before I give you both hidings! This is a place of God not a bloody treehouse! Out!'

We ran outside so quickly that we barrelled into Ted, who was leaning against the door frame, waiting to sneak up on us. He watched us sprint towards the cake table with a deeply con-fused look on his face.

'Found you,' he called after us.

When I told Clare this story, I left out a few things; the next part in particular. I didn't know how to say it without coming across like a madwoman. But I can tell you. You were there.

The priest chased us out of the building. We ran past the cake stand and up to the edge of the scrub. I placed your hand against my rib so you could feel my heart galloping. You sucked on your lower lip and your hand tensed. My heartbeat only upped its pace. And with that, a sort of light seemed to surround us. A warm bitterness like wine. I became aware that the stories I told were enclosing us like a second kind of air which I was learning to breathe.

We were only small, and can't have understood a thing about it. I still don't know how to tell this. It is too close to the shape of a dream.

If I know one story that is both true and false, it's the one I have begun. I wonder if I am brave enough to make the parts whole, to fill in the gaps, to call your name. But I have already made my choice. Your letter is only the first handhold knotted into this rope. The other end of it has sunk to the ocean floor. I must heave away, haul away. I must see where it leads, even if I know what I will find. I am raising a whole shipwreck from its resting place. I am disturbing an ocean full of sleeping ghosts.

ten

I can hear music today: that generic, mournful acoustic guitar so favoured by surfies. It must be coming from one of the cars parked by the beach. Sometimes the wind is selective, picking up a single sound and carrying it all the way up the headland. The music could be in the room with me.

It's still just warm enough for tourists. I walk onto the concrete porch and watch the surfers out there in their black wetsuits, coasting lightly along. It looks effortless, though it must be hard work. The waves are crashing mightily today. I can almost feel the headland shake beneath my feet.

I return to my kitchen and try to pick up this letter where I left off, but it's getting harder. Memories are fickle, stories downright cunning. I hear so many yarns in here, and each one seems to stretch the truth a little further. The fishermen are the worst of course. Tick and Fish, old mates of Ted's, often spin me stories about their catches. They've been doing it for years, their three strong right arms taking turns to wind me up. The three of them used to be inseparable, but now there are two.

Today it's not the one that got away. It's the one that didn't.

'See that surf?' Tick asks.

'Yeah, it's rough today,' I nod.

'See this big solid feller?' He slaps Fish on the shoulder. Fish looks obligingly solid. Both of them do, brawny and big as overgrown boys.

'Nearly snatched him,' Tick says proudly. 'I had to grab his pants or the waves would've picked him right up off the rock.'

'Bastard gave me a killer wedgie,' Fish complains, rubbing the base of his spine.

'You could do with a beer I reckon.' I pour them both frothing schooners. 'On me,' I add.

'What for?' They're suspicious. I usually only offer them freebies when I need them to help me lift something.

'Failing to drown,' I say. And then, because I have gone soft, I add, 'Looks like I have to give you an incentive. I need those Friday prawns, don't forget.'

It isn't yet lunchtime, too early for most people to start drinking, but they've been up since dawn, and they swallow their draughts gratefully. They carry on telling the story, giving it more detail and colour, fleshing it out. By early afternoon they've escaped a tsunami.

'Oh yeah, massive waves this morning,' a young backpacker pipes in. 'Nearly got smashed into the rocks myself.' He looks at me hopefully.

'What can I get you?' I ask.

Occasionally, it strikes me that this is all I ever say to people.

It's not just the fishos. To hear some of these surfers talk you'd think they were superheroes. I have to listen to little Joe talk about what a good woman Mercy was, what a help to him. Then there's Louie and his plans, his ridiculous ambitions and illusions of success. I'm surrounded by recreational liars. Even the ones who try and get it straight can't help exaggerating. So how am I supposed to get this all down exactly as it happened?

The fishos know how to give a story chase. A hook, some bait, a length of line, and then the long struggle. They know how to sneak into another creature's element and beat it at its own game. I would never catch anything, the few times I went out on the boat. It was Ted's place.

I'm not very patient. I want everything to make sense, to happen in the right order. I want to be in control, but my memory has a mind of its own. The words spilling out of this pen aren't in my charge at all.

In the evening, Clare asks me about the collection of postcards on the wall, and I don't lie to her. I admit that I've never left New South Wales.

'They're from friends,' I say. I'm still not lying to her.

'You never wanted to travel?'

'I never needed to,' I reply, though I wonder if this is true. I turn around and scrutinise the collection. I hardly look at them any more.

Now that I see this frenzied international wallpaper through her eyes, I can't help thinking it's insane. So many cards fading and curling away from the wall like peeling skin. I wonder if Clare sees me as an elderly collector, harmlessly weighted down by junk. I wonder if she sees the stories pinning these scraps together. But she doesn't judge me, not aloud.

'I can understand that,' she says, 'living here. Me, I spent three years travelling the world. I was looking for something, I guess. The diamond in my pocket.'

A knife blade runs the length of my spine. I twist back to face Clare. 'What did you say?'

'The diamond in my pocket. It's an old story.' She opens her mouth to share it, taking a breath to blow a lock of hair from her eye.

'I know it,' I interrupt.

'Oh, of course you would,' she says, smiling at me in all innocence. She's apparently completely unaware that she is quoting you. I don't know how she is doing this, but I don't press her. It's a coincidence, I think. Coincidences happen all the time.

'Did you find it?' I ask.

'No,' she says. 'But I learned a lot. Mostly about here. It's funny, the concepts of Australia people have overseas. Kangaroos, crocodiles, the desert, the beach. I always used to get asked about Aboriginal culture, like I had any idea, let alone any right to explain it.'

'You should meet Aunt Betty,' I say. 'She's from here, it's her country, but she lives up in Sydney now. Her and a few others came down to fight when the point was up for development. She tells good stories.'

'You should know,' says Clare. I blush at this, shrug and pick up a spotless glass to polish.

'Ah, I don't know all that much,' I say. 'I'm just a simple local.'

'All right, local, fill me in,' she grins. 'Tell me about the point.'

It was the women who started it. The first meeting was organised right here in the bar, as soon as a few locals found out about the plans. We haven't had a women's auxiliary for decades, but some kind of group seems to form every time there's a need for it.

Council let the development application through by a narrow margin. Someone was mates with someone else, the usual story. A friendly handshake was all it took to grant permission to bulldoze a patch of earth that had lain green and wild for centuries, even through the mining boom. The unbroken stretch of wildness from the top of the escarpment down to the coast was a highway for possums and wallabies, a bushwalk for us, and a sacred place for the Tharawal.

Locals from a long time ago showed up once we got a little group going. Betty was one of the first. She's Tharawal, and would have been called an elder if there was any continuity; as it is she's proud to claim the Aunty tag.

I hadn't seen an Aboriginal face in Coal for a long time, which was another unfortunate result of the gentrification. They'd been scattered up to Redfern and down south to the cheaper suburbs. Families always go where there's work and housing, I guess.

It was work enough for us just trying to keep the developers away. We built a tent out on the point with a couple of tarps and some two-by-four, outfitted it with posters, petitions, a primus stove and a kettle. We decided someone should always be posted to watch for bulldozers. Joe used to do double shifts with his easel. Me, I'd sit there in the morning and think. You and me with the moon rising over the edge of the sea, walking out to the point in the coal-dark night. That wet and sudden hold.

Mostly, though, I just provided a meeting place. Every second Tuesday, the bistro filled with the old sounds of planning and laughter. Sometimes Aunt Betty would stay on afterwards and tell us stories her own mother had told her about this country. Ted was still here then, and he would nod quietly and listen carefully, fidgeting in his lap as though he had to turn his thoughts over in his hands.

We tried every avenue we could. We found lawyers. The local people put up a native title claim, but this country has changed hands so many times that they had no hope of regaining it. I tried to get my head around land use agreements and all that, but wasn't much good. It was a relief when we realised direct action was the only option left.

When the first bulldozers came, we locked ourselves together in a line to stop them, using whatever we had: bicycle locks, chains from the mechanics, even old lifebuoys. We sang some heartening songs and did our best impression of standing firm, but when the police arrived they dragged us out of the way like so many children. City cops, not from around here. We still only have one cop in Coal and Alan was conveniently absent that day.

I was chained to Aunt Betty when the bulldozers came in. Much to my dismay, she threw herself at the police and begged them to arrest her.

'Take me in,' she shouted, 'take me in!'

I tried to stop her, as we were locked to each other and if she went to jail so did I. But she wouldn't hear of it. She'd obviously done this before.

'Think about what we could do to them,' she said. 'Arresting a couple of old ladies!' She winked at me, and I had to let her drag me into the fray by my arm. In the end the cops must have had the same thought about bad publicity, because they let us go.

We kept fighting even as the row of houses grew, beige boxes staggered mechanically against the earth. The protests fired everyone up for a while and even got some of the younger ones interested. We got our pictures in the city papers with sympathetic captions. Despite all this, we lost. The point has been shaved bare except for a few patches of neatly planted shrubs.

Progress is supposed to be inevitable. You can't keep things the way they were, even if you want a patch of old wild country to walk your dog in. I wanted my grandkids to be able to chase wallabies down there like we used to. I wouldn't mind if I could see the odd moonrise, either. They've got streetlights in just this month. They take away the stars.

I have no right to complain. I make just as much of a mess of this place with my big lightbox signage, asphalt car park, and noise. It's not as if I was here first.

Clare listens intently, her head slightly to one side. I watch her face change with my words, enjoy the shifts in her eyes. I feel like I could talk all night. For a few minutes I've actually enjoyed the telling.

The door swings open and some tourists wander in. They stare around at the room and sidle nervously up to the bar. The trance is broken, and I retreat into my role with relief.

'Anyway, that's enough,' I say. 'Things to do.' I wipe the bar in front of her with a wet cloth and turn to the newcomers with a smile.

'What can I get you?'

I am neglecting those things to do right now, sneaking these words in behind the bar. They can't see what I'm doing, but I write slyly anyway, my left hand curled around the page. You are taking over, Grace.

Tonight some heartbroken surfer is playing every sad song he can find on the jukebox. His pool-playing mates move languidly in the syrup he's made of the air. I open some windows, careful to make a bit of noise, and look around for Runner. They're just his type of customer.

I spot him leaning on a wall outside, sipping from a bottle of water. Runner doesn't drink beer. He only comes in here to sell pot to the tourists. I know this, of course, but if he knew I knew he wouldn't be half as entertaining to watch. If I didn't keep my mouth shut, I'd be forced to admit that I need him. The stoned ones sit there for hours, keep buying beers, and never get into fights.

Besides, it would take all the fun out of his day to think I'd been letting him win all along at his small-time swindle. And it's good to have something on people, just in case. He does his rounds in tourist season, October through March. He takes a seat with a group of young people and chats to them for a while, then swaps something under the table or follows one of them to the bathroom. Or else he walks them outside where I can't see, out to the grassy clifftop in the wind. Then he moves to the next group.

He knows everyone around here is relaxed about the law. Even if Alan had the fibre to bust a local, he'd be hard-pressed getting any evidence out of the rest of us. Not to mention that he'd be barred for life. I've been tempted to do that already, just on the strength of the uniform. Coming in here making everybody nervous, he's bad for business. Shame I can't get away with it, really. Not because of the law, but because of the fact that he's as local as they come.

Runner's not, but I don't give him a hard time. He's had a pretty tough time of it already. He ended up here from Queensland, where he got done for running dope down to Brisbane from a plantation in the far north. He spent a couple of years in the big house for that. They bashed his ears in the lockup, trying to get information on some big-time dealers. Runner came out deaf as a post and thought he'd come down here and go on the pension for a while and learn to surf. Because of his hearing, everyone had to yell at him, which didn't do his line of work much good.

His hearing's fine now. He's had it fixed. Sometimes people still shout at him though, out of habit. He just shouts back until they get the picture. It's handy for him, especially if he doesn't want to hear what someone has to say. I've seen him play his little Helen Keller routine at the bar when Louie's blathering in his ear. It works so well I've thought about going deaf myself.

Alan comes in, asking me something about a stolen car. Louie claps him on the back – Alan was at school with his son – and dribbles in his ear.

'Yer a disappointment, son. You always were bright. You had a good head on your shoulders and wheredya put it? Up that arsehole of a hat.'

Alan smiles wanly and ignores the affront. 'You heard anything, May? I don't want to ask, but we haven't got any other leads.'

'Now, Al, do you think I'd let them drive anything out of here in their condition?' I nod at the small pile of car keys I've collected behind the bar. Everyone lives within a few minutes' walk anyway.

He glances at Runner, who looks as if he's about to act like his name and do one.

'You know anything about this stolen car, mate?' Runner ignores him, conveniently deaf.

Alan looks past me at the plastic clock. 'Guess I knock off around now anyway,' he says. 'Give us a beer then.'

'You're paying,' I say, placing the cool glass in front of him. 'If my da knew I served you he'd turn in his grave.' He looks put out but hands me a fiver.

'They said this job would have perks,' he mutters.

Louie nods sympathetically. 'I'll perk you in the eye if you want,' he offers.

I laugh, though I could have said it myself. I know all the jokes that are going to come out of their mouths before they open them. I know this place too well. I'm like Mallee; I recognise them first by their cars, then by their footsteps, or the unique sound each one has of pushing open the door. If I have a language, it's in the Danker.

It follows that if the Danker has something to say, it's me it will tell. And this morning, it does. I sit down to this letter and hear a mouse run across the floor upstairs. I've been trapping them for months, but as it's getting cooler they seem to be everywhere at once. It's a personal quest to rid my bar of them, and probably impossible.

'Fat lot of use you are,' I say to Beth, who is asleep on Ted's chair. She twists an ear and pointedly ignores me.

I go upstairs to find it myself, opening cupboard doors, turning out drawers that have long been jammed shut. I don't find the mouse. What I find instead is a piece of paper which has fallen behind a dresser and been crushed. I tug it out thinking it might be part of a nest, but it's not. It's a page ripped from a scrapbook, a cut-out woman glued from catalogue parts. She has a veil. In a corner, in a childish scrawl, is a drawing of a snake.

eleven

One minute the Americans were blowing up their atom bombs, and then suddenly, the war was over. We had come out the other side. You and I were nine – almost ten, I insisted – and had no memory of peacetime. I wondered if the whole world would be re-arranged, and specifically if someone would go looking for my lost brother. Despite my guilt, I couldn't believe I had murdered him completely. I couldn't ask Mam; she'd only ignore the question and find me some job to do. I couldn't ask Da because he'd either cry or get drunk again, or both. Brendan was no use, too busy poring over his textbooks. I tried to ask Callum, but all he said was that I was worrying Mam and Da with my talk, so I gave up.

At least school became a sort of holiday. We helped put up British flags in the portable classroom and sang 'God Save the King'. Mrs Gowan had to bite her tongue to stop herself from making cynical remarks about the patriotic display, but she took us through it cheerfully enough.

The celebration at the Danker was far more serious. Thorne

had generously given the men a half day, and the pub was full by the time I got home from school. Tom Cullen shouted for open bar, and my da obliged. He brought out his fiddle and played until he was too drunk to make more than a scraping noise. There was singing and dancing until well into the morning. We were allowed to stay up late, and we took advantage of the rare treat to get under people's feet and eavesdrop.

Tim, the oldest of the Cullen boys, had come back unscathed with a medal pinned to his chest, but he didn't appear to wear it very proudly.

'What are you going to do with that?' Da asked him, fingering the weight.

'First thing tomorrow I'm going fishing,' he said. 'Reckon it'll make a decent sinker.' There was a sadness in his laugh. His next brother Daniel was still missing.

Ration coupons were burned in the fireplace. Widows, and mothers whose sons didn't return, were comforted by the flames. Sylvia Cullen gathered her clutch of boys around her. My own mother, though, didn't seem to need any comforting. She was steel-eyed where others wept. I was beginning to think she was heartless. My da wasn't afraid to cry, even if he did so a little too often – and publicly, in the middle of 'The Wind that Shakes the Barley'.

You and I eventually wandered out to the headland. We walked to the edge and looked down at the rocks, where the sea was smashing itself. The height of the cliff meant instant death if one of us tripped, but we weren't afraid of the place.

'I wish he would come back,' I said. 'Or I could just fall into the sea and find him myself.' I wiped at my eyes, blew my nose, and sat down heavily on the ground. 'It's smoky in there,' I lied.

You knelt beside me and took my hand. 'If you fall, I'm falling too,' you said. 'I'm a better swimmer than you anyway.'

'Are not,' I protested, though I knew it was true.

Your words didn't hold water. In the end, you let me fall without you.

At the first post-war picnic, you stroked my arm. The families were spread on the grass, inert from eating. Indulgences were suddenly permitted.

'I'm bored,' you said. 'Tell me a story.'

'True or false?' The hairs on my arm prickled under your fingertips.

'Both,' you replied.

'Okay,' I wriggled, warming to the challenge. 'See Mrs Cullen's mole?'

'Yeah.'

'Well do you know how she got it?'

'How?' Your fingers were now playing with my sleeve. It was as if you thought that my arm was a part of your body. I let it rest in your lap.

'Tom Cullen was once an international blow-dart champion, a sport he learned sailing in the tropics. Locked out of his gymnasium the night before the big final, he resorted to practising at home. Little did he realise his wife was in the next room ...'

You were laughing. Your light shakes ran through my body as well. I remembered a picture of Siamese twins I saw once, an illustration from the papers. I wondered if we would ever be separated.

★ ★ ★

My stories were the first cure for boredom. At other times we would run and play around the yards of our neighbours, or go looking for beautiful things on the tide line. You loved to swim, I merely enjoyed it, but when I think about my childhood the first thing I see is the ocean; an endless source of life, games, bright refreshing waves, and drama.

I remember running everywhere at that age. You and I and a cloud of boys would race up the headland to the Danker's porch or chase each other along the beach. We would run out onto the point, get lost in the low scrub, and look for wallabies. We would lie in the grass and invent things about the clouds. When there were no clouds we'd look up at the sandstone rocks that ran along the top of the escarpment and find shapes in the shadows. Our eyes always returned to wonder at the pattern of a human body marked into the rock.

We were both tomboyish and strong runners, but pursued other interests too. Scrapbook magazines taught us about ladies, which didn't seem to have much to do with the bush and the beach and the sea. We mocked them together, but we mocked the boys together as well, forming a tight army of two and embellishing the world with our conjoined imaginations. We were indivisible, or so it seemed.

When the tide had just gone out, it would leave a line of shells and pebbles along the beach to mark the place that it had reached. We would walk along this line hand in hand and stoop to pick up pieces of glass, some the same amber as the bottles that we sold in the pub, others vastly different, greens and blues from another world.

The shapes were smoothed to a deep matt finish, and I would hold them up to the sun to look at the light. I would tell you stories about where they came from. A single artefact was all I needed to invent a whole world. It was a kind of addiction, I think.

I remember you looking out to the horizon, searching for the tales: the shipwrecks full of treasure, the drowned sailors hanging on a plank, the island out there populated by transparent people made of glass. Transfixed. I tugged at your hand.

When you held it out to show me a piece of glass polished almost round, I took it from you, examined it, and frowned.

'It's not ready yet,' I said, and threw it back into the sea.

Housebound on a rainy summer afternoon, we were cutting up women's bodies. Mrs Thorne had given her old catalogues to the miners' wives at Christmas, and we were busily destroying them.

I sliced through a pair of legs and stuck them carefully in my scrapbook under a mismatched body. You were clumsily cutting around a skirt. I looked at the woman I had made out of scraps. She wasn't complete without a story.

'This is Carlotta,' I said. She had a Spanish veil for a head. You continued diligently around the pleats, accustomed now to my habit of invention.

In Carlotta's story there was a lot of trouble and woe. Trouble and woe were an interest of mine by that stage. Her trouble was imprisonment in a castle, and her woe was a visiting snake.

I drew a careful serpent in one corner of the page as I told the story. I thought about the snakes I'd seen. The living ones were few, and only glimpsed. But there was Eve, and Mary always has a snake at her feet. On Mam's little statue it was grey. The snake's eye had fallen out. Sometimes I'd catch her looking at the statue the way she looked at the sea, like she could see through it.

There was some discussion, I can't remember it now. My

heroine lost the argument, and the snake bit her. I stabbed the picture's leg with the scissors to make my point. You had finished the skirt, and it dangled in your hand while you watched me.

The snake was magic, of course. Its venom gave Carlotta incredible strength. She kicked the castle door down and escaped. She ran until the power wore off and she could run no more. She found her way out of her prison and into the real world.

'And she lived happily ever after,' I concluded.

'She should have married a prince,' you said, 'so she could live happily ever after in his palace.'

'She would have been bored,' I explained. I was annoyed that you didn't like my ending.

'Now tell me a true one,' you said.

I complied as best I could. I gave you fleetness of foot, a handkerchief wrapping an apple and a sandwich, a torch and a bottle of water. I gave you the power of running, made you the fastest thing in the world. Stupidly, I left the castle door wide open.

Great black storm clouds were bearing down on us, and the Danker was thrown into general panic. Mam and Da were busy trying to close the doors and windows. It was my job to get the animals in. I ran outside to save the chooks and barrelled in with four or five squawking, struggling bundles in my arms. I dropped them and fled upstairs to help my brothers secure the balcony doors. When I came back down the chooks were standing around in the kitchen like awkward guests.

You must have thought the bombs had finally come, because you ran for cover as you had been taught. But instead of seeking it at home or, as you often did, with my family, you ran into the bush.

When your absence was discovered, your parents ran out into the thick rain and shouted for you, but the wind was too strong for their voices. The water lashed their bodies at a sharp angle. They were drenched within seconds. Finally they slammed their door and decided to wait out the storm before they tried again.

At the first sign that the rain was abating, Jack and Faith hurried up to the Danker to look for you. I remember the glowing shapes thrown by headlamps in the dark afternoon. I followed them into the bush.

'Grace!' echoed up the cliff in many voices. We fanned out, stepping over the snapped stems of silver gums and telegraph poles. The bush had ripped itself to pieces. Massive trunks lay like split toothpicks on the ground.

I imagined your body lying crushed under a log in the mud, or fallen, swept off the cliff and dashed upon the rocks like a ship. Your white limbs snapped, your skull cracked. The images were a guilty pleasure.

I followed my brothers into the wild darkness of the escarpment to call your name. The mud was slippy and I grabbed at handfuls of bracken to steady myself. My voice echoed dimly against the blackbutts, their trunks slick with rain. It was a small sound, and it did not carry in the undergrowth.

Torn bracken sprang back and the rustling sounds made me think of the things that were haunting the place. I stuck close behind Callum and watched my back for the swagman. I swore that if you weren't dead, I'd be furious with you.

Tom Cullen found you, and then only with a miner's headlamp and a hunch. You didn't answer any of the calls, though they must have echoed loudly down to where you crouched against the concrete walls of the railway tunnel. You let yourself be swaddled in an army blanket and carried into the light. I watched your body hang in the man's arms like a sack of flour.

You weren't hurt at all, not a scratch, but something had changed. There was a strange triumph in your eyes. You looked right through me. I was left standing by the gaping mouth of the tunnel, my eyes unable to adjust to the darkness inside.

As the storm cleared and the clouds dissipated, the light became sharp, almost cruel. The bush was dripping with green and crowded with ecstatic birds. It was like an extra day, the light that followed. It made the world look fresh-sprouted. I walked home as slowly as I could.

When I returned, my brothers and Da were back already, circling the place, inspecting the damage with some admiration. Mam was watching them from the porch, busy pushing the tables and chairs back into place.

'Haven't seen a storm like this since the night you were born,' Da remarked as I joined them.

'I'm surprised you remember, you were that pissed,' Mam rejoined. 'Hate to interrupt the reminiscing but are you going to give me a hand?'

The headland was a mess but, for the most part, the Danker had managed to weather the storm. A few scraps of corrugated iron lay bent and awkward on the hillside like broken wings. We bent them straight and nailed them back on the roof. We knocked the chook house back into shape and Mam returned the hens before they made themselves at home in our kitchen.

When I'd finished helping with the chook house I stood from the exertion with fists still stiff and clenched. The wind might have died and the tempest gone, but I was no less furious. You had taken my imaginary world and made it your own. Suddenly,

I was locked out of my own kingdom. And you had only taken a first taste of the attention granted to those who dare.

Mrs Gowan had been the teacher at our school as long as we knew, and at least as long as my oldest surviving brother could tell me. I never would have called Callum that then. He was the oldest; it was said as if Patrick had never existed.

She'd been around almost as long as the school itself. During the war she had married Victor Govedaska. She kept her name not out of principle, we simply couldn't get our little Anglo-Celtic tongues around Victor's surname, and in the end he adopted hers. Soon she was taking time off to have children: a daughter, Polly, a sweet, black-haired thing, and a baby son. She used to bring them to school with her, laying the baby on her desk where he gurgled distractingly. We were all ages at that tiny school anyway, so it made little difference.

Victor Gowan had arrived during the war. He was a reffo, according to Callum, and this gave him an air of mystery. He worked down the mines like anyone else, though. He was almost a local by the time of the accident.

Alfie Cullen, I think it was – those boys are almost inter-changeable in my mind, there were so many of them – burst into the classroom just as we were beginning to let ourselves float off in the afternoon drowsiness that led up to the end of the day. It was hot, and he was covered in sweat and black dust. The combination made him shine like a wet pebble.

'Scuse us, Miss,' he said, that having been Mrs Gowan's name when he was at school. He took off his hat. We all woke up and watched him with far more interest than we applied to our grammar books.

Alfie glanced at his shoes as if he'd written cheat notes there. 'Miss, I . . . there's been an accident,' he said. 'You better come.'

Mrs Gowan remained calm, barely a fluttering eyelid revealing her inner panic. She took the baby up with an automatic sweep.

'Wait here, Polly,' she instructed the little class pet, who was engaged in having her hair braided by Mercy. 'I want you all to stay in your seats until I get back,' she said.

For a reverent moment, we sat still and good, then all but Mercy and her charge raced to the windows to watch our teacher disappear. There was a great deal of discussion about what was going on. Perhaps I took too much hold of it, but I felt I had to settle everyone, and I saw my chance.

I could see the man lying prone under a weight of rock, locked in by a barred cage that was supposed to protect him. His torch lit the bloodstains on his overalls, and I could feel the absolute solitude of his separation. I could see the men drilling through to him, hear their calls of reassurance. I had everyone's attention. I did my best, but I couldn't save him.

Despite the fact that times were good, the company was still denying the men the time to put up enough supports for their excavations. Too expensive, it was claimed; they needed coal fast and bugger the structural work needed to get it safely. Of course there were going to be collapses. When the rock caved in on Victor, he was cut off on his own, his buddy having retreated as they were blasting a section. They said he died instantly, but it took half a day's work to get the body out.

When I got home that afternoon, the pub was empty but for a few tired-looking men, the ones who'd come off the first shift at digging him out. I wandered in behind the bar and hung off Da's leg and listened.

Jack was already drunk and rambling about a strike. Da, by

contrast, was in a quiet mood. He liked Victor, and had often enjoyed the young man's company. They'd shared a few songs of an evening, Victor singing his slow, Eastern European laments as Da listened with wet eyes.

'Once a man has taught you a tune,' he said, 'you can't forget him.'

Jack said nothing to this. He'd had his share of arguments with the young Balt about the promise of the Eastern Bloc. Jack didn't like his ideals to present themselves like that, in the shape of refugees from a society he considered immune to criticism. However, he put all that aside after the accident.

'It's an opportunity to do something about the conditions,' he said. 'We can turn this around, make things happen. Now they've got to listen.'

'A man might be dead, Jack. Leave it.'

I held onto my da's trouser leg with one fist until he shooed me away.

Thorne gave everyone a day off for the funeral. They weren't grateful. The older men, even the ones who didn't go to the war, had seen enough funerals already.

We weren't allowed to attend, still considered too young. Undaunted, you and I snuck around the back of the railway line and hid in the bushes behind the churchyard. Father Percival, the Proddy one, made a speech and waved a solemn Bible over the hole in the ground. Our teacher wept copiously all over the baby in her arms, and we watched her with morbid fascination.

The wake afterwards was better. We always had the wake, and because it was a man swallowed by the mine there was a right-eousness to the grief. The bar rang with angry voices. You came over to watch the proceedings from behind my kitchen door.

'Teacher's not here,' you observed, scanning the room through the sliver of an open door. 'Do you think there'll be school tomorrow?'

'Nah.' I shook my head. 'You want to come over?'

You nodded. 'I'll ask Jack.' You went to look for him in the bar to see if it was a good time to ask.

It had been years since there had been an accident, and this one wrenched the town out of its complacency. Anger at the long hours and low wages, and frustration at being proved right too late, made the men thirsty. There was talk enough about industrial action to get old Thornbag worried. A journalist had come down from the city paper to interview him about the conditions and talk anonymously to the workers. There was a lot of attention on coal that year, as the union had already been making demands for better pay and safety. I almost felt sorry for the boss in his corner as the men glared at him, slamming their empty glasses down. They were only prevented from violence by the fact that he was buying.

Jack tried to rally people into action, but was dismissed.

'Not tonight,' Tom Cullen said, a hand on his shoulder. 'Talk about it in the morning. Now's not the time.' He leaned into Jack's ear and whispered something. Jack fell silent at last, and moved around the room making ideological consolations. I watched you approach him, and watched him dismiss you with a wave of his hand. You recoiled as if physically struck.

'It's not a good time,' you said, reappearing in the kitchen. 'I'll ask him in the morning.' Your eyes were downcast. I should have asked you why you flinched from your father, but I didn't have the words.

'Okay. See you then,' I said instead.

'Goodnight, May.'

You slipped out of the Danker and off down the track in the dark. I watched your shape move in the moonlight until it was swallowed by the trees, until my mam came to tell me it was high time I was in bed.

I sat up on the balcony, wide awake under the bright moon. The bar was too noisy to sleep, and the excitement of the day had fired me up. I saw Thornbag shuffling nervously away, having made his presence felt. I thought of Victor crushed under the pile of rock and knew that my attempt in the classroom had been part of what had dragged him into his grave. I was ashamed. I might have tried to pray if I hadn't heard the call for a song that rang out beneath me, the happy sound of banging on tables that accompanied the cry for music.

My da obliged with a song or two that stripped me of any need for prayer. Love songs, goodbye songs that I knew would have even the angriest of them leaning on each other with tears in their eyes. 'The Fields of Athenry', which all the men joined in on for the last verse: 'I rebelled, they cut me down.'

You came over the following day, bright-eyed with the excitement of having a day off in the middle of the week. It was still hot enough to swim, and we went down to kneel in the shallows, pushing the tiny waves away with our hands.

'Tell me a story.'

'I don't know, Grace,' I muttered. I was tired from my late night. I ducked my head under the waves, feeling the freshness of salt water and the sand grabbing at my scalp. When I came up and wiped my eyes, you were still looking at me expectantly.

'I don't know if I should. It feels like everything I say comes true.'

Now, if I am to be honest, I must admit that I was proud of this, as much as it scared me. I was no murderer, but the level of culpability was just enough to convince me of my powers.

'Mr Cullen didn't really hit his wife with a blow-dart,' you pointed out.

'He might.'

'Please?' You addressed this to the water, or your own submerged hands. 'What if it's a good story, I mean a story where good things happen?'

I wasn't sure I knew how to tell that kind, but I could not resist the challenge. With the sight of the ship out at sea before me, waiting to dock at the jetty down in the town where the steel mill stood, the smokestacks burning holes in the sky, I used the materials available. I knotted ropes of seaweed in my hands as I spoke. I wove.

I began an adventure for you. I wanted to show you what lay beyond that blue, haze-blurred horizon. To prove that all the stories start and end right here, I sent you out to sea. I gave you a pirate ship and pushed it out into the waves, sent it in search of treasure and glory.

You listened with a stillness that was so unlike you, I looked into your face to see what you were sad about. But your eyes, so far out to sea, were dry, and tense with a quiet, defeated rage.

I kept on telling, in the hope that I was tying knots. The sea tricked me into an illusion of connection. In fact, I was loosing your moorings. I was mapping your next escape.

Shortly after Victor's funeral, Da took to slipping out at night after closing without telling anyone where he was going. From the balcony, I watched him wobble off on his rusty old one-speed pushbike. I suspected him of participating in some clandestine revolutionary activity. I romanced secret meetings in a darkened hall, coded messages and plots. His obvious stress, a failed secret, was irresolvable.

Sometimes I would catch him making a guilty mess of paperwork in the kitchen, crossing things out and rewriting them, a muddled frown creasing his forehead, a hand cradling his stubbled chin. When he saw me, he would lock the paperwork away in a drawer, sigh, and begin one of his stories. I was too old for them, but I listened, knowing it was more for his own comfort than for mine.

I can't remember my parents ever arguing, but I knew Mam was angry with him about something. It wasn't her way to shout. She'd ignore him, then let fly with a bitter remark. As I didn't have a clue why, I would immediately side with him, attach myself to his arm and stand as if propping him up. I'd pull faces at my mother behind her back. I had no respect for stoicism, in those days. I thought she had no heart.

For the most part, though, they took care of one another. It wasn't rare to find them leaning on each other behind the bar on a quiet night, his arm around her waist, her eyes far off somewhere, perhaps looking back on country dances, on the promises of diamonds that had brought her here. Or perhaps she had not forgotten, and her sailor's eyes were out at sea, casting nets for the body of her lost son.

Your parents argued properly, in broad daylight, and were sometimes audible from the headland. But this fitted neatly with the idea that they were passionate, driven people; and besides, it was the sort of thing nobody mentioned.

★ ★ ★

The second time you ran away, you ran into the dark.

The escarpment hung over Coal like a bad debt. The long-abandoned mine sites had never been filled. The pits carried pools of brown water in their bellies, and in the unlit shallows swam the rusting, broken pieces of redundant machinery. We could walk through that place, but climbing down the holes was forbidden. We learned to fear what might lurk in the honeycomb of darkness. The earth we met could swallow a grown man whole.

I can still see you running through there in a white dress, a slight, golden-haired child crushing leaves underfoot. In your wake, the bracken springs back weakly. Fallen trees break the track, their shadows laid down like thick brushstrokes. Particles of life dance in the patches of sunlight that thrust through the canopy. Each trunk tells its functional name: stringybark, scribbler, blackbutt.

Those shadowy blackbutts raise themselves like bushfire scars, seeping out great hunks of sap which are as red as human blood. You disappear behind them, following what might be a path. Careless and noisy, you are noticed by every bird and insect. Somewhere up ahead, a lyrebird calls out to you in stolen songs.

You rest beneath a frame of young strangler figs that are eating each other's limbs in such a way that it creates a small house bedded with moss. The track you followed isn't a path. It is a dry, silent creek, and it has narrowed into nothing. As you lie still, staring wide-eyed at the web of branches above you, the insects descend to investigate the stranger in their midst. They drone in the quiet, comforting and close. Somewhere further down the ridge you hear a cockatoo scream across the sky. You are lost.

I remember this in such detail. It seems strange that I can't have been there.

★ ★ ★

At first you looked out for a hole in the ground at every turn, but you soon realised that being careful slowed you down. You walked as straight a line as you could, parallel to the sea. Shadows that might have hidden pits loomed before you, but you pressed on bravely.

You made it across to the pass that zig-zags its way up the escarpment. Recognising the road you began to walk down it, not home exactly but towards the safety of the sea. The afternoon was growing cool. The sun had already passed over the top of the cliff. Sunsets come early here, behind the shelf of rock that studies us and halves the sky. With the sea beside you, it sometimes feels a little like the world has tilted, the horizon foreshortened on one side, extended on the other.

The pass had no verge and was still dirt then, so when the milk truck stopped you had to scramble out of the way. It was a dangerous road to stop on, all hairpin bends, and there were no houses for at least a mile in either direction. The milkman pulled up in a gap between trees. You reached his truck, leaned against the passenger side door. You had no fear of strangers; none of us did.

'Where are you headed, little lady?' he asked you.

'I'm going to the city,' you said. 'I'm going to get a job and a flat.' You were twelve years old. Who knows what kind of job you were thinking of? To you, it was simply a given that you were at liberty. The milkman smiled.

'The city's the other way. Hop in, I'll take you home.'

Back in Coal, school was finishing for the day. You had told the teacher you were sick and gone home early. I came straight over after school to visit you. It was me that told your mother you were missing.

'Come to see how Grace is feeling,' I said, loitering on your doorstep.

'What do you mean,' your mother said, 'how is she feeling? Isn't she at school?'

'School's finished. She was feeling sick this morning, Mrs Harper, and she said she was going home.'

'Bloody hell,' she said, 'where's the little headache got to now?' I thought that might have meant you were sick after all.

We quickly arranged another search party. I say we, though I was left behind this time, posted to wait at your house in case you came back. Your parents, tense and tired-looking, went out with the volunteers to find you. I sat at your kitchen table and swung my feet and tried not to rearrange anything.

I sat still and waited. My books stood in a hard lump in their calico bag on the kitchen table. I twisted the strap around my hand. I knew with pure conviction that you would arrive before your parents got back, that you would come to me alone. I could see you lying in the mossy frame of figs and vines, moving your arms and legs every now and then so the flies didn't think you were dead. And then in the seat of a milk truck, riding down the pass. I had absolute faith.

It was late by the time the truck's lights came along the road. I had moved to the back porch as it was still light enough out-side to see, despite the shadow the escarpment cast.

When the truck pulled in I didn't get up. You ran over and up the couple of steps and sat down next to me. The milkman tooted his horn and you waved as he drove away. I asked no questions and at first you said nothing. We sat slapping mozzies stubbornly for a bit, but eventually I capitulated. One of us had to break the silence.

'They're all out looking for you,' I said.

'Oh,' you said, smiling quietly to yourself.

'Probably be back soon cause it's dark.' I didn't want either of us to run and tell them you were found. I wanted to start today over again. You flicked your hair and slapped a mozzie and looked quite satisfied.

'I saw you,' I whispered, 'you were lying down. You could have told me you were running away, I would've come. I know how to get to the top from the fig tree place.' I felt a hot wound swell in my throat, a lump the size of the massive wasps' nests that hung off the trees in your yard, buzzing a sullen threat. I felt tears coming and didn't want you to see them, so I looked down the road in the direction the milk truck had gone. I stood up and watched for your parents to come.

A small voice raised itself from where you sat. 'How do you know where I was?'

I shrugged and leaned on the post.

'I didn't plan it, I just got bored of school. It's so slow.'

I frowned at your unapologetic tone.

'Anyway, there could be, I don't know, snakes and spiders up there. Dangerous things. I was just looking. Next time you can come with me?'

'I know where to go,' I repeated. 'Not through the blackbutts, you go up the track, to the top where the shape of the giant is, you can climb up to the road.'

'Oh. Right.' You seemed to have accepted that I knew exactly which track you'd taken.

'When?' I said, but you hushed me, because your mother and father were running up the road in the wake of the bright glare of their miner's lamps.

'The milkman, oh for shame, Grace, would you promise me never to do that again.' Faith was so flustered, she seemed to grab you with about three or four arms. Jack just stood there on the porch looking tired. I watched the scene from outside it, waiting for my moment, but the milkman had passed them further down the road and told the whole story. It turned out he knew your father from the union.

'If he hadn't stopped, you'd still be walking,' said Jack. 'It's a long way down by that road. Lucky, eh?' he smiled and reached out to touch your head. Faith glared at him.

'I'd better go home for my tea,' I said, and Jack nodded, one arm still outstretched, not even looking at me. Your mother called her thanks after me, though, as I tumbled briskly out of view.

'Thanks for waiting,' is what she said.

As I reached the fence, I heard your father say 'I thought he could have let us have some milk, don't you?'

That evening, I was the centre of my family. It was as if I'd run away by proxy. I told them the milkman found you hiding in the scrub as he went in to relieve himself. I told them you were terribly afraid of snakes and the dark up there and Mam nodded and said, 'Quite right too, that escarpment's full of holes.' I ate away at your fearlessness and it tasted bitter. I told them you were so weak that the milkman carried you up to the house and I had to revive you.

We all knew that I had no idea, at twelve, how to revive a person. But my family appreciated the entertainment, and I was proud of the glow.

I didn't say I saw you there in the bush and I didn't say a word about next time. I couldn't sleep properly for a week afterwards because everything felt complicated. I didn't want to make plans. I wanted us to keep being inseparable, to go on as we were. I didn't want either of us to run anywhere.

★ ★ ★

There were good times though, in those days. That complicated feeling didn't last. When the strike was called, more than a year after Victor's death, it was like a party. I loved to go down to the picket line, stand with you and your parents around a forty-gallon drum full of fire, and listen to them talk politics.

The union had asked for a 35-hour week and a thirty-shilling increase in wages. It was a good time to make demands; productivity was at a high.

Chifley responded by setting up a board that could wrest control from the union in an emergency, and then created that emergency by attacking the unions as dangerous organisations, full of communist sympathisers. Red was becoming a forceful accusation. The Cullens even changed their new dog's name to Ginger, just to be on the safe side.

Within a couple of days of the strike starting, the government made it illegal for shops to give the striking miners credit. Our tick list was promptly hidden in a locked drawer under the bar. We only had one cop in Coal but Mam and Da didn't trust him.

Some of the top union officials in Sydney were arrested, and your father grew nervous. They were mates of his, card-carriers all, and he knew that if fingers were being pointed, sooner or later one would end up pointed at him. He could no longer trust his connections. Once-strong bonds of solidarity were snapping like twigs under his feet.

The railway workers caved in after a couple of weeks and transported the last of the black-banned coal, but still no one was working. Times were tight again, but this time by choice. People took the time to repair their homes, talk to their neighbours, fix up the park and, of course, spend all their free time at the Danker.

Mam crossed out 'tips' on the big jar next to the beer taps and wrote 'strike fund' in its place. The Danker opened earlier and stayed open longer, functioning as a meeting hall, childcare centre and soup kitchen.

It was lean and hungry for most of the workers, but for us kids, the strike was fun, just as if we were given an extra Christmas in the middle of the year. You celebrated your thirteenth birthday on the picket line, waving your red flag and smiling as your mother divided the cake up amongst the strikers. I helped you take the plates around, glowing in the fire and the warmth of mutual support, and watched you proudly. It seemed like we were getting somewhere.

At the end of the third week, the troops arrived. These strangers in uniform with rifles on their shoulders burst through the picket with ease, waved in by old Thornbag with the reluctant assistance of Kev, the local copper. The men shouted and tried to hold the line, but the guns had raised stakes they couldn't meet.

The troops were supposed to be here to work the coal, but there were other ways to get scab labour. They were really there to intimidate the miners out of their militancy. It was said that at the bigger mines they even carried machine guns. Suddenly, we were at war all over again, and this time the fascists had arrived on our doorstep.

The dozen army boys were camped on Thorne's property, guarded day and night. No one could touch them without an instant trespassing conviction, or worse, a bullet in the leg. The miners tried to think of a way to get at them, but they'd busted through their line, and it was too late, the coal was starting to be processed again.

The people of Coal gave up for the moment and slunk off up to the Danker for a consolatory drink.

My da was furious. He refused to admit the military. 'This is our place, and they can't tell us who to serve,' he said, and wrote a bold sign in his solid, clumsy handwriting: *No Scabs No Troopers*. He stuck it on the door and locked it.

Kev, who had grown up in a local mining family but earned the distinction of being Coal's only uniform, banged on the door that night. The Danker was full to bursting with striking miners planning their next move. Jack was busy holding forth about the ALP's traitorous actions.

'Labor is a party of the capitalists,' he shouted, 'and at least now we know where we stand!' For once everyone was happy to listen to his speeches.

My da excused himself through the group of cheering men and headed for the door. He leaned on it and pointed at the sign, shrugging and grinning his apology. Da and Kev were fishing buddies, but this was war.

'I just want a beer,' Kev yelled through the glass. 'I'm off for the day.'

Da clicked the lock, pushed the door open a crack, and examined Kev through the gap. 'How do we know you're not a spy?' he asked.

'Come on, Sean, you know whose side I'm on.'

'If I let you in I can't guarantee your safety,' he said. 'There's a meeting.' He looked over his shoulder to check the state of the men. 'They're not happy with what you've done today.'

'I didn't help them, I bloody tried to stop them!'

'Hang on a minute,' Da said. He closed the door in Kev's face and went behind the bar to get the soundproof earmuffs Callum wore when he worked down the pit. Mam eyed him with suspicious amusement as he returned to the door.

'Here,' he said, 'put these on. Can't have the likes of you

listening in on our plans, now, can we?' He handed Kev the earmuffs and let him in.

The poor copper did as he was told. He sat quietly on his stool and signed to Mam for a schooner. More than one comment about the nature of his job was made that night, but he heard nothing.

You and I were watching all this from the bistro. Mam had enlisted our help in getting the men a feed. She shrugged away the no-credit rule.

'If we can't lend it to them, we'll give it to them,' she said.

We prepared a feast for the strikers every evening, fresh-caught fish and fried potatoes, Irish stew from a sheep brought up from my grandparents' farm, and even some of our chooks. It cost us nothing but the labour.

'I'm worried about Jack,' you said, when the potatoes were all peeled, sliced, and in the fryer and Mam was off tidying up the bar. I envied the way your parents kept you on first-name terms. They were intent that you would grow up independent, aware of your equality with any man or woman of any class. It made you seem strangely adult, while I was forever the baby of my family, and learning to be satisfied with my chores.

'He seems to be enjoying himself,' I said. He'd finished his speech and was sitting at a table by the fire along with Tom Cullen, Greg Barrett, and a handful of younger men. They were conspiring in low tones. When Jack spoke, he had the whole table's attention. You ran the tap for the washing up and watched the suds blossom in the sink.

'He's going to lose his job,' you said. 'The union has to get rid of the communists. They can't go on like this.' You pulled the rubber gloves on and turned off the tap.

'I don't know what will happen to us,' you said, thrusting

your hands into the sink and leaning there. 'If he loses his job, we'll have to leave Coal.'

With a sharp intake of breath, I smelled danger, like something burning.

'Leave?' It wasn't possible. Did you not realise that you were needed here? I couldn't let you go to Sydney. That was nearly two whole hours away by train.

'They can fire him from the union,' I said, 'but he can still work at the mine, surely.'

You shook your head. 'He reckons it's impossible. They'd never hire a Red now.'

'And what about your ma – your Faith?'

'She can get a job, easy. So can I, soon. And Jack would find something. We can't go back to Sydney though, he still has too many enemies there. We'd have to move interstate. Faith has a sister in Adelaide.'

'South Australia?' That might have been Siberia, for all I knew.

That faint smell of burning hung in the air. I remembered the potatoes and pulled the basket out of the oil just in time. I shook it and set it to drain, then took a towel and wiped the dishes, passing them to you to put away. If there was no Grace at the other end of my arm, I thought, these plates would fall and smash to pieces. How could I explain this to you? It would be like losing my own arm.

We served up a feed to everyone, and not a moment too soon, because things were starting to get a little rowdy. Kev was sitting at the bar, oblivious to the noise but not to the smells, trying to make eye contact with Mam and score a bit of tucker. She shook her head and leaned over to uncover one of his ears.

'You still have a job,' she said. 'If you could call it that.'

He rummaged in his pockets and handed some money over. 'Keep the change,' he said, 'you know, for the cause.'

'All right,' said Mam, 'thanks.' She deposited the change in the jar and handed him a plate with a smile. 'You can put those ears back on though. They suit you.'

I helped clear the plates from the tables and thought hard about how I could make you stay. I ran over my options. We could run away together, just the two of us, but where? All my ideas of the rest of the world were stupidly unrealistic. The imaginary places that had once seemed so solid to me were just pathetic fabrications.

I looked around the bar. The Danker was full of happy activity. Da was throwing a log in the fire. Mam was taking up plates in a stack against her hips. Callum was leaning on the bar, already one of the men, and Brendan stood by his side, trying to match him. I couldn't leave them. I would have to think of something.

Faith took you home when she decided Jack had had enough. She told us we were good comrades for all our hard work, and I would have felt proud if I hadn't been too busy willing her not to leave. I moped around the bar, tidying half-heartedly until Mam sent me up to bed. I was too worried to sleep. Which was lucky, because I'd have missed all the fun.

That night, one of the men went down the mine in secret, slipping over the back fence and past the guards. He came out with a small sack, which he carried carefully in his arms like a sleeping child as he walked silently up the headland to the Danker.

From upstairs I could hear the buzz in the bar, vibrating through the floorboards. It was as if the building itself were excited. I knew the strikers were planning something. To judge from the belly-laughs and shushes echoing drunkenly up the stairs, it was something interesting. I slipped out of bed and went to the balcony to watch.

A wobbling caterpillar of men emerged from the pub. Some carried small packages under their arms. I could hear them shushing each other loudly down the track as they headed to the shelf of rock that jutted out under the headland. I could smell their excitement mingling with the healthy weedrot of low tide. I hid my face in the curling shadows and waited.

There was silence after they disappeared behind the rocks, and I started to wonder if they were simply drinking down at the beach, or slipping around in the rockpools for fun. We used to walk out on that rocky shelf to spot sea slugs, which my brothers would throw at us if we weren't careful. We'd stick our fingers into red suckers, get them stuck in anemone tentacles, move snails out of their tracks and try to prise limpets from their strongholds. It was fun, but I couldn't see how grown men would enjoy it in the dark.

An explosion rocked the land. I felt the Danker lurch gleefully beneath me. Water shot up towards the pub, so high it crested the headland. I felt a faint spray land on my face and my eyes grew wide. I thought someone might be hurt. But the line of men returned up the hill, laughing and boisterous. And down on the rocks below, something had changed.

First thing the next day, I ran across the back of Cullen's place to get you, shirking my chook-feeding duties. This resulted in a talking-to from Da, but it was the kind where he ruffled my head halfway through and said away-with-you. His trousers were out on the line, recovering from knee-deep seawater. I'd seen his shape in the line of men. In the usual hierarchy of such things he got a talking-to from Mam, who grumbled about the washing, though you could see she was pleased, even when she said they were all bloody stupid fools and did they want to kill themselves dynamiting in the middle of the night.

You met me halfway along the path the two of us had worn across Cullen's yard. The old yellow cow eyed us sleepily and munched her grass as we bolted past. The not-red dog followed us down to the beach.

A section of the rock shelf was gone, but in its place was a new kind of marvel. The pool was rough around the edges, but perfect for swimming when the sand settled down. The blasts must have been powerful to break up all that rock; it's a wonder the pieces didn't fly up and break the Danker's windows.

By the time we got there in our bathers, the Cullen boys and my brothers were already treading gleeful circles in the captured sea, dunking each other's heads. On seeing us, Brendan and Callum swam to the edge and splashed us with wide sweeps of their arms. The water was icy, but the pool was too good to resist.

They've evened out the sides now, and concreted the edges. Every morning the swimmers, braver than me, are down there at dawn, watched over by a few idle cormorants. It would do me good, but I never got the hang of the cold. Joe goes every morning, and sometimes comes up after his laps for a cup of tea, especially when he sees me walking Mallee or out feeding the chooks. The rest of them are mostly new people, Sydney people I call them, though some of them have been here half their lives.

They never caught the man who stole the dynamite, but we knew why Tom Cullen was shouted beers for the rest of the week. To this day, Joe's never admitted that it was his father, but it's one of his favourite stories. I hear him telling it evenings, his stocky little legs tucked up under his stool and his arms animated. He tells stories in colours. I listen and nod and remember my own way.

The first thing you did in the pool was swim to the bottom and come up with treasure. A stone that had split so you could see the lines of sediment that made it over the years: sea washing out, earth setting in, stripes of black and red and gold. You left it on the edge of the pool, and when you went home for your dinner I retrieved it. The colours had faded in the sun. My brothers and I were called up to eat and I carried it home in two salty hands. I placed it on the shelf beside my bed.

'Adelaide,' I said, and shook my head.

In the end, there was no Adelaide. Faith solved the problem of your father's job by getting one herself. This was considered by half the town to be a ridiculous and foolish experiment, by the other half a brave and honourable gesture. No one thought it was practical, and everyone assumed it wouldn't last. Faith was just doing what she had to, as she had always done, cleaning up her husband's messes, making ends meet.

It would have been all right if she'd taken up nursing or teaching or secretarial work, but she went down to the steelworks and got herself a man's job, punching holes and sinking rivets, melting great pots of metal in the furnaces. She got a pair of overalls, tied her hair up under a cloth cap, and started smoking roll-your-owns.

I adored her for it, of course. I had my own selfish motives for admiring her. I didn't realise that the sister in South Australia was part of a family that had disowned their second daughter out of shame when she decided to pack her education in and become a defender of the proletariat. They had sacrificed a lot to educate their girls in the hope that they would marry up a class, and Faith had denied them the satisfaction by dropping out in her teens and heading resolutely down.

I was overjoyed, you were quietly relieved, but Jack, when the strike ended and he got his letter from the union in a big brown envelope which told him that his services were no longer required, was a lost man. He threw his full weight into the party as a means of dispelling the sense that he, as an individual, had failed. Failed to adapt, failed to see the crunch coming, and failed as a man to provide for his household. As Faith let her committees slide a little, understanding the need for covert operations and enjoying the laughs and comradeship of the new work, Jack committed himself to every regional meeting he could find, and perhaps a few that he had to invent.

After a while, he seemed to enjoy the freedom. But he was never the same man. His pride had taken a beating. His eyes became shifty, as if they were looking for a chance to get back at the world.

You, on the other hand, seemed as glad as I was that you were here to stay. Disaster had been averted, for the moment.

twelve

If I could draw a map of this story, it would be made of rough circles. I come back to the present, only to find that it is still full of the past. I turn a page of my pad and begin to outline the place my memories might be. When I look at what I have made, it is a meaningless scribble. A tangle of fishing line found on the beach. I throw the page away.

About a week before your letter came, I saw something I haven't seen in a long time. I was walking Mallee on the beach at night. The gibbous moon was bright enough to see by. I don't often walk out after closing, but when I do I find it soothing knowing that everyone is asleep, that there is no more work to be done until morning.

I heard the car approach from at least a kilometre away. I heard a movement in the scrub, the usual rustle of nocturnal creatures. Mallee growled at it, but I held his lead. The rabbit sat up and looked at me in the dark. I could only see its shape, but when the car came closer I could see that it was black. Its eyes lit with a mysterious green, like two electric signals. I watched its silhouette tense and take flight across the road, watched its edges grow sharp and fade in the looming headlights. I was glad when the creature made it across.

I am not superstitious, I keep telling myself. I am too practical to be convinced by a normal genetic mutation, a throwback. In the darkness after the vehicle had sped by, I stood still for a moment, watching the scrub for movement, but found none.

It's not even a superstition, is it, when you invent it yourself. I am playing tricks on myself, only seeing the things I want to, drawing connections where none exist. Anything can be a coincidence, with hindsight. I don't believe that objects have a will of their own. Clare's told me about the idea of manifesting things. That your thoughts can bring them. But I think that only works because if you wait long enough, everything happens again.

For all that these coincidences leap up and yank at me, it is probably nothing. It is probably just a result of my own head going around and around this story like a spin cycle. Sometimes when I walk around the whole place is so heavy with meaning that I am exhausted by it. I don't want to go out into the burdened country. I haven't been up the escarpment in weeks, and I love walking. Those old pits were filled in years ago, but it still feels as though there are too many shadows up there. Too many holes.

It's just that it's not any one thing, Grace, it's an avalanche of them. Your ghost, these memories, the artefacts that surface from our past. All these stories and memories and inventions crowding back into my life. I look at this letter from you on my kitchen table, the one I'm still trying to answer, and feel that it's a symptom. Some dam has burst. Some pressure in the sea has released a tidal wave. It's no accident the surf is higher than usual for this time of year. King tides leave a lot of junk on the shore.

I can see no explanation, no clean way out. All I can do is face it head on and hope that my feet are planted firmly enough that I will not wash away in the next storm.

The irony is that you are asking me for some kind of truth to hang on to, an anchor of fact, a rock of yourself. That you can't trust your own memory any more, after all that you've been through. But I have nothing real to throw to you, no proof, only the way things happened for me. I have only my stories and all these things I had thought buried and forgotten.

All that fiction. I grew out of it. I refused to cling to you as some kind of sustaining fantasy. I had no realistic choice but to think of you as a dear but absent friend. I had too much work to do here. What did I deny but a fiction that we could never inhabit? It wasn't possible. I lost my faith in it. I learned to trust nothing but the earth beneath my feet, the hand in front of my face as my da used to say. But that was a lie.

That night I walked on the beach barefoot, the sand cold between my toes. I thought about the night I told you the rabbit story on the edge of the porch, too young to know what I was messing with. I thought how different my life would have been if I hadn't begun. The sea crashed at the rocks, its passion anything but pacified. I walked to the edge and let its smallest waves reach over my feet, let it drag at the hem of my skirt, let it call to me.

'Grace, where are you?'

The sea has no echo. It was a long time before I realised I had spoken aloud.

★ ★ ★

I'm trying to resist updating you on all that has changed in the landscape, which would be a life's work in itself. To keep track of all the little shifts and growths and collapses, that would take another teller. The land we once danced all over in a circus of risk, a game of follow the leader, has altered. It feels too much like a refusal of your existence to mark time in this way.

The lantana has gone, bulldozed to make way for houses, and it's probably a good thing too. The council hires people to do bush regeneration. Authentic plants only. The bush is being restored to its former glory, as much as it can be with us here at its edge. Eventually there will be no trace of you save for my own memory.

But the map hasn't changed. I still know the stones and the stories, the secret tracks we marked up there. I've learned some of the older stories too. The stories of how this country was made, why the tracks trace certain lines. I don't let on that I know. I only tell them to myself sometimes, when I'm walking up there.

Last night, Clare asked me if I knew any of these stories about the country. I shook my head slowly, but her clear eyes didn't stray from mine. She wasn't fooled.

'Wait,' I said. 'Wait until you meet the right people.'

'You won't tell me?'

'It's not my place, and I can't promise I will get it right. Anyway, Betty drops around from time to time. You'll meet her eventually.'

'It's just that I love it here,' she said. 'I want to know everything.'

'Curiosity killed the cat,' I smiled.

'True,' she said. 'But the cat has eight more questions.'

'Go on,' I said, 'I'm counting.'

'In that case, I'd better save them for another time,' she said. 'I've just been thinking. I've been all over the world, but this is the first place I've ever wanted to stay, to get to know. Why is that?'

'It does that to some people,' I said, 'but getting to know it takes a lifetime. Maybe more.' She downed the last drop in her glass and I poured her another. 'It changes too slowly to see. And it changes too quickly,' I added. 'You turn around and the place you thought you knew has gone, replaced by a row of houses.'

'If there's any bulldozers to be chained to, I'll be first in line,' she said.

'Let's hope it won't come to that again. That part of it was crown land, see. They could sell it off. The rest of the escarpment is state forest, it'll be picked up by national parks when the mining leases expire. I don't see why they can't just give it back, but at least they've finally worked out how important it is to look after it.'

'I hope someone has,' she said.

'Part of me thinks it's too late for us. When I was a kid, there were wallabies, even the odd koala here. There used to be fleets of whales on the coast. They've come back a bit, but you're lucky if you see half a dozen in a year.'

I picked up the bottle opener from under the bar and flicked the corkscrew out in my hand. The heft of it was so familiar, I might have been holding a part of my own body.

The door swung open to let in a few straggling, late-season tourists, bronzed from their day on the beach.

'You have seven questions left,' I smiled, and went to serve them.

★ ★ ★

If I could draw a map of this story, if I could chart the course of it, I might not feel so lost. I think of an old map my father once showed me, from a time when Australia was an idea.

The cartographers that drew this country a long time ago, before anyone sailed around it taking measurements, engaged in a speculative fiction. Just like my childhood self making a mirror world in the haze of a horizon, the mapmakers presumed the world had balance. If the earth was round, they thought there must be something there, a counterweight for the north. The southern land on those maps is round and ambiguous, like a child's drawing. It is bigger than the real country. Such symmetry only exists in the mind. The real world is always less satisfying.

How true can this be? There are too many things we don't know. I can deliberately leave parts out of this story, I can keep going despite the gaps. But I can't invent you, not now, not from nothing. Not alone like this.

thirteen

After the strike, the world seemed to shift its shape. Our bodies changed as if in sympathy. We shared our first blood, a few weeks apart. We shared our fears about what this meant. I came to rely on your house for information, because your mother wasn't shy about answering questions. Where my own mam would impatiently sideline my curiosity or tell me to get out of the way, yours treated me as an equal. I came over with invented requests for cups of sugar and waited for Faith to come home, hang her cap on the door and unbind her hair. I listened to her tell us, with patient bemusement, what was really going on.

Faith smelled interestingly of sparks, now. The liking I had taken to her when she got that job was the start of a friendship that, in a way, outlasted yours. Faith leaned on the kitchen table and told us that there were no stupid questions, that information was power, that we were a new generation of women who didn't have to accept the roles that men dictated for us. She was quite charged with the thrill of her role. It was only when Jack came home that she would wink conspiratorially and herd us out of the kitchen to get his tea.

According to the more conservative social codes of Coal, we weren't supposed to take any active interest in boys in those days, so it didn't matter if that hadn't happened. Boys had become interested in us, though. More to the point, they had become interested in you. I found that I no longer enjoyed the rough and tumble games on the beach, or hide and seek in the bush on the point, when I had to fight a line of Cullens for your attention. Even my own brother Brendan followed you around with a hangdog look. You'd grown beautiful, losing some of the ready sprinting ability of only a year before, but gaining something akin to your name.

I took comfort in the fact of our ongoing conspiracy. You still mocked everyone but me, only there was a different light in your eyes. You liked the attention.

When I was fourteen, my mam, in her steady, taciturn way, decided that instead of explaining anything she would take me up to the city. We went to Mark Foy's department store to get some devices that would upholster and restrain my growing body. No more hand-me-down jumpers and homemade skirts. I was to be born anew in elastic and bone.

The city terrified me. I think I still blamed the place for taking my brother away. Everything smelled intimidating. I had never seen so many strangers. I was dragged unwillingly through the big glass doors on Liverpool Street, pushed through the hall of mirrors and told not to whine. I was fitted for beige-coloured garments that laced or snapped my body into shape and stiffened me. As compensation, Mam bought me a pair of white kid gloves. They were the most beautiful thing I had ever touched. Their soft leather was exactly like living skin.

Afterwards we visited an accountant in his office upstairs. The man was a distant relative of hers, and she'd called in a favour. I didn't realise the significance of this at the time. I was still too busy worshipping my father to think about what he was doing when he slipped out at night. Despite her near-omniscience, I doubt even Mam knew the full extent of the problem. I waited in the foyer, watching the secretary stamp forms and lick envelopes, and wondered whether I could get away with leaving my bag of shopping in this stale office.

As a full stop to the day, there were fish and chips at Circular Quay. The fish was rubbery and dry, not fresh-caught as we were used to, and we both threw most of it back in the harbour. Standing there on the cobblestones laden with my new burdens of womanhood, my mother finally steeled herself and gave me the Talk.

What followed was a vague but terrifying exposition of things men do in alleyways, of the city, and of blood, more blood than anyone rightly deserved. The curse had something to do with Eve's mistake. I felt myself go pale and decided I preferred my mother when she was aloof. I didn't want to break her heart and explain that I'd been visiting Faith, eating my own apples on the sly.

We watched the ferries come in and ate our chips. Mam frowned at the boats. She had gone very quiet. I knew she was thinking of Patrick, but I was too shy of her to offer any sign of the sympathy I felt. We said nothing more until the train was due and I had to haul the heavy bags of corsetry up the stairs. I was relieved when I arrived back in the safety of the Danker, where I could close the door to my room and lie in my own bed and tell myself stories until I put myself to sleep.

Coal is not normally susceptible to bushfires. There are worse places in the west beyond the top of the cliff, dry valleys with tinderbox summers. Here we've got the sea breeze pushing cool, damp air up the wall of rock.

It was a particularly hot summer the year of the fire. We wilted at school. The old portable tin classroom made snapping noises as it heated. The flies hung off us in clouds. I swatted at them all morning as we sat learning English poems about a tidy, friendly natural world. Wordsworth might have been from Mars as far as I was concerned.

It was Joe Cullen who spotted it.

'Mrs Gowan, excuse me, look,' he said, without putting his hand up, an omission usually punishable by ruler. His hand was too busy pointing out the window. A plume of smoke rose dark and thick not far from our schoolyard.

'Oh, I see,' said Mrs Gowan. 'Perhaps someone's burning off. Now what do you think he means when he says that he's lonely as a cloud?'

'It's a metaphor,' said Mercy in her best voice.

'That's almost right. It's a simile.' You rolled your eyes at me from the next desk because of course it was a simile, and you hated sharing a classroom with people who didn't know this already. I shrugged; not being as clever at schoolwork as you, I was far more patient with it. We were all in together with the little ones in the mornings, which wasn't as unruly as it sounds, mainly because us older kids did half the job of keeping the younger ones out of trouble. There were more young kids now that the post-war babies were growing, and the school had expanded to a sizeable thirty students.

We still didn't have a bell, though. Mrs Gowan simply looked at her watch and said, 'All right then, go and have your lunch.' When the hour was up, she would stand on the veranda with her arms folded until we all lined up at her feet.

That lunchtime in the dusty grounds, it was far too hot to run around. We all sat under one of the scribbly gums to wilt quietly, watching the plume of smoke get bigger.

A dry wind picked up from the west, but we didn't think much of it. You and I were sitting a little apart from the rest, on a bench particular to our habit, the privilege of older girls. Mercy went home for lunch most of the time because otherwise someone would steal it off her. You have to hand it to her parents, they could have sent her to a boarding school but they were trying hard not to alienate themselves any more than was necessary.

As it happened, that little patch of bush to the south was where Alice Gowan had her house. Fortunately her children were both at school, even Victor Jr. He was only three, and really too little, but Mrs Gowan had nowhere else to put him in the daytime.

You and I watched the smoke as the other kids ran weakly in the heat. I was telling you a story, a false one. A fire story, in a castle I had built from the poems. You drew in the dust with a stick: castellated towers, moats and drawbridges. We had more in common with the romantics than we would have admitted. You interrupted me halfway through my description of burning ramparts.

'May, where's Polly going?'

We watched the twin black pigtails of our teacher's eldest child disappear behind the portable.

'Ah, she must have a meeting with her secret society,' I began, but you were already up and tugging at my sleeve. By the time we reached her, Polly was halfway over the fence.

'Where are you going?' you asked her.

'My house is on fire,' she said, calm as anything. She had the dark, sad eyes of a cow.

'No it isn't,' we chorused, and then we saw our teacher running up the road in a panic. Polly bolted over to her mother, grabbed onto her, and they ran together back down the road.

You looked at me meaningfully.

'We'll be missed,' I said.

'Five minutes,' you replied.

'All right, but it's your fault if we get caught.'

We snuck across the fence and around the perimeter of the school, ran behind the shop and up the hill. The bush above us was blazing in sections, and ash fell from the air like black snow. We walked to where Mrs Gowan's wooden house perched above the point, where it shoulders the escarpment. It was not on fire yet, but we could feel the heat coming and our eyes were already watering from the smoke. There should be firemen, I thought, maybe the road is cut off. At that moment the truck came roaring up the hill and we had to jump out of sight behind someone's garden wall.

'Look,' you said, standing to see over the rough brick. 'It's coming.'

I felt the blast against my skin as the fire crested the hill and swallowed a tree whole. I was quiet and still, mesmerised by the speed of it. You had to drag me away from it. We ran the quick way down the railway line and back to school.

We were, of course, missed. We found the rest of our classmates lined up in the dust by age and being counted by Kev. The copper frowned at us and herded us into line. I wondered why you always thought you could get away with this kind of thing. Two out of thirty is a fair percentage.

After half an hour, Mrs Gowan returned, visibly shaken and glancing over her shoulder. I would have liked to have done something for her, but the fire must have swallowed everything by now, and besides we were busy watching her develop a second air of tragedy.

Thankfully she was too distraught to give us the ruler. We listened instead to Joe caw about his find. 'I was the one that spotted it,' he said, as if it was a gold nugget.

We were given the rest of the afternoon off. 'Go straight home, all of you,' Mrs Gowan said.

We all promised we would, then ran as fast as we could to the line where the volunteers were fighting. They had put up a bit of rope to deter us from running headlong into the flames. Da was there, and your parents, standing together in a little cluster around the hose. Nearly all the others in the group were women.

I wondered if the men were all still down the mine. I wondered if you could be trapped and cooked down there, like in a pitfire. I thought of roasted potatoes dug out of the ashes in their jackets. Callum and Brendan were down there in the dark. I wanted to ask Da, but he was busy helping with the hose and I didn't dare interrupt him in case he made me go home. We had a magnificent view of the fireys in their red hats disappearing into the smoke up ahead.

The wind must have turned in their favour, because they fought the line back as far as the creek. The exposed strip of burned bush looked like sticks of drawing charcoal stuck in the dirt. The trees were black and bare and dead-looking, the ground suddenly flat and naked without its undergrowth. The houses were all right after all. Mrs Gowan was better without another air of tragedy, though it was a good story either way.

'Praise the angels,' she said, as if they had anything to do with it. She kissed all the firemen, who were blushing red from the heat.

Finally, my da noticed us standing in the line of kids and came to take me home. His eyes were bright with the fire, his face dark with smoke. I followed him back to the pub, but made sure I arranged to meet you at our tree in the morning.

In my memory, it's not the fire that stands out. It's the image of the strange unseasonal springtime that settled in afterwards. Late in the summer the place looked like a 'real' winter, meaning European. Trees stood bare and white ash covered the ground like snow. Out of this, the green began. First, the grasstrees sprouted overnight and stuck out tentative crowns of green spines, then the gums spread new branches from strange places along their bodies and cascaded with leaves.

I can see this growth occurring before our eyes like a time-lapse film. It can't have happened that way, I know, but it's what my memory tells me. You shot up too, an inch taller than me. Your hair spread long tendrils down your back.

We walked in the new green. Familiar with every rock and tree, I was shocked by the shift that had occurred. I stared hard at the bush until I could make out the old landmarks. The places where we normally hid had been thrown bare, almost brutalised. I felt the country's bruises.

You stared too, but if I thought you felt the same way, I was wrong. You smiled at the bald bush and touched a spray of fern with your hand.

'Life looks like it comes out of nothing at all,' you said.

I opened my mouth to answer, but no sound came. Instead, a thunderclap resounded against the cliffs.

We hurried back through the stricken forest. Black patches in the sky threatened to beat us home, and I followed your lead. Drama against drama, the sky cracked open to bless the bald earth with its next shot at living.

The rain came down just as we got to your house and ran inside for cover. We ran down the hallway that divided it neatly in two. I could see the world on either side framed in a doorway. Your house was bare, but lived in. Tin cups stood on the kitchen table amidst a scatter of crumbs and an unwashed pan with a crust of yellow egg. Your father's papers were scattered on every surface, some in piles, some tied up with string, but all maintaining an air of urgent disarray.

Your room was plain, but decently sized. A dusty, crocheted bedspread was thrown over the bed, its colours faded to shades of grey in the light of the storm. The rough floorboards creaked and threatened splinters. You leaned and pulled one from a bare foot with expert fingers.

The particular, living smell of rain filled the room. You crawled onto your bed and lay back across it, your head propped against the wall, your feet dangling. You kicked at the air and pulled your knees up to your chest.

'Tell me a story,' you said. 'I'm cold.'

'True or false?'

'Either one will do,' you said, but considered it, scratching an ankle with a bare foot. 'True.'

I sat cross-legged, perched on your wooden chair. I told you a story from before we were born, one my da had told me many times, about the freight train robberies of the early Thirties. I tried to conjure the desperation of the night my father injured his knee. I had to raise my voice above the rain, which came down on the tin roof in heavy sheets. When I finished, I saw that your eyes had closed.

'You asleep?'

'Jack told me that story,' you said. 'I thought he made it up. Is that really true your da was one of them?'

'So he says,' I replied. The story was as true as I'd ever heard it.

'The thief,' you muttered. 'No wonder you're a liar.' You were lying down the length of the bed, staring at your ceiling. The roof above was thunderous. Rain wrapped us in a blanket of sound. Even now, revisiting this moment, I feel a sympathetic ache in my joints.

I moved myself out of the pose I was in. I crawled in beside you, between your body and the wall. I stared at the ceiling, trying to imagine I was gazing at the exact same place, trying to discover your thoughts in the cracked plaster. It was growing dark, but impossible to tell if that was due to the clouds or nightfall. Your skin felt cold against mine, and I wriggled closer.

'May?'

'What?'

There was a pause the size of a house, and then a small voice crept in my ear, your breath a brief warmth against the chill.

'Will we always be friends?'

'Yes,' I told the ceiling. 'Definitely. Always.'

Your hand found mine and we lay like that, sleeping intermittently as the rain went its way out to sea.

When I awoke, I had fallen between the bed and the wall, and had to pull myself out of the crack. My movements must have woken you, unless you'd been lying there thinking. You turned your head to face me, so close as to blur your features.

'What do you want to be?' you asked me.

'When? I already am.'

'You know what I mean. How come you never tell stories about yourself?' You turned your head away in irritation, stretching out a warm neck. I nestled my forehead against it. I can't remember if I gave you an answer.

As I write, a currawong lands on the back step, eats a convenient caterpillar, waddles sideways, and spreads its tail into a black and white fan. Mallee raises an ear and flutters an eyelid but pays it no more heed. The air's too crisp and still. It has no substance, only light. I wonder if I dare proceed. The unravelling, once begun, cannot be undone. I am a bird pulling at a tangled string.

What did I want to be? Did I ever think I could be someone I was not? When I try to remember my dreams from that age, I can only recall the lies. Maybe I always knew where I belonged, or maybe I was never bold enough to question it. It was you I made futures for. You were brave enough to fill them.

You and I were sitting in a hollow in the rocks above the pool, watching the sea. Your dress cast crisp shadows on the sandstone. The tide was on its way out. Two shoeless girls, we sat in broad hats that shaded our faces. I was sturdy, tanned, and work-strong. Your slender body coiled with some urgent energy; you had no substance, only light.

'I'm going to swim out to the rock.' You pulled a long gold strand back into place under the hat's straw ceiling and pointed at the outcrop a mile or so from the headland. Breaking waves raised calm white flags, surrendering to the sky. The horizon was a perfect line; I could see the curvature of the earth. We weren't wearing our bathers, those shapeless suits with stiff shorts, jelly-fish frills around the hips to conceal any hint of what happened at the tops of our legs.

'Do you want to go up to the house and change?'

'I'll miss the tide,' you said. 'It'll turn.'

I didn't believe you were really that bold, even when you thrust your hat into my hands and stood to wriggle out of your dress. Stays and girdle held you together despite the slightness of your growing curves. Your dress fell softly beside me, like a breeze had dropped it. The body beside it towered, teetered, and tensed. Parts of your pale skin were exposed between the bones of these practical undergarments from a catalogue, mended by hand. There was a tight, cursive bend in your back, pushing the hip-bones out.

You didn't strip naked, to my uncertain relief. You tiptoed down the rock, surefooted, never a glance at the world that might be watching you scandalise yourself. It was a performance for my benefit, as though I'd been the one to dare you. My eyes followed you like a compass needle follows true north.

You worked your way past the pool to the edge of the shelf. The water lapped subserviently at your feet. Out past the break-ers the ocean was a fathomless dark blue, the blue I associate with music. You slipped into it like a pointed fish: first hands, then face, shoulders, waist, legs and feet.

I inhaled again when you surfaced a few strokes out. We must have taken gulps of air at the same time. You turned one back-stroke, I suppose to make sure I was watching, then rolled onto your belly and swam overarm in a straight line. You did not rest, nor glance up to check your progress. I watched you shrink. As you became smaller, the waves grew bigger. You were lifted over the rolling hills and sank into the troughs, only to rise again and again.

Finally, a distinct shape came out of the water. You clambered up the rock and stood holding your chest, one tiny hand raised in triumphant greeting. I waved and smiled, though you couldn't have seen my face; I couldn't see yours. You lingered there, staring back at me for a long time, longer than you would need to catch your breath. You looked lost out there, like a miniature of yourself. A tiny, porcelain Crusoe. I took my eyes off you for a second to scan the coastline for observers, remembering to be embarrassed. By some miracle, we were unobserved.

I turned my face back to the horizon. You had vanished. I stood up too quickly and my heel nearly skidded out from under me. I held onto the rock. I scanned the water until I could see thin arms striking at the sea. You were swimming back to shore, a pale arrow streaking through the blue.

I scrambled to the edge to meet you with your clothes bundled under one arm. As you stepped out of the water in your dripping undergarments, I held out your dress. I clutched the hat against my side and waited. Your face was pimpled with the chill and you wiped your hands over your eyes to get the water off. You twisted your hair to wring it out.

'That was bloody freezing,' you said.

'Grace.' I was still clutching your dress at arm's length. I was trying not to stare at the texture of your skin. Finally you let your hair fall, shook yourself off, and took the dress. I crushed the straw hat in my hand, pressed it against my leg.

'That was reckless,' I said, blushing. I should have been more impressed.

'One of us has to be reckless,' you replied. You looked back at the ocean with longing. 'Everything looks so neat from out there. Like a postcard.'

'Wish you were here,' I said, and straightened the crumpled hat in my hands.

I might not have been as smart as you, but I was the one who read. My love of books was stimulated by my brother Brendan, who always left a small pile of discarded biographies on the floor of his room. Eventually I'd tired of his stories of great and noble men – inventors, usually, or explorers – and read every book my parents owned, which didn't take long. There was a library in Wollongong, and I begged to accompany Mam when we went down to buy stores. They eventually got a bus and brought the library up and down the coast but, before that, my supply was limited.

When I walked into the library, I always felt a rush of the illicit. Perhaps this was because the librarian used to follow me around the room. She was there to make sure I didn't pick up anything inappropriate for a young lady. DH Lawrence had lived in the neighbourhood years ago, but his books were not available. I didn't mind. I would read anything. I grew to love the flawed heroines I was allowed: Scarlett, Jane, Elizabeth and Anna.

I always lent you the books I borrowed. Perhaps it was your intelligence that made you impatient with them. You'd get bored, throw down your book and exclaim, 'Why can't they just get on with it?' You wanted to be in their position, as you'd have done things better. I merely wanted to be in their world.

We were lying on the beach, reading my latest collection of novels. A basket half-full of biscuits lay at my elbow, a broad hat on each of our heads to protect us from the sun.

I always read the book before you, and knew what was going to happen next. I watched you out of the corner of my eye and waited for the inevitable moment.

About halfway through, you turned the book upside-down and leaned on your elbow.

'What happens next? Does she get rid of him? Does she marry him?'

'You wouldn't,' I replied. 'You'd be off. Take the money and run: blackmail him into it, or steal if you had to. You'd travel the world.'

The novel stayed upside-down in the sand while you listened to me put you in its heroine's place and do far better.

'You never tell me what's going to happen next,' you said. 'Only what you think should happen.'

'It's the same thing, isn't it? My version is usually better.'

'Yes, but I want to know what really happens.'

'Read your book then,' I said, throwing a biscuit at you and missing. A seagull came to scoop it out of the sand, glancing at me as if expecting a catch to its fortune. Your eyes were on something behind me.

'There's Ted,' you said. 'He's watching you.'

'He's watching you,' I replied, but I turned around to look for him.

'Are you crazy? He waits around the pub for a chance to say hello. I think he's in love with you.'

I thought about this, watching you watch him. Your eyes reflected the sun's glare, but the blue in them was yours alone and piercing. I shook it from my head.

I thought Ted Barrett was kind of handsome, in the way of boys who are shy and strong. Red hair and freckles meant he'd never had the vanity of a really handsome boy. He often loitered around the Danker. I'd always assumed he would get over me and follow you around like everyone else. He was older than me, old enough to be working in the mine, but he was trying to make a living by doing all the jobs around the place that hadn't yet been automated, like chopping and delivering firewood. He was good with his hands. You hardly noticed him, but he'd appear at just the right moment to fix something. He was around so much, he got to be like one of my brothers.

I didn't mind him, especially as my real brothers were making their own plans.

Callum quit the mine shortly after the strike, citing exhaustion. He wanted to go to sea, he said, and did not say like Patrick, though we all knew that's what he meant. He worked behind the bar for a year before he found a job down at the docks, and took it eagerly, hoping that he'd get his chance to sail away.

We lost one behind the bar.

Brendan was down the mines after him, but he always had his nose in a book and was fired for a lack of concentration on the job. The fact was, he was too shy to tell anyone he hated it. He was far too clever for the work, and besides, he had a girl up in Sydney he'd been visiting on the weekends for months. She worked in a hat shop in Petersham, and he wanted to go to one of the technical colleges, learn something different from blasting and digging; like most of my family he had a head for invention, I suppose, but of a different kind. He left shortly before I turned fifteen. Carrying his black bag of treasured tools onto the train, he looked like a kind young doctor.

Which left me, as expected, the last in line. As soon as I turned fifteen I was introduced properly to the trials and joys of life behind a bar. Mam instructed me with minimal communication: a frown here, a cough there. Da was different. He held forth on the philosophy of it. I think he loved the attention he got from teaching me as much as I loved learning his secrets.

'It's all about timing,' Da told me. 'Never take a glass away unless you're sure it's empty, that can wait. Never interrupt a decent argument until one of them rolls his sleeve up. Never ask anyone if they've already paid, because they'll lie to you.'

After a whole day of such functional wisdom, he walked around to the other side of the bar and ordered a whiskey. I poured an imperfect measure over ice and passed it to him. He held it up for inspection.

'Not bad. Always pour a little over, like this,' he said. 'It keeps people coming back. Makes them feel special.' He leaned in and lowered his voice.

'Guess what?' he said. 'Nothing I've told you today is of any importance whatsoever. There's only one thing you need to know about this job, and that's how to listen. Ninety per cent of it is listening, and it can't be taught. You'll have to learn the discretion of a priest and the patience of a saint.'

Mam appeared at my elbow and frowned at his glass. 'Saint Sean, patron of the single malt,' she said.

'And the other ten per cent,' Da muttered, raising one thick finger to indicate his wife, 'is doing what she says.'

I took to it with the near-instinctive knowledge that came from growing up here. I hardly had to be told what needed doing, having watched it all my life. I still had another year at school, but I rushed home afterwards to clean glasses and wipe floors and laugh with the drinkers. I would lean on the bar at closing and smell the sea on the night air. I would happily take my father's place when he slipped out on the quiet.

The Danker was my whole world. Anything that happened in Coal happened here first. I knew I was at the centre of things, and I felt safe and happy working alongside my parents, blessed by their attention for the first time in my life, though I knew I was still second fiddle to the old pub itself. I quickly learned to mould my days to its demands.

I remember the night I began to suspect what Da was up to on his jaunts. I was bailing out the icebox with a plastic cup, pouring the water down the drain.

'Looks like we're sinking,' Da joked from beside me. 'Hope you can swim.'

I hit him with an iceblock.

'Hey! Put some glasses in the fridge would you. Tom'll be up directly. His wife's having another one.'

'How many's that?'

'Oh, must be hundreds by now.' We laughed.

'I'm never going to be like her,' I said, though I always wanted children. I was superstitious about having too many, knowing what happened to the one that came after me.

'Oh, you will,' Da said. 'Children are a bane and a curse and a headache, but you'll find that out for yourself well enough. There's blessings, for all that.' He sighed into the middle distance with a secretive smile until Mam loomed into focus.

'Tidy this place up a bit would you,' Mam urged him, 'I've got the women's committee coming.'

'A clean bar's an empty bar,' Da quipped, but he got the rag out and whistled a tune as he wiped the tables down.

'And what are you so happy about?' Mam frowned.

'Oh nothing, nothing at all,' he said.

When she left the room he passed me a pound note.

'Buy yourself something,' he said, 'and don't tell your mother now.' He skipped away before I could object to his generosity, or question it. I sniffed the money and decided I would have to find out for myself.

For my sixteenth birthday, Da gave me pearl earrings. I had investigated the books by then, and had an idea of the level of red in them. I knew we couldn't afford any such luxuries. He handed the box to me sheepishly as he wiped the glasses dry.

'I can't take these,' I said, fingering the tiny, beautiful lumps of sea. 'We can't afford them. You have to take them back.'

'Can't,' he said, 'they're not from a shop.'

'Mam will murder you,' I said.

'Let her. I can give my only daughter whatever I like.'

'But where did you get them?'

He flicked me with the teatowel and his eyes danced. 'Just because it's your birthday,' he said, 'doesn't mean you can stand around idle all night. Get down and change the barrel before the work whistle.'

I did as I was told, and I kept the earrings secret from my mam for as long as I was able. When she finally discovered them I told her they were a gift from Ted, a story she accepted with gratitude. His older sister Bernadette had just got married to Tim Cullen, and Mam had been dropping hints at me ever since.

It was easier to hide things now that my brothers had gone. I had taken out the partition and had a proper-sized room of my own, albeit with the unusual quality that it had two doors. The spare beds were kept there for a brother, grandparent, or other visitor, who were rare. You often slept in my single bed, pressed against me until I woke between the wall and your body. I had nothing to be ashamed of, but something always made me mess the sheets of the adjacent bed in the morning.

You came into the bar with a solemn air and a gift of a predictable size.

'It's a book,' I said, without even hefting the weight of it.

'I found it,' you said. 'The dandelion woman. It's in here.'

'What are you talking about?' I unwrapped the package carefully, trying not to tear the plain brown paper.

'These dark satanic mills,' you said. 'It's Blake. See?' You opened the page in front of me.

I ran my eyes over the words, turned the pages carefully. The book was second-hand but it was beautiful, bound in blue leather with the edges gnawed away and the embossed title sunk illegibly.

'Faith says he's a fine supporter of the working class, even if he is a bit of a religious nutter.'

I read the poem through twice before I remembered the phrase being called out after us as we ran from the madwoman. The fact that you remembered such a detail was your real gift.

'We should never have teased her,' I said. 'She was only being literary.'

'In her slippers,' you added. You tore your hair out of its clasp and crowed like she had, running around the empty bar until I grabbed your wrist and stopped you, and myself, from laughing. It wasn't, after all, very funny.

'I still think she was a witch,' you said. 'It makes sense.'

'She was a sad old lady,' I countered.

'Story's better,' you replied. 'Tell me one?'

'It's my birthday, not yours.'

'Come on, I'm no good.'

I let go of your hand and motioned you to a barstool, reinstated myself behind the bar, and leaned on it. 'True or false?'

'True.'

'A true one. All right then.' I thought for a while, rearranging the objects behind the bar as if physically ordering my thoughts.

'You will be literary one day,' I began.

'And crazy?'

'No. Well, maybe a little. You will be beautiful, and have a thousand lovers. You'll travel the whole world with books in your pockets. A great success story, from coalminer's daughter to cultural queen. You'll live in some distant city like Paris or London and read all day long, and you'll forget all about me.'

'No I won't,' you said. 'How could I?'

Our little school let us go free shortly after my birthday. The graduation from schoolgirl to young woman was no shock to me. I was already becoming an old hand at the bar, and I was more excited about graduating to pulling beers than my school certificate. I considered I had learned all I could from that old tin portable.

When we finished our last day, we were suddenly, as if by magic, allowed to sit in the bar. Though I'd been working behind it for over a year, I hadn't touched a drop beyond the rare special occasion. Da poured us shandies, which went to our heads and made us laugh.

Boys came to congratulate us and linger beside you to watch your bright hair shine gold in the fading sun. Ted clapped me on the back like a mate, but took your hand like a gentleman.

'What are you going to do now,' I asked, 'go down the steelworks like Faith?'

171

You smiled. 'I'm going to do the correspondence course. Do my Leaving.'

This was the first I'd heard of it, but I bit my tongue. Nothing about it seemed unnatural. I added it to my list of your fictional aspirations. You would never actually leave Coal.

'You always were too smart,' I said, because it was true. You had finished top of the class without effort. You nodded in agreement. Humility was never your problem.

'What about you?'

I made a gesture of affectionate resignation at the bar around me.

'I live here,' I said. 'They need me.' I tried to put a note of reluctance in my voice out of solidarity, but I couldn't disguise the love I felt for this place. The love I feel for its story, for the fact that it requires me.

I felt shy, and got us another drink each. When I returned, you were looking around at the bar with curiosity. I thought you were trying to see in it what I see. Your hair hid your eyes, but when you raised them, they were far away, not in the room at all but out to sea.

'It must be good to be necessary to something,' you said.

'Yeah,' I murmured, but I was thinking: Shouldn't you know what that feels like?

Our second shandies made us sleepy. The sun had slipped behind the escarpment and the last light threw a red glow into the sky. I felt my body glow along with it, brimming with affection: for you, for my home, for the whole world.

'Hey, it's full moon. Let's go down to the creek and watch it come up,' you suggested.

I nodded, trying not to wobble. I couldn't tell if it was from the drink. My whole body was shaking. It felt as if someone was pulling on a rope that tied my scalp to my belly. I steeled myself, rearranged my skirt, took charge of my internal organs, and realised I had to pee.

I walked to the bathroom a little unsteadily. It wasn't the drink. You'd made me nervous. The affection I felt was somehow embedded in my body, I realised as I washed my hands. It was just a desire to be close to you. To feel your skin. It is normal to love your friends, I reminded myself as I fixed my plain face in the mirror.

The creek ran down from the escarpment and through the block beside the shop. It emerged at the place where the point jutted out to sea, in the crook of its neck. It's dry now. With so many houses up the top, the water has hidden itself somewhere like a snake that's shy of human footsteps. To get there, we followed the track down to the beach and walked along the sand, carrying our shoes in our hands. Reaching the place where the water trickled into the sea, where a curtain of slime had formed on the rocks, we clambered up and stood beside the stream, looking out to sea.

You sat down on a rock and I sat on another, perched on opposite sides of the stream. Dusk shrank the world. The outgoing tide shushed against the rocks and let up wafts of warm, comforting stink. The darkness brought the shrill notes of cicadas, hitting a collective pitch.

The moment of semi-darkness between sunset and the rising of a full moon still gives me vertigo. That night it was as if the sky grew skin. Venus shone, a bold puncture in the space above the sea. The stars emerged, pressing through the membrane. Our limits are an image, a conceit.

I couldn't say a thing. Anyway you wouldn't have heard me; the cicadas were too loud. I could feel the presence of your body, a little out of arm's reach. I concentrated on my own weight against the cool rock. We waited in silence for the moon's white lantern to save us. I couldn't even look at the stars.

When it slipped up out of the sea, the moon was preceded by its aura, like a halo which shimmered in ascent. It had never got dark enough for us to disappear completely. I shivered with relief, could almost feel the sun's reflected warmth in the moonlight.

'Are you cold?'

I shook my head, but I was shivering. Yes, I was cold, like someone who has walked away from a fire. The cicadas faded out one by one, a gesture of respect for the light. I felt a sadness wash over me as the blue-white light greeted the bush and lit the trees like ghosts. Perhaps it was only time, the fact that we were no longer children. A kind of premature nostalgia for my youth, or a feeling I have placed there now, knowing what I know.

You stood on your rock. You could see more of the moon than me this way, I thought, but I was patient. Besides, I felt almost immobilised by the spectacle. It lifted its fullness up out of the sea with an effort, as though reluctant to leave its bed, and the yellow reflection on the waves grew stronger and spread towards us in dancing slices, crests and troughs. In another moment it would disengage itself from the water altogether. At its last heave, the bottom swelled out flat like a drop. Surface tension. I remembered that it was the surface tension of the water that breaks your neck if you fall. You should drop your keys, Da told me once, if you're going to jump off a bridge.

By the time the moon let go of the horizon, I was in a dark, private place. I could almost hear the sound of it disengaging. I looked, as I always have, for the rabbit in it, the comforting shadow of life in the cold stone ball. I remembered pointing it out to you, then remembered where I was. My hand looked for your hand, but you were gone.

'Grace!'

Beside your rock, wet footprints glistened in the new light. Panic rose like acid in my belly, and I stood. My eyes found a movement in the darkened scrub of the point. Your shape fizzled out in the circles I had burnt into my eyes from gazing too long at the moon.

I thought I should follow you, but instead I watched. I was waiting for my eyes to readjust. I was waiting because I could not change what was to come.

The south wind pushed your dress out like a sail. A night bird spooked itself in the bush behind me. The rustle and the aching song insisted on being heard. It made me lose concentration, and when I searched for your shape on the point again it was gone.

'Grace!' I called out, unsure if I had made a sound; the sea has no echo. I stepped through the rough grass shakily and walked down to the shore, unsure of my feet in the dark though I'd walked every inch of the track a thousand times.

When I came to the edge of the rock I could hear a sound from beneath the water. I remembered the mermaid stories my father used to tell me, the way that Patrick would repeat them, and felt a pang of loss.

I scanned the waves for a sight of your head, or worse, your body floating off like a clump of weed, but the water was blank. I could still hear the muffled sound beneath me. It pained me that I couldn't make out the meaning of it.

Something cold came out of the sea and grabbed my ankle. I screamed.

You laughed and climbed up, using me as a handhold.

'Shit,' I said.

Your laughter bubbled away in the back of your throat, like a kettle that had been taken off the flame. A currawong called out its night-time litany of minor slide-scales. I took your hand and did not let go.

'Got you,' you said, grinning.

I wanted nothing more than to hit you in that wide mouth of yours, split those perfect lips against your moonlit teeth and draw blood. Instead I put a hand to my heart to feel it racing. Steadied it in a cradle of my fingers. I was shaking.

Your face fell serious, but you made no apology. Instead you pulled me against you in a stiff collision. Your hands on my back, my waist, held me to you. I was helpless. My hands were stiff, one jammed between our hearts and the other hanging awkwardly by my side. I was so paralysed that I might as well have been electrocuted.

'Shhh,' you said, pressing my head into the curve of your neck, 'shhh, I'm sorry. I didn't mean to give you such a fright, it's all right now, it's all right,' and the envelopment soothed me. There was nothing left in the world but the absence of space between our bodies.

I don't know how long we stood like that before I remembered where we were. The lights of houses began to break the black escarpment with their bright, square eyes. I watched them come on over your shoulder, unable to move.

When you let go, I didn't feel any power return to my body. It remained numb and stiff, as though I'd spent too long in the water.

'Are you okay?' you asked. 'I . . .' Then you kissed me, with pert propriety, on the cheek.

'It's late,' I muttered, trying to find my bearings. At the sight

of the Danker's lights on the headland opposite, I caught gratefully on the small domestic responsibilities it offered me.

'I have to get the tea,' I said. 'I have to get home.'

We walked back along the beach in silence, carrying our
shoes in our hands. There were no farewells. At the point where
the track meets the road, our paths separated. You walked your
way, I walked mine. No gesture necessary. No words spoken.

In a town this size, there is never any sense saying goodbye.
You will see everyone within a day or so. We all know where to
find each other. I still find this comforting about Coal, the way
nothing ever stops to start again.

Above me, the Danker glowed with warmth. The place
seemed to have grown. I was smiling as I clambered up the hill
towards the light.

fourteen

Autumn is always windy, as if the air is angered by its own chill. The Danker is louder than ever, but sometimes the wind drops and stillness returns to the earth. When that happens, if there's no one here, I stop time.

I slide off my stool and fade out the radio. I reach behind the fridge for the switch to cut the hum. I close the door on the ocean and the animals and take a long look at the place to prove that nothing changes. I walk into my fortress and reach up to flip the plastic clock face down on top of the shelves, like an unwelcome photograph. I stand so that I touch nothing but the floor, and close my eyes.

Complete sensory deprivation. Self-hypnosis. I can stay like this for minutes. Then the troubles come in like flies through an open window. They buzz at me: bills to pay, fixing I should get to, have I done the ordering or haven't I. I wonder how dusty the rooms are getting. I worry about the kids.

But if I focus I can freeze them too. I can stop the details in mid-air. I can empty the room of these concerns, of any evidence that time is passing. I can stand like this indefinitely, or at least until, in the space outside my body or from somewhere within it, I think I hear the shadow of your voice.

Tonight I want to stop time. There are nights when I've had enough of this place. Frozen, I could walk around it freely, neither of us decaying. But I'm afraid of your ghost. Instead, I make the fire, piling twigs then logs, twisting last week's newspaper into a hard fuse. It's not really necessary. The wind outside is gently breathing the last warm breaths of summer. It's all right though. Lots of things I do are unnecessary. If I restricted myself to the necessary things I'd have bored myself to death by now.

So I enjoy the familiar rituals. I enjoy the flames licking the logs, the tension of not knowing whether it will catch and the joy when it does. Not everything works the way you intend it to, but most fires seem to like me.

The paper flames lick at the sticks with the rich thrill of youth, an adolescent energy. I smile at them. Fire knows time. Its urgency, its fall towards a slow and beautiful death. I won't stand still, I won't shut down today. This is a relief in itself. Fire is forgiving. Though of what, I don't know.

I don't know what I could have done differently. I couldn't have left the Danker. My family needs me and the Danker needs me and the regulars would probably be a damn sight better off if I shut up shop and they had to go out and get their shit together, but until that day, they need me too. I'm everyone's listener, therapist, pharmacist, conscience and comrade, and it's enough. It's more than enough.

You will read this and hear the regret in my words. You always saw right through to the truth of me. You will shake your head at all this self-justification. Hey, someone has to listen to me argue with myself.

The fire dies down, the flames cease their dance, but the coals are still alive. I remember my father telling me that to kill a fire quickly, you spread the coals out. Separated from each other, they'll die faster.

I found out that Clare's real name is Clarity. Hippy parents, she claims, though I think it sounds like an old spinster's name from the deep South, a thin, cheerful old lady in black crepe. When I tell her this, she laughs.

'In a past life, maybe,' she says, and thinks about it. 'Hey, that's a good idea. I could do a series. Self-portraits throughout the ages.'

'Why don't you paint Coal, like Joe does?'

'I don't need to paint real things. They're already here.'

'Real things can go away,' I say, glancing at Joe's painting of the point pre-development.

She decides to consult a psychic in order to find out more about her past lives, even though she doesn't believe in them. I find this willing curiosity of hers charming.

She comes in straight after the appointment. I guess she hasn't had much time to make friends here. It's hard in a small town. I don't mind. I pour her black beer before she asks for it.

'What did the psychic say?'

'He said I was a new soul. That I didn't have any baggage.'

I raise an eyebrow. 'Oh yeah?'

'Then he asked me out for a drink,' she says, frowning. 'I always get this from the most random guys. Can't they tell?'

I take in her short dyed hair, the pierced lip, the wide, dark eyes. I shrug. I never picked her preferences, or only from what she's said. Maybe she picked me.

★ ★ ★

The wind collects in my face. It's an unfortunate barometer. I've always been readable. I resent my face, from its distracted gravity to its encroaching age, its wrinkle and sag. I avoid mirrors. I once read of a man who injured his brain in a car crash. His arms would move against his will unless he watched them carefully. I've sometimes wondered if I'm the same, because I can't control my expression. I have to concentrate, and even then the effort only shoots more creases across my forehead and people ask me what's wrong.

'Nothing,' I have to say, 'it's just my face.'

More recently, my hands have started doing the same thing. They wander off on their own like grown-up children. I've caught my fingers crossing, or reaching for something, when I haven't told them to. When Mam had the Alzheimer's she would deny knowing what her hands had done. Maybe it's that, but surely I'm not old enough yet.

It's madness, the wind today. I half expect pieces of the Danker to fly off like car parts in one of those old comedies. I hope it's all noise. At least it'll keep the people away for a while. More often these days I find I want this place to myself. What the hell for, I ask myself. I tell myself I am brooding. The Danker croaks at me unsympathetically.

The truth is, I am a little afraid someone is going to interrupt me writing this thing and I'll have to slip it under a pile of invoices. I'm afraid, in my neurotic small-town way, of everyone knowing what I'm up to. You've become my secret again, Grace.

The Danker is protesting. It's trying to sabotage me. I spent this morning rehanging the swing door between the kitchen and the bar, and when it was done I heard an almighty crash from upstairs. I climbed into the attic to find that a beam had fallen down, collapsing a pile of boxes I had stored up there.

Repacking them, I found a bundle of papers. I've brought them down and put them in the kitchen drawer, but that's as far as I've got. I'm not ready to untie that knot.

A small army of these objects has mobilised against me: a bundle of papers, a drawing of a snake, a stone, a piece of polished glass. You can't have moved these things because you are not here. I know it's not your ghost. It's the Danker. We're like an old couple who finish each other's sentences.

The Danker gives these things back to me, and sometimes I examine them. More often, I put them away. I keep the evidence hidden out of habit. It should mean I have locked you away in a corner of the house. Unfortunately, this place is too much like my own mind. It's full of memories and distractions and in some disrepair, and hiding things in it is no use at all.

I am not arguing with you. I have no point to prove. It is just that bringing up all these stories – my own set of past lives – is eating up all my time. Time doesn't run in a line any more. It runs in circles. I am making myself dizzy trying to follow its unruly thread.

I try to reconstruct you like a historian, from these materials: a memory here, an artefact there. Brushing dust from submerged bones, speculating from clues. Maybe I hope that if I find your shape with these investigations, you will be brought back.

History is useful. It is supposed to prevent us from making the same mistake twice. Mistakes are not like lightning; they can recur. What if I'm wrong, and history is learning to make the same mistake, over and over again?

The trouble is that I'm not a historian. I don't know where stories end and real life begins. I fall into the crack between truth and fiction too easily. I wake up between the bed and the wall. It's hard to break old habits.

fifteen

I was singing as I hung out the sheets I'd spent the morning washing. My own were bloodied, but Mam conspired with me over the laundry, much to my relief. She was busy in the bar by the time I got all the stains out and started to spread the sheets on the ropes that ran diagonally across a corner of the fence. I was careful not to drag the ends in the dirt. The sunlight shining through showed where the stains were, but the unknowing eye wouldn't see them. A few soft cirrus clouds stroked lazily overhead. The air was crisp, the sky insistently blue. I couldn't help whistling.

Your head popped over the fence beside the jasmine and its humming cloud of bees.

'Morning,' you said casually. You were wearing your straw hat. The sun shone through the holes into your hair and made it glow like a golden mane. I stood dumbly, a wooden peg in my mouth. I plucked it out.

'Come and help me get these out,' I said.

Your head disappeared and reappeared around the corner,

complete with body. I felt none of the doubt or discomfort of the moonlit night before, just happy to see you. We were comfortable and neighbourly, giggling as we spread the sheets out along the line. You moved between them as if they were curtains on a stage. When you bent to pull a peg from the basket, you even held on to your hat theatrically.

'What do you say to the city?' you asked, straightening up.

I thought about this, leaned back on my heels and tilted my head.

'I'm trying to convince the old man that we're mature and capable enough for an excursion,' you said.

'When?' I chewed my lip. I was trying to remember when you'd started calling your father 'the old man'.

'Next week. Monday.' You stepped out from behind a sheet. 'What do you say?'

The city. I had been there twice before, but only with my mother. I remembered waving Patrick off to sea and the frightening hall of mirrors that scissored off my childhood so cleanly. What would we want to go to the city for? I wasn't ready for another excision. Still, with you beside me, it would be exciting.

Standing uncertainly between the white sheets billowing against us in a growing breeze, I relented. 'I'll ask them,' I said, gesturing towards the house. I took a step and then turned back. 'Do you want to come inside then?' You dropped the corner of a sheet, which fell closed behind you.

Mam raised an eyebrow. Sensing we were about to ask a favour, she went straight for the kettle. I hesitated, looking at your face, and made a little gesture with my eyes. You coughed.

'Mrs McCabe,' you opened bravely, 'we were wondering if you'd spare May next Monday? Faith says we can go to the city, if it's all right with you.'

I nodded at her. 'If you can manage without me,' I added.

Mam poured us out cups of tea and hummed tunelessly to herself. She pushed the milk and sugar at us, frowning imperceptibly when you took three lumps from the bowl with your fingers. Eventually she looked from one to the other of us and her face seemed to relax.

'I'd ask your father if I was you,' she said. This was in the vicinity of yes, and I grew excited. 'He's in there, pretending to fix something.' She indicated the bar with a tilt of her head. We leaped up and bolted through the door.

'Your tea will get cold,' she muttered after us.

In the deserted pub, we found Da crouched under a table, clutching a hammer.

'Mornin', ladies, how'd ye be?' His voice was garbled by the nails he held in the corner of his mouth.

'Mam says we can go to the city on Monday if it's all right with you,' I said, as casually as I could.

He pulled the nails out of his mouth and looked at us.

'Sure, you're young women, free to do as you please,' he said. I caught the spark in his eye that meant he knew he'd been a little tricked, and rushed to hug him.

'Thank you, it's just for the day and we'll be back for tea and everything,' I said in his ear.

He struggled out of my grasp and waved the hammer at me.

'Get on with you,' he said. 'I'll swallow my bloody nails in a minute,' and we went back through the kitchen door to tell Mam it was all set.

We stood and smiled at each other over our mugs until Mam drifted back into the laundry.

'What are we going to do there?' I asked, imagining a hundred possible adventures.

'I have to enrol in my course,' you said. 'You know, for the correspondence. I want to get started as soon as I can.'

You were serious then. I'd almost forgotten. My hands went to my sides.

'Come upstairs,' I said, and then added without thinking, 'I have something for you.'

On the way up I tried to think what it could be. The pearl earrings Da had given me were too precious for you to accept. None of my dresses were any good, and anyway they would have to be taken in. A seashell or a piece of polished glass from my windowsill would be too like the treasures of our childhood kinship, and were we not something else now? Then I hit on it, the perfect thing, intimate but not banal. Besides, I had out-grown them and your hands were finer.

The kid gloves were folded neatly in the bottom of my drawer. You perched on the bed as I rummaged for them, quietly pray-ing they had not been eaten by the moths. You'd coveted them only recently, a day when I'd met you on my way to church with Mam.

'Here!' I found them and passed them to you with a nervous little bob. I felt as if I was making a formal presentation, sud-denly shy with the thought that you might reject them. I knew your family had pride about charity, but your face lit up with disbelieving joy.

'I can wear them?'

'You can have them,' I said. I laced my hands together. 'I don't – they don't really fit me any more any way. And your hands are so . . .' I could say no more, and bit my lip.

You slipped the gloves on and splayed your fingers to look at the backs of your hands, turning them over to admire them, then leapt up and kissed my cheek.

'Thank you,' you said, 'I'll wear them forever,' and you kissed my cheek again.

You see, that's how we got started finally. I bribed you. I didn't know what a difference it would make to pass you a layer of my skin. The next thing I knew, your hand was on my shoulder in as much of a caress as you would dare. You looked at the floor.

'They're perfect. So soft,' you said, and found my eyes. There it was again, a secret, a dark pulsating thing around us. A thrill, an electrocution, my arms immobilised. My body estranged from me.

It must have been the gloves, the fact that you wore my skin, so it wasn't really your hand touching me. I remember it all, every detail. There were squares of light on the wall behind your head. The bottom left one was not quite square because it crossed my bedhead, making an indent. There was a fly caught in a web in the window frame behind me and I could see its shadow vibrate like a taut string on Da's fiddle. There was soft white leather against the hollow of my shoulder. A speck of cotton lay on your cheek where it must have fallen, spindling like the motes I could see in the light. I brushed it away.

You can't fault my memory, Grace. You pressed your lips against mine. I was too startled to close my eyes. I watched yours, two blonde lines in the blur of proximity.

I stood back a step, blushed, and muttered, 'Really my hands have grown out of them.' I looked down at my hands. They were bleached white from the laundry, burned between the ridges.

I look at my hands now. Raised blue lines mark the passage of my blood and time. The flesh sags; it stays where it is if you pinch it. My skin has become inelastic. I can still see my hands as they were then. Never beautiful or delicate, but useful. Working

hands, even-skinned but for a nick on one finger from the potatoes of the night before.

You can't fault my memory, Grace. I stared at my raw hands
as you turned and walked to the door. I gazed down at the short,
pared nails bleached clean by the sheets as you paused. My eyes
remained glued to them as you started to say something.

'May,' you said, 'I . . .'

I felt your body shake with the pause. I did not lift my face to
you, afraid of what it might reveal.

'Monday then,' you said, and your voice resonated thinly in
the light.

When you left the room, there was a white impression on my
retinas in the shape of my hands. When I closed my eyes I could
see it. I listened to the sound of your feet going down the stairs.
The fly buzzed in its prison and went deathly still. I turned on
one heel and stepped to the balcony to watch you run across the
lawn and disappear around the corner of the garden. A gull passed
over the headland, calling. My hands were still frozen into the
shape of a holding, holding something lighter than air. The sea
crashed and broke and beat itself against the wall of stone, wore it
down. It was trying to break the earth out from under my feet.

I would like to say: See? You started it.

I would like this to be simple. Either true, or false.

Something tiny and brittle snapped in my chest, as if I had
swallowed a wishbone. I heard it click; a fragile question answering itself. I went down to see if the sheets were dry.

'The wind's died,' my mother said as she stepped outside to
press her hands against her kidneys and crick her back unbent.
I didn't reply. We looked at the sea for a while with our sailor's
eyes, standing side by side. I wondered if she saw in it what I saw:
the temptation of distances unknown.

★ ★ ★

We went to town together the following Monday. You wore the gloves and your patched yellow dress. I had a woollen skirt that sat discreetly below the knee and itched my skin, too hot for the day.

We walked hand in hand to the station. We would have looked like two friends out on an excursion, but I slipped my hand away when I saw the station master's eye work you over. The engine pulled in, loud and cloudy and smelling enticingly of grease, and the man waved it down with a small flag.

The train gave us a perfect view of the sea, spread out invitingly beside us like a huge, blue picnic blanket. It was another crisp, clear day, but the wind had come up from nowhere.

We talked about small things for a while, but the conversation petered out after a short time and I was left with my thoughts, wishing I'd brought a book. Normally, our silences were comfortable, shared; this was two separate silences. I watched you straighten yourself and look out to sea. Your face was already adult, your cheekbones defined. You had taken on a sharpness.

The train was full of workers on their way up from the docks, and women and their children running errands. Everyone seemed to have a purpose. There was something furtive about the two of us, as if we were skiving off from everyday life.

Without warning, you snatched my wrist and broke the trance. You pointed out to sea.

'Look,' you said. 'Whale.'

My eyes ran over the surface of the water until I found the speck of black in the distance, the solitary raised fin of a giant. We watched it dance in silence until the train slid into the tunnel and away from home.

The train pulled into Central and we changed for Circular Quay. We walked down to the ferry docks where I had sat with my mother two years before. The tram yards on Bennelong Point were huge and ominous. The bridge raised itself behind us, a grand gesture in imperial iron. We walked south down George Street, past shops and hotels. Their bright facades mocked us as obvious provincials. It was all so flash that I was frightened into silence, but you spoke expansively. The seagulls, the tripping waves, the raucous city cockatoos, the light, all these things permitted you a new kind of energy. You waved your arms around, a part of the business of things, and walked so fast that I had trouble keeping step.

We crossed over to Hyde Park and sat in the shade to watch the city people strolling. There were old women with parasols, men without hats, vast families of vaguely foreign extraction, a young couple rolling unashamedly in the grass, and one madman with his socks off, muttering to himself under a tree. We stood awkwardly in the shade of an enormous fig and took it all in.

'I'm going to live here,' you said.

'What, in the park like that man?'

You laughed, pushed me playfully, and resettled yourself like a bird.

'In the city,' you said. 'And I'm going to get a job, and go to university.'

'University?'

'Why else do they call it the Leaving Certificate?'

'You'll come back,' I said.

'I can't wait,' you said. 'I've got to see all this. Real life. I'm going to learn everything!' You span in a circle, your eyes blazed in the sun, and I looked around for a post I could tie you to.

'You see that man,' I said, picking a suit from the crowd at random. 'He's having an affair with his mother-in-law. They meet in secret at the fountain. He's waiting for her right now.'

'Stop it,' you said, 'stop.'

I played with my ungloved hands, my skin raw and worn. 'He's waiting,' I faltered.

'May, don't! Can't you just be happy for me? Here and now?'

I didn't know what else there was to say, so I left your side and walked over to watch the men playing chess in a corner of the park.

You appeared beside me and leaned your head against mine. 'May, I'm sorry. Listen, I have to go to the office. Do you want to wait here?'

I smoothed my skirt and straightened my hat. 'No, God no, they'll eat me alive,' I said. 'I'm sticking with you.'

I waited for you in the foyer of the education building. My back cooled gratefully against the sandstone. Intelligent people came and went, carting books and folders full of knowledge, and as I watched them I thought of the whale dancing in the morning light, its fin leaping free of the water. It was a creature perfectly contained in its element.

Now that we were older, Sydney was more accessible to us, but I still needed a decent excuse to leave my work. The Queen's visit provided the next one, and I begged to be allowed to go. I was surprised when Mam invited Faith to accompany us, and even more surprised when she agreed.

'It's the spectacle of it I'm interested in,' Faith explained.

'Her interest is purely academic,' you teased.

In fact, she was probably glad of an excuse to escape her husband. Jack had been irritable ever since Stalin passed away the previous year. His commitment to the party was stronger than ever, and he was unable to accept any criticism of his beliefs. I can only imagine what it must have been like for him, living with two such strong-willed women. At any rate, I was glad to be able to take you and Faith away from that dogmatic environment for a day.

The streets were hot and crowded. Girls turned as red as the stripes in the bunting and fainted under their flags. We stood all day in a crowd ten deep to catch a glimpse of a passing car between the hats in front of us. When it approached, we could hear the roar of the crowd from the next block and see the waving of tiny Union Jacks in the distance. Finally streamers began to fall on us, thrown by people watching from the balconies above. The crowd made more noise than I'd ever heard.

We stood on our toes to see. Loyal to our parents' views, we stopped short of waving the flag. When the car slid slowly past and I glimpsed a hand protruding from the black chrome, my own hands dangled by my sides.

'Is that it? Not a bad job she's got, if this is all she has to do.' You mimicked the waving hand.

'We should have brought some rotten tomatoes,' Faith quipped.

Mam frowned, but I could see a smirk hovering on her down-turned lips. She leaned into Faith's ear.

'Some would have suggested dynamite,' she whispered.

'Shhh, you'll have us all arrested,' Faith whispered back. The two women looked at each other and began to laugh.

I don't believe I'd heard my mother laugh like that since the war. It was a strange and reckless sound, and it startled me. She pulled off her hat and let her greying hair out of its net. Infected, the four of us exploded in riotous hysterics, causing a small circle to widen around us.

Mam wiped a tear from her eye, patted her dress, and began to apologise to the people nearby. When her back was turned and Faith was looking up at the balconies, I squeezed your hand.

We walked back to the station that afternoon, carried along by the crowd, past drunks, boys selling flags, schoolgirls in uniform, and endless decorations. You and I walked ahead of our mothers, holding hands and chattering excitedly. On the train home, we sat together and dissected the things we had seen.

I caught Mam watching me, and she turned her eyes away. Any trace of that momentary laughter had gone from her face.

All the local families were gathered at the Danker for Ted's sister's baby shower. Even Mam was out from behind the bar for once, as Callum was home to visit. We ate a late lunch with Bernie and her friends at the picnic tables in the shade of the pine tree, and listened to them gossip. You and I gave each other daring looks and let our feet touch under the table.

Faith was there too, and Ted's mother Francine sat between her and Bernie, a huge pile of Sylvia Cullen's home-made cupcakes in front of her. Ted himself was around the back with Da, being useful. I think they were fixing the fence to avoid the women.

Bernie glowed in the midst of the group, her hand around the small form she held against her belly, so new it was still a part of her body. They talked about the baby – she'd called it Greg after her father – and drank wine mixed with lemonade until they started talking about the part that came before the baby, and your looks and your feet intensified. I had to smooth my dress to stop from giggling.

I wanted to extricate myself, find some refuge in the cool

house, and you read my thoughts. In a break in the laughter, you coughed and spoke loud enough for everyone to hear. 'May, did I leave my purse in your kitchen?'

'Excuse us,' I said, and we walked too quickly into the house.

'Oh thank Christ,' you sighed as we entered the back door. 'I thought I'd never escape.'

'Wait here,' I said, when you had seated yourself at the kitchen table.

I leaned on the kitchen door until it swung open, just far enough to see that Callum was busy clearing tables. I got down on my hands and knees and crawled through, careful to let the door swing shut behind me silently. I crawled to the fridge, grabbed two bottles of beer, and crawled back on all threes, reminding myself of the dog they used to have at Cullen's. If Callum saw me, he made no comment. I made it back into the kitchen and grinned to see you sitting patiently at the table, watching me curiously.

I motioned to you to follow and carried the bottles up to my room. When we got there we'd been keeping silent for so long that we both fell on the bed in a fit of hysterics. My bed is where we stayed for the afternoon, while the women got tipsy outside and the men beneath us sawed and hammered away.

I didn't judge myself then. We were having too much fun to worry about the consequences. It felt right to be with you, our bodies pressed together like two slim fish in a bowl. It was secret, sacred, unlike the lewd allusions the women had been making before. You opened your eyes mid-kiss and I saw in that blue the thrill of wonderment they held when I had entranced you with stories.

Hours passed; I might have slept. You crept from your place

beside me with stealth. We had not undressed, not properly. We slipped our stockings and shoes on and tiptoed down the stairs to the kitchen, wondering if we were missed. The women were still in the garden, but the men were filling the bar. I could hear Da's loud voice calling his son to him, drunk already before dusk, and the other men laughing nervously at his boister and excess. The women on the lawn, in a cluster of white, grey, and pink, resembled galahs, a group of which were feeding at the base of the hanging pines. It was still the afternoon, and nothing had changed.

I took it in from the kitchen, relieved and sobered by the seeming permanence. You were in the doorway, watching me. Framed with the green headland beyond and the blue sea and sky so perfectly reflecting each other that I couldn't see where one began and the other ended. There was so much light in you.

We stepped back onto the lawn to rejoin the women. I was conscious of my body's movements, but we slipped right back into our places. Your mother asked if you found it, and you raised the purse in one hand, a hefty alibi. The women's voices wrapped us in warm laughter and Bernie sat self-satisfied, her hand under the baby. You looked at me so long and hard that I wondered I didn't break like glass under a high, sustained tone.

The sun stole behind the escarpment. The picnickers headed inside for the warmth. I could see Callum shifting chairs around the fire. I could see Mam fighting Da for the newspaper and matches, and imagine her teasing him: 'You're that much whiskey you'll set yourself on fire.' The affection in their gentle banter almost made my eyes water, because I loved them, and because I knew I could never duplicate their commitment.

You and I stayed outside until the sky turned pink and gold, until the last reflected glow of the hidden sunset faded from the eastern sky. We stayed until the rabbits were out and the cockatoos called last drinks.

'I love you, Grace,' I whispered. I wasn't sure if I had said it loud enough for you to hear. You bent your head close. Your breath against my neck was heavy with silence.

I was already a veteran behind the bar, well enough installed in my place to relax and laugh with friends. You were usually seated on a stool, distracting all the young men. Tall, blonde, full of life, there was no hint of the submissive about you. It was natural to be in love with you; everyone was.

On this particular night, however, you were at home studying, and I was enjoying the relaxed company without you.

It was a golden year. The mines were raking it in and so was the Danker. A flood of new settlers had come into the area, bringing new stories, interesting cooking smells, and more young people to fall in love with you.

Stalin's death had released a steady trickle of immigrants from Eastern Europe. The Szolosi family had escaped the Hungarian Uprising, travelled through a dozen countries, and ended up here. People no longer changed their names to English ones when they came, but Szolosi proved too much of a mouthful for Coal. It was Mr and Mrs Shorty before they'd been in town a week. They were hardened, but for all they'd been through they weren't prepared for red Jack Harper.

While I was laughing and joking with Ted, your father was arguing with the newcomers. He must have grown tired of fighting big, impossible battles; these days he drank and fought small, pointless ones. When even Khrushchev had denounced Stalin, Jack seemed determined to be his last defender.

Shorty listened to Jack's discourse patiently, with one eyebrow raised.

'It's a plot,' Jack said. 'The East is better off than we are. They're lying to us for fear we'll match your revolution. All that bullshit about the repression, it's just propaganda.'

Shorty put his glass down slowly on the bar, lowered his eyes, and inhaled like a bull. He turned to Jack. 'They murdered my parents in cold blood,' he said. 'I am lucky to be alive. And you, my friend, are an idiot.'

Jack look dumbfounded, but he swallowed his whiskey and quickly regained his composure. 'It's not true,' he said. 'No one was murdered without just cause. They had to weed out the counter-revolutionaries.'

'Please repeat that,' Shorty said. He rolled up his sleeves with the calm patience of a man who was accustomed to fighting. I remembered what my da had told me and decided it was time to intervene.

I put my dishcloth down and went over to talk them out of it, but it was too late. There were already a few blokes around to back up Jack, who'd fought for them for nearly twenty years, and the group moved outside. Jack wouldn't have a second mate in but wanted to settle it like men, and the scuffle began.

Mam sent me down to get your mother, but when I arrived at your house it was silent. One small light was on. I crept to your bedroom door and stood in the shadows.

You were bent under an electric lamp with a pencil in your mouth, your hair a halo. I watched you for a moment, but remembered my mission.

'Where's Faith?' You looked up when I spoke, and smiled.

'Meeting at the steelworks. Why?'

'Jack's got himself in a fight again,' I said. 'You better come get him before he gets hurt.'

You frowned, irritated. You finished the sentence you were writing before you stood up, then snatched a jacket from a nail and followed me up the headland. We walked briskly towards the lawn and found that the group of men outside had grown. They were huddled around two bulky shapes that approached each other with sidesteps, like crabs. The group was strangely hushed. You shoved your way through it with your elbows.

'Stop it,' you said, stepping so close to the two men locked in battle that they must have felt your breath against their skin. Jack's shirt was torn. He wasn't keeping up. The other man was stronger and less drunk. The circle around them buzzed with murmured remarks when you appeared in its centre.

The fighters froze. Their stances seemed foolish in suspension. I watched from behind the men, terrified for your safety but too nervous to break inside.

'You,' you said, pushing a hand against Shorty's shoulder. 'He's sorry for whatever it is he said to you.' Shorty raised his hands and shrugged.

'And as for you,' you said, pushing your father in the chest, 'what do you think you're doing?'

Jack glared at you. A little blood trickled out of one nostril. He wavered, unsteady on his feet from the grog. He looked like he would turn on anything.

'This is my own business,' he slurred. 'Go back to your bloody books.'

You took a step back and cocked your head, then ran at him with fire in your eyes, flailing a fist hard into his stomach.

There was a moment of stunned silence as Jack fell slowly to the ground. He hit his head on the earth and closed his eyes.

A cheer rose from the crowd. It was hard to be sure if they were laughing at you or with you. Either way you had everyone's attention. The circle of men advanced, and I pressed myself between them. I knelt beside your unconscious father while they slapped you on the back and called you a good sport. Jack came around, dizzy and breathing shallowly, but all right.

'Let's get him out of here,' I said, and a dozen hands emerged to carry Jack back to your house. He refused them all except for yours. We helped him up.

'Run in and tell Mam I'll be five minutes,' I said to the nearest face. It was Ted, hovering by us. He smiled at me and started inside.

Jack walked happily between us, whistling the 'Internationale', but we had to support him to stop him from toppling. He was surprisingly light. We must have looked a sight, the three of us stumbling down the hill to the wobbling sound of a drunken proletarian anthem.

'Miss Grace the boxing ace,' someone cried out after you, and the crowd laughed.

When we got him home we dragged him into the kitchen. We arranged him in a chair, where he promptly went to sleep. I put the kettle on for want of a better idea.

'What are we going to do with him?' It wasn't late. Your mother would still be at her meeting. You waved a glass of water under his nose and shook him gently.

'Here Jack, have some water. You'll be right.' I shivered at the maternal tenderness in your voice. It was so adult. It also failed to rouse Jack, so you lifted the glass and tipped it over his head.

He seemed to be unwakable. We met eyes above his wet snore.

'Better put him to bed,' you said. 'Faith won't be happy.'

We dragged him between us to your parents' dusty mattress and pulled off his mud-soaked boots.

'What was it about this time?'

I shrugged. 'The usual. He was fighting for Stalin. I hope Uncle Joe appreciates it.'

'He's probably too busy burning in hell,' you replied, and giggled. 'I'm sure it's all true, about the murders. Don't tell him that though.' You pulled a blanket over Jack and sighed.

'He's getting bad,' you said. 'It's the grog.'

'Mine too. Not much we can do about it.'

'Can't you water it down?'

'Oh, sure, and that wouldn't start any fights.'

We went back to the kitchen and sat there listening to the snores coming from the next room. The silence was broken by the whistle of the kettle, which made us both stand and speak at the same time.

'Do you want a cup of tea?' / 'I'd better get back to work.'

'You're unbelievable,' I said, shaking my head. 'I've never seen anything like it.' I mimed the punch you'd thrown. We both laughed.

'Yes to tea,' I said. 'I think I can get away with another five minutes. Weren't you scared?'

You shook your head, but I could see that you were shaking. I touched your hand. It must have been your night for rash movements and snap physical decisions, because you turned and kissed me on the lips.

I rucked your skirt up against your legs, pressed you against the kitchen table, and had my hands up your shirt before I knew what I was doing.

I must have known what I was doing. In my memory, it's as if someone else had control of my body.

'You'd better go,' you said, prising my hands from behind your back. 'You'll be missed up there.'

Reluctantly, I let go of your body, which was flushed with heat. I wanted to freeze time. Instead I backed out of the room without taking my eyes off you. I can still see you standing there locked in eye contact, staring at my retreating shape with your head at a weird angle. Your ears were cocked, listening to your father's drunken snores. Your dress was pressed against the bench like an afterimage. Your lips were swollen and your eyes glistening, a flush of red trying to break out from under your ghost-pale skin. I retreated slowly, charging myself on the energy of your image, and at the last minute, just before I would have tripped and fallen off your back step, I turned and ran.

It took no time at all to get back to work. No one had noticed my extended absence. They were still telling the story of the fight to one another, as if I had only been gone a moment. But I held a secret in my body, sharp and unbreakable as a diamond.

That night, I soaked myself in the bath. Afterwards I stood looking in the oval mirror. I examined my body for signs of the sharp stone inside, but it told me nothing.

Now that I have broken into the part of my story which most frightens me, the part where we learn to be bound to one another, I can feel it there again, like one of those lodged pins you hear about in women who sew without pincushions. If that is where the aches have come from, it is my fault. I swallowed something I shouldn't have.

You finished your Leaving, passing with the expected high marks in everything. After a week or two of waving your certificate around, you quietened down. You realised it wasn't enough, as it didn't yet amount to a ticket out of Coal.

The trouble, of course, was money. Jack still wasn't working, and your mother didn't earn as much as a man would have in her job. Sending you to university was out of the question. Even if Faith had cared for intellectuals she would never have been able to afford to make her daughter into one. You realised that you'd have to earn a place there on your own terms.

I thought about asking you to come and work at the Danker. Now that the boys had gone, there was plenty of work to be done, but something stopped me. I would like to think it wasn't an urge to sabotage your freedom.

At any rate, I couldn't consult my parents about it. They were stressed enough by their own tight finances. I noticed that the margins in our orders had gotten thinner. The few choices on the bistro's menu dwindled to one a day. The bitter remarks my mam made at my da were growing sharper, more acidic. In this climate, I couldn't suggest you work for us. I didn't get paid myself, and we were starting to rely on the money my brothers were bringing in from their other jobs. Brendan was working in engineering by this time, fixing farming machinery, and Callum still hadn't made it any further out to sea than being a wharfie. They both came back on irregular weekends and hid their earnings under things so Mam wouldn't be angry with them for helping out. I remember her lifting the fruit bowl off the kitchen table once and swearing openly at a small bundle of notes. She always tried to give the money back, but my brothers would just deny ever having put it there.

I tried to help too. I decided I would sell the pearl earrings, the only possession I had that was worth anything. But when I looked for them, they had disappeared.

I didn't understand why times were tight. We were busier than ever, even attracting a few guests in the hotel. Then again, some weeks we would have more money than we'd thought, and Da would arrive home with a brand new refrigerator or a gift for Mam.

In the end, I didn't have to ask them, because you talked yourself into a job in Charlie's shop across from the beach. By then it was run by the Kourmastis family, though they didn't change the name. Recent immigrants, they were nervous of disrupting Coal's staple foods of white bread, chips and burgers, but if I went around the back I would find you making coffee in a briki, and Mrs Kourmastis rolling pastries filled with spinach, fetta, and a dash of cinnamon, offering me food with a 'please, call me Soula'.

Soula had a daughter a little older than us who lived in Sydney with a husband and a new baby. Soula was talked into employing you occasionally so she could visit them, but you quickly charmed your way into regular hours when you found they were the most educated people in Coal.

You and Mr Kourmastis discussed Socrates while frying fish for the customers, Aristotle while restocking the mixed lolly counter. You argued about fate and acquired a dog-eared copy of Homer. It wasn't quite university, but you seemed happy enough, and at least you learned a little Greek.

You also discovered rock'n'roll. By summer you were well versed in ancient and popular culture. I dug out the transistor radio Brendan had built as a teenager, and we lay on the floor in my room, trying to keep cool. We both stared at the crackly little speaker intently, as if we could hear better with our eyes.

★ ★ ★

The Danker always opened on Christmas Eve, mainly because my family were all together. My grandparents no longer came up from the farm, being too frail, but my brothers were back on their brief holidays and I was happy to see them.

'You grew,' Callum said, jabbing me in the ribs. 'What have you done with my little sister?'

Brendan came down from Sydney in a new car, honking the horn to announce himself. Da and I came out of the bar to see what the noise was.

'What's this?'

'Company car,' he said. 'Got a promotion.' He tossed the keys in his hands. 'Want to take it for a spin?'

We drove up and down the coast laughing. The beach zoomed past in the window and the Holden rattled like a tractor.

'I'm moving into sales,' Brendan explained, 'so they gave me this to drive out into the country.'

'I thought you liked working with your hands,' Da said, hiding his pride.

'Got a few ideas,' Brendan said.

'And what about your girl? She coming?' Callum teased.

'Nah, Lucy's got her own family. Might be asking her something soon though. When I've got enough for a deposit.'

That afternoon, Da sang as he worked: 'Cocaine makes you lazy, champagne makes you crazy.' It was an old tune he had picked up travelling. I thought he must have them mixed up, because the champagne was making me want to go to sleep. You and I were seated on bar stools, sipping from highballs. We only had three kinds of glasses in the Danker.

'Eighteen,' Da said, looking at me strangely. 'Eighteen,' he told Mam, taking her waist in his hand.

'If that's how many whiskies you've had, you're fired,' she said.

'Oh, don't be like that, my love. I was just thinking. Brendan here's about to make his millions and marry his sweetheart, and my only daughter's all but grown into a lady. And Callum, what are your plans? Still going to sea?'

'I might be foreman next year,' he said. 'Old one's retiring.'

'Good for you, son. Avast and belay, is that it?'

'Something like that, Da,' he smiled.

'They grow up and leave you,' he said, wiping an imaginary tear from his eye. 'They make their own plans.' No one asked me about my plans. Everyone always knew I would never leave the Danker.

'That's enough,' Mam scolded, turning off the tap he'd left running behind the bar. 'You're more in the way than of use, you bloody drunkard.'

'Come and see the car, Da?' Brendan offered. The men wandered outside, Da still singing his tune.

I got rid of Mam for once, saying I'd tidy everything up. She looked relieved, and went upstairs without complaint. I shooed the last straggling customers home to their families and turned the chairs onto the tables to sweep the floor. When I finished, I spun around in the middle of the empty bar, excited. I had made plans, if anyone had cared to ask. I had a million of them.

'I've got plans,' I said. I listened to the Danker grumble happily in the warm summer night.

'Come on then, what are they?'

I turned around with a start. You were standing in the doorway, watching me with a smirk on your face.

'Haven't you gone home?'

You shook your head. 'They're arguing again, so I came back. Go on, tell me.'

'Tell you what?'

'Your plans.'

I took a deep breath. 'I want children,' I confessed. 'When this is my place, I want my kids to run around like we did. I'll get rid of that damn piano off the balcony, and I'll halve the bistro and put in a pool table and a jukebox. Wouldn't that be fantastic? Maybe I'll even make a little stage, and we can have a band.'

The smirk on your face was a bitter line. 'Where are you going to get a band?'

'Joe Cullen can play the trumpet,' I faltered.

'In the scouts,' you pointed out. 'He hasn't picked it up since.'

'People play music here. My da.'

'A couple of old men playing sea shanties like it's eighteen hundred and something!' You mocked. 'It's hardly rock around the clock.'

'Grace. Don't be like that.'

You looked at your shoes. I took your shoulders in my hands and kissed the top of your head.

'We'll be together. You're still my best friend.'

'You too,' you said. You kissed me on the cheek, but your skin was cool and taut.

'Hey,' I said. 'Come here.' I put my arms around your waist and tried to hold you still, but you wouldn't look me in the eye. You twisted out of my hold and danced across the room, a slow, mad waltz, with your arm stuck out comically for an invisible partner. I whistled a tune for you, but my breath grew dry as you danced out the door without saying goodnight.

I sat in the empty bar afterwards, trying to figure things out. I concentrated on my future, trying to draw you into my pictures of it, but they flickered like firelight.

Christmas Day dawned with an unseasonal cloud cover, which was a relief from the heat but made me wake with a sense of foreboding. I went through the motions of the day, finding solace in cooking, but spent most of it worrying about you. I decided I would visit you after dinner.

Jack hadn't been well for some time. There were days he wouldn't get out of bed, and others he would pace the house. Sometimes he'd take the household money and go up to Sydney for days, coming back bruised and penniless, forlorn and apologising. Faith still did his washing, even though she was the one with the day job.

I didn't get a chance to visit you. That evening, you burst into the kitchen as we were tidying up after our Christmas dinner. You came across the room with tears in your eyes.

'May, I have to talk to you.'

''Scuse us,' I said.

I took you up to my room and you handed me the letter solemnly.

'Read that,' you said.

'I love you both,' I read, 'and that's why I've gone to Victoria to see if I can make something of myself. I'll come back when I've worked it out.'

'Jack's gone?' You nodded your head.

'Come back when he's worked what out?'

'I don't know. Whether he loves us I guess.' Your voice wobbled. You rested your head against my shoulder.

'He says he does.'

'My father says a lot of things he doesn't mean.'

'He'll be back,' I said. 'I'm sure he's just gone to drown his sorrows in a bar where he can still throw a punch without you coming in.'

You smiled, but your face was sad. You lifted your head and moved to the balcony doors to look out to sea. Shafts of moonlight fell through clouds in the distance, beyond the horizon.

'Maybe that's why,' you said. 'It's my fault. I shouldn't have hit him.'

'Of course you should have,' I replied, thinking more of what had happened afterwards. I stroked your hair, which was as fine as a child's, and tried to comfort you.

'How's Faith taking it?'

'You know what she said?' You turned and took on your mother's face: 'Oh good, less washing. Must be Christmas.'

I couldn't help laughing, but when your hand crept up my dress the laughter turned to something else and I pulled you against me, seeking the sorrow in your body.

I let my hands fall.

'Can't,' I said. 'My brothers are here, remember? You should go.'

Your eyes widened and you looked over your shoulder at the doors of my room, both of which were closed. It was still early in the evening. I could hear my brothers laughing with my father outside, checking out Brendan's car for the fifteenth time.

You crept down the stairs in your stockings, then put on your shoes at the kitchen door. I followed you outside and leaned against the wall. The moonlight was strong, and it cast bold shadows. I watched you disappear into the darkness beyond.

'Bit old for sleepovers aren't you?'

Callum leaned against the wall beside me and lit a roll-your-own.

'Jack's buggered off,' I said.

'Well, you could have seen that one coming.'

'They didn't.'

'True.' He dragged at his smoke, then looked into the kitchen to check it was empty.

'Listen, May,' my brother began, 'I don't want you to think I'm being nosey, but people are talking.'

'What about?' I said, pretending innocence.

'You know,' he said. 'It's not doing anyone any good. Mam's stressed enough without the stories going around.'

'What stories? I'm allowed to have a friend aren't I?'

'You're dreaming,' he said, 'if that's all you think this is. I know.' His voice cracked and he dragged on his smoke. He coughed, which seemed to settle him. The combination reminded me of my father. Frightened by his words, a part of me had time to realise that my brother had been a grown man for some time. That he would one day grow old.

My heart crept into my throat. I shook my head, but I couldn't give voice to false denial.

'I had a mate who was like you once,' he continued, forging on. 'He disappeared off the pier during work hours. No one saw it happen.' My brother grimaced, then patted me on the shoulder. He dropped his smoke in the grass.

'He was a good bloke,' he said quietly. He lifted his hand away and shrugged.

Callum stepped around the corner and into the light of the house. I watched the red dot of his cigarette fade in the grass at my feet, and the sound of my heartbeat faded with its light.

★ ★ ★

On a hot January day I was whistling to myself, tidying the kitchen, when you came around with an armful of spinach and a hunted look.

'What's wrong?'

'Nothing.' You separated out the leaves, your white hands dealing delicately with them as though they were fragile flowers. You placed them on my kitchen table, leaned on your elbows and sighed.

'I can see something's up,' I said. 'Just tell me.'

'I can't stand it. I can't bear it any more. I have to get out of here. Faith will be all right, she's got her meetings. Now that Jack doesn't need us – has proved he doesn't need us.'

You took the parted leaves and began to rinse them under the tap. 'I've applied for a scholarship. I came to tell you. If I get in, I can go and live in the women's college.'

'Oh,' I said. 'What about us?'

'There's a world out there, May. I want to see it for myself.'

I dragged you by the wrist to the kitchen door, scattering spinach in my wake. I pointed out to sea, to the vague horizon and beyond.

'Look, there it is. Now you've seen it.' I dropped your arm, and you faced me.

'It's not enough. You're the one that showed me there could be more than this. Look at it, May.' You gestured to my kitchen. 'Are you going to spend your whole life being satisfied with this?'

'Yes,' I said, feeling pain well in my throat. 'Excuse me.'

I left you in my kitchen and ran. The only place I had to go was down the headland to the beach. I threw off my dress and walked into the ocean. The cool water soothed the work-sweat from my body, and the push and pull of waves gave me something to fight against. I turned in the water and looked up to see your shape standing on the edge of the headland. You were dwarfed by the pub behind you. You raised a hand, in greeting or farewell, and walked away.

I felt the undertow pull at me, and thought about letting go. Pulling anchor and drifting out. But I am a strong swimmer. I know where my shore lies.

My mother's parents passed away that summer, both at home, weeks apart. Mam took care of selling the farm. We put the money into the pub, upgrading the bistro and rebuilding the bathrooms with their ancient plumbing. After the renovations were over Mam was still hectic with grief, so she set about organising other things.

Ted asked me while we were carrying the vegies up from the shop. It was distinctly unromantic. I was holding two big pumpkins, and he had potato dust all down his shirt from the sack. He didn't take my hand or bend his knee. We were just bringing the vegies as we always did, except that when we got to the pine tree at the edge of the headland, he stopped. A couple of cockatoos hung upside-down eating pinecones. They watched us with their cheeky eyes. Ted cleared his throat.

'I reckon you and I could get married,' he said.

'Do you?' I walked past him towards the house. I wasn't sure if he was just speculating. Sometimes we did that: 'I reckon I could hit that tree from here', or, 'I reckon it's gonna rain today.' But when we got into the kitchen, Mam was there, and she gave me a look.

'I better get that washing on, I'll leave you to it.' She smiled at me like a cat and took her mug of tea out with her. I knew then that he had asked her first.

'The kettle's boiled,' I said.

'I'm serious,' he replied.

I watched him across the table, thinking how different his body was from yours: sinewy, heavy, almost clumsy. I was aware that I had expected him to become my husband for a long time, but I didn't have much of an idea what that was going to involve. In the images of my future, the husband was a vague shape, a necessary object. I wasn't sure I knew what I was supposed to do with him.

'I better put these away,' I said, lifting the sack of potatoes onto the bench.

'Is that a no?'

'It's a maybe,' I said, turning around and leaning my back against the bench. 'I don't know Ted. You're like my brother.'

'Oh.' He traced a line in the potato dust on the table with one grubby finger. 'What if I don't want to be your brother?' His brown eyes were dense and liquid.

'Just give me some time to think about it. It's too soon.'

'All right, mate,' he said, and put his hand on my shoulder. 'I can wait.'

I walked to your house the long way, down the road and in the front gate. I was on official business, not for shortcuts. You were reading on the porch in the early sun and didn't look up from your book when I arrived. You turned a page and frowned when I sat beside you.

'What are you reading?' I interrupted.

'Blake.'

'Hey, that's my book.'

'I borrowed it. He's on the list of readings for my application.'

You shrugged and smiled your innocence. Your expression changed when you saw my face, my traitorous face. You found a gum leaf for a bookmark and slid the book closed. You lifted your eyes to mine with an expression of expectant impatience. I couldn't bring myself to speak.

You put the book on the floor and let your body relax. I rested my head in your lap, where the leatherbound volume had been a moment before, and stared into the morning sun. Its warmth felt cleansing, and I closed my eyes.

'To see a world in a grain of sand,' you recited, 'and a heaven in a wild flower.'

'You should keep it,' I said. 'It's yours anyway.'

'Hold infinity in the palm of your hand,' you continued. You placed two fingers very gently behind my ear, where the hair started, and traced a line to my neck and back. Your fingertips were cool against my skin. If they hadn't been, I don't think I'd have been able to tell where you ended and I began.

I should have told you then, but I kept Ted's proposal to myself. That summer I learned that I could keep secrets from you. That I had to. This isn't the whole story, and we both know it. There was another reason I had started to reserve a place for myself alone. But why bring that up? Isn't it better to leave our wrongs forgotten?

Some memories live in the body. The skin can hold what the mind can't manage. My face won't lie, and my neck won't be silenced. Absently, while pausing in writing this, I have moved the pen onto my skin and made a line. I can forget the hurt, but it is already mapped into me. A scratch on the back of my hand that won't stop bleeding.

sixteen

If history can be etched in skin, then the body is a country. It has borders, a distinct language, a culture. When I look at my body now, it's hard to believe it ever betrayed me. It's solid, dependable. Apart from the aches, it works for me most of the time. It's my mind that seems to have lost its sovereignty.

I am becoming more absentminded since I began this letter. Or should I say since your presence came back? Because there were dreams, I'm sure of it, before your letter arrived. Why now? That's what I don't understand. Why now, when I have already let you go?

I find myself staring at the wall behind the bar. I imagine seeing it with your eyes, and I am ashamed. The plastic clock, the tacked-up currencies from other countries, the postcards of faraway places I have never been. It's like a map of the world made of lies. If there is any sense in that map I have forgotten it.

★ ★ ★

I walk the perimeter of my land, comforted by the lay of it, the familiar footholds on the rock, the known form of the headland. I take pleasure in knowing exactly how my life fits into the shape of this country. But this is not my land. Da won it fair and square, but who knows how Parson got the title in the first place? It was granted to someone way back, before the mines came, but we now know it wasn't any government's to grant.

We used to think we'd earned our place by settling, by hard work and building, fixing, making something of the place; but it's the place that makes something of us. I belong here by default, but that belonging is contingent on the country itself, and I know not to push its tolerance too far.

The world is in these few acres. Every square inch of this town is a memory. I walk through Coal and am drenched by the droplets of stories suspended in the atmosphere like winter fog. Every rock and tree has a particular history. There are layers and layers, and sometimes I feel I'll never be free of it.

That flowering gum is slowly eating a fence post. You can't see it happening, that kind of change, but if you don't look for a while you notice the swollen trunk has swallowed another inch of dead wood, taking it into itself patiently, as though in sympathy.

You can stay in one place for years and still see things that are new. Did you know that? I want to know if you miss home, not just here but the broader notion of staying somewhere, developing that slow intimacy with a place and finding things to wonder at after a long time. It's like a marriage, and I mean one that goes on for a long time. The complexity of detail saves us. You see, you don't need to travel to see the world.

I might be talking to myself here, but I like to think I've earned the privilege.

I can smell the workmen next door raising the sharp scents of sawdust and electricity, hear their grunting trucks drown out the birds. The Danker rattles angrily when they drive their earth-movers up and down the road.

It's almost noon. I should open the bar. Every day I consider staying in the kitchen a little longer. If anyone comes up at this hour they're local, they know to come and get me from the house-half, to knock gently on the screen door. I never stay long though. That would be admitting defeat. If I'm old and tired enough to take one afternoon off I'm old and tired enough to let the place go and the bloody developers can have it.

The workmen are building another glass house against the hill to catch the view. The staggered Lego homes along the point stare across at me with their grey, flat eyes. The real estate sends me ads for free appraisals. So I will open precisely at noon as I have always done and let the lot of them go to hell. Even if it is just stubbornness, holding on to a certain pattern, afraid of progress, I don't care.

When I do open, no one comes in. Winter is official. The caravan parks are closed, the beach is deserted except for a few locals, the brave old lap swimmers, and the birds. I can't be bothered fixing things, and the Danker is as clean as it gets. I make the fire and sit with it, with your letter.

I think of my regulars sitting at home by their own heaters, Louie spending time with his wife, Clare painting perhaps, and Joe asleep on his couch in front of the TV. Runner will be smoking on his porch, Alan hanging up his hat in the tiny police station. They all have roles and purposes, but thinking about them makes me feel lonely.

★ ★ ★

Spending your whole life somewhere is no guarantee that you'll know it. You just know a series of habits so familiar you can't even see them. I'd say it was my generation, that we had less choices, if you weren't a shining counterexample. It's my anchor that attaches me to Coal and stops me seeing it as an outsider must: as just another coastal town, set in its ways, resisting the inevitable changes. Redevelopment, tourism, the bloody sea changers. Last time I walked Mallee down to the point, the real estate had a sign up that said 'God's country for sale'. I almost growled at it. Who thinks they have the right to hand this country over to their god? Then I remembered Aunt Betty begging the coppers to take her in, and I was humbled. Even the country I think of as solid under my feet has thousands of years on me, and who knows how many stories.

I must still have faith in something. This telling, then. The uncomfortable fit between God and country, between story and present. I want to belong here, not just in this land but in the stories that have made it home for me.

When I began this letter I was trying to find you, but it goes on and on and I am still no closer. Perhaps I am trying to find a way to rid myself of you. A conjuring trick: now you see her, now you don't. A vanishing act.

Last night was so quiet, the place is spotless. A clean bar's an empty bar, as Da would say. I will myself to keep busy. I restock, straighten chairs, polish clean surfaces. While I work, I think. I wonder whether I need to get the stools reupholstered or if they'll last another season. I think about the floor that dips in the middle and when I last got the termite man in. Eventually, I am exhausted by this mental inventory. My thoughts go back to the kitchen table and your letter sitting there, waiting for me. So I sit down, I take up my pen, and I keep going.

I've hardly begun when Pat comes crashing through the door with a dead fish in his hand, yelling.

'Mum!' His eyes are full of the ocean, thrilling blue and sprayfraught.

'Eeew.' Eight and boss, Lisa wrinkles her nose from her place at the kitchen table where she's laid out her homework. '*More* fish.'

Pat and I swap winks and he presents the animal to me like a cat, sure of glory but reluctant to part with treasure. 'Can I clean it?'

I pretend to consider this and wait for Ted's boots to scrape on the step, the cough that always precedes him. But the kitchen's empty. Only ghosts. The thousand little waves of the lost and parted, and beneath them always the swell, the rising tide of your absence. I forget for hours, sometimes days, but it's always there. It's the sound of the ocean.

When no one comes in for three nights in a row I finally close the bar, but instead of brooding I decide to visit Clare. I get halfway up the hill before I realise I am breaking a code, that I am her publican and not her friend. I change direction, head back down, and call on Joe instead.

I glance in the window to his front room. He's asleep on the couch with the TV on, just as I imagined. He's the only one left here who would remember you. I could talk to him. I knock on the window and he sits up and squints at me.

'Come in out of the cold, you fool,' he beams as he opens the door. 'I made chocolate chip biscuits. I was going to bring some up for you. They're still warm. Have a seat.' Joe pulls a stack of magazines off a chair. The house is too big for him, but he manages to clutter it with city art glossies. Canvases lean on every wall. Under the sweet aroma of baking, the place smells sharply of linseed oil.

'These are delicious,' I say, when I've taken my third warm biscuit from the tray.

'I'm baking every night 'cause the heater's on the blink, but I can't eat everything on my own.' Joe looks sheepish. We both stare at the TV, which is showing an old black and white movie. The sound is turned down. The silence in the room is comforting because it's not mine.

'Why didn't you ever remarry?' I ask him abruptly.

He takes a biscuit from the tray and examines it for the answer. 'That's funny you ask,' he says. 'I was thinking of getting a dog, for the company. But a wife? Nah. I only ever had two loves in my life, and Coal can't up and leave me. Besides, I keep busy enough.' He gestures at his easel.

'But you could still meet someone.'

Joe shakes his head and swallows his biscuit. 'I like having myself to myself. A dog though, that'd be all right. Take him for bushwalks, and that.' He appraises me with sharp blue eyes. 'Course, I could ask the same of you.'

'I've got Mallee,' I say. I suddenly do not feel like talking. Joe's neat life, his art, put me to shame. He's complete.

I walk home a roundabout way, past the war memorial in the park. My brother's name is etched there, on the side facing the old coal mine. I don't read it, or any of the familiar names. The fat obelisk, the lawn around it mown cautious by the council, bothers me. It's too much and not enough at the same time.

At my kitchen table, chewing the pen, I am filled with a sudden impulse to demolish my work. I could burn every word of this letter. I could take down the curling postcards and destroy them. I could rid my house of the objects it proffers me. But I'd still carry the mark of this story, carry it like a eucalypt damaged by fire. It's too late, if it was ever possible, to excise the part that went wrong.

Even from inside the Danker, I can feel the escarpment leering at me. Betty has hinted that the place is inhabited by something, something that doesn't want us here. Further inland, there is a place where fourteen Aboriginal people were driven off the cliff at gunpoint, to their deaths. That gorge is supposed to be haunted, but no one can say that the massacre is to blame. The haunting might have come first; the country might have drawn the violence out of people. That kind of story keeps itself in place.

I don't know if anyone was murdered on the escarpment, or if there's some older guardian we have offended. I don't know if I believe in spirits. I don't know if I have to, when I have your ghost to blame. But I do know that I am not ready to go back there. Allow me the luxury of the storyteller – to walk around the dark pits in the rock as if they are not there.

seventeen

When you won the scholarship, your mother laughed. 'Literature as befits a lady,' she said, and shook her head.

I could tell she was proud of you. She was just trying to disguise her fear of losing you by making jokes about intellectuals. You couldn't see it. You fought with her at every turn, and told her she had driven your father away.

'Jack would be proud of me,' you said as we stood in the heat of your room, packing the small red case. I nodded, wiped the sweat off my face, and folded a white skirt. It dangled in my hands like a dead butterfly.

'He'll be back,' I said for the hundredth time. I stopped myself from pointing out that you liked him much better in his absence.

'Maybe. I'm too much like him to know what he'll do.'

You were always unpredictable, true, but even the ocean has a pattern. Sudden rain that falls on our bodies in the night has a reason. Even a storm has a cause. I put my hand to my neck where a bruise the colour of a thundercloud lingered. I wore a scarf despite the heat. I handed you your folded skirt and it weighed nothing. Our hands did not touch.

Your body flickered like light over your weightless things. You had accumulated so little: a pile of books, a few clothes, some trinkets. I watched you stuff your possessions into the small case and press them down with your hands. I watched your delicate hands crush the fabrics together, gentle but firm. You could not meet my eye.

'Do you want these?' I held the kid gloves up in front of you, waved them in your face.

'Of course,' you said, and snatched them out of my hand.

'You're leaving all the rest?'

'I'll only be an hour away on the train, you know. I'm not dying, for God's sake. How come you always have to be so bloody dramatic?'

I stood to be near you, reached out my hands, but you pushed them away.

'Don't,' you said. But you changed your mind and took my waist in your arms, held me to you. The familiar smell of your body was not enough to make me forget you were leaving. It would change, it would shift its shape when you were gone, and I would no longer know its contours, its thundercloud shadow.

We separated. You patted me lightly on the shoulder, and your hand did not linger.

'You must promise you'll visit,' you said.

'Of course I will.' I might have offered to come with you if I had had any confidence in my own existence. But I have always been contingent. When I leave Coal, my borders shimmer like flat country in heat.

You smiled, but your eyes were cold. 'You don't *have* to,' you said. 'I'm not going to *make* you.'

'I said I would.'

'Fine,' you said. 'Promises don't mean anything anyway.'

I turned away from you. 'You don't have to be like this.'

'This is what I'm like,' you replied.

I walked out of your room to hide my tears. After what you did I should have hated you more. Instead I hated myself for being so quick to forgive. In the kitchen, your mother was filling an old cake tin with scones. She turned, her eyes wide with anxious sympathy.

'It's not you she's leaving,' I said.

Faith smiled sadly. 'Thanks, May. I know. She's just . . . like her father, I guess. Great things.' She shrugged and handed me a bundle of half a dozen scones wrapped in a teatowel, the ones that wouldn't fit in the tin. I stood in her kitchen, balancing what felt like a bag of warm rocks against my stomach, and tried to imagine what it would be like to live in an empty house.

The scholarship provided you with a shared room in the women's college. You telephoned me to complain about it. It was too small and cloistered for your liking, what with the curfew and your fellow students being hardworking country people, the children of station managers and landowners, the children of another species.

I could visit you there, you insisted, and when I declined you offered to meet me in a café down the street or in the library. I made excuses, though. I had plenty of work to do here.

The telephone was in the laundry. I would sit in the shadow under the stairs, holding the heavy bakelite phone to my ear with both hands. The crackle and delay had a strange kind of intimacy, disturbed only by the fact of my mam always standing by, one ear cocked to the door or pointedly passing back and forth with a basket of dirty sheets.

Our conversations were strained by distance. The delays were just long enough for every phrase to be an interruption. I preferred to write long letters that I could compose in private, and once I started, you stopped calling. It got so that we wrote nearly every week.

I wrote you long stories about Coal, true ones and false ones, stories about the landscape changing, about my parents' arguments and the nights you were missing at the Danker. I tried to respond to the ideas in your letters, to raise myself up to poetry or philosophy, but always came back to the world around me. The letters all ended with 'Come home soon'.

You came in winter, with your red case. You stayed with your mother, but she was so rarely home that it was as if you were living alone in that little house. I stayed there with you, telling Mam it was to keep you company. I forgot all about my anger and slipped straight back into familiar patterns.

There is something perverse in taking comfort from the person who has hurt you.

I suppose I held off telling you about Ted because of that hurt, though I told myself it was just that I didn't find the right moment. I forgot that the right moment can be contrived if you want it. I suspect you'd have preferred it if I'd told you straight away, you would have been less angered, but it didn't feel definite yet. It still didn't even when we were married. We just sort of slipped into the spaces in each other's lives. I've said he was like another brother around the house. Isn't that better, to bring someone into the family who is already like family? At least with him, I knew where I stood. It was never a contest.

It was not until the last day of your visit that I finally got the courage to tell you. We were walking along the beach, fighting a harsh winter wind.

'Ted wants to get married.' The air hauled my voice out of my throat and threw it away.

'Well, are you going to?' Your mouth was a painted line. Now that you lived in the city you wore lipstick and high heels. Your cityness had enveloped you in difference; you even had a new smell. I was still plain mouthed and sensibly shod. On the beach, however, we were both reduced to the simple equality of our bare feet.

'I'm not sure,' I said, though I'd already told him yes. I gave you this lie as a gift because I thought you'd be envious. But I could see from your expression that you were not concerned, not even surprised. You pitied me. Poor May McCabe would do no better than a local boy. I pulled the ring from my pocket to show you. Proof.

'You're going to spend the rest of your life here,' you said.

'Yes, I am, and what's wrong with that? You're the one who read me that poem: the world in a grain of sand. At least we have millions of those.' I kicked at the sand with my toes, sending a spray of it up into the wind. 'World, world, world,' I said, enunciating the word with every kick.

'It's only a metaphor.'

'Oh, stuff you Grace. Stuff your education. I know what it is. Why do you read, if it means nothing to you?'

'For the same reason anyone does,' you said. 'Because it makes me into someone else.'

We walked a little way. The wind coming in from the water

was icy. It made tiny sandstorms at the level of our shins which stung my skin. I couldn't breathe except in short, careful gasps.

'What's wrong with who you are now?' You looked out to sea. The skin on your face was taut in the wind, your arms thin shapes under the windblown sleeves of your jumper, like two crowbars in a sack.

'You know exactly what's wrong,' you murmured. 'You of all people.'

That spring, after you'd returned to the college, Jack came back from his year away. He had little to show for it in terms of money, but he certainly looked fitter. He'd been working on a station in the Territory, out under so much space and silence that his voice had quietened, his movements grown subtle, his muscles wiry under browner skin.

Faith took him back in with a list of conditions. He had to promise that he would get a job and take on an equal share of the cooking and cleaning. She pointed out how much easier her life had been without him, and told him if he wanted her back he'd better have something to offer.

He called in a few favours and trusted some people had forgotten his trouble, and within a month he had work in the new car parts factory near the steelworks. With you gone and both of them working down south, Jack and Faith started talking about moving away from Coal. There were many locals who had been shocked enough by Faith taking a job, but making Jack share in the cooking and cleaning was taking things too far. Despite her cheerful fortitude, even Faith was tired of the looks that some of the neighbours gave her. It seems ridiculous now. I guess she was ahead of her time.

After you went to Sydney, I visited her regularly. I took comfort in her company, the honesty of her kitchen table, and the unassuming way in which she treated me as family. I spoke to her more than I spoke to you, and offered my support for her stance with Jack. I'd like to think I was ahead of my time, too, but it was probably just my training. Mam had always ruled our house.

When Faith mentioned they were thinking about moving down south, I was devastated. I would miss her, and you would have one less reason to come back. In desperation, I used the only trick I knew. I manufactured reasons why my mother needed her around.

'Da's taken ill,' I said. 'Not that he'll tell you as much. But there's something wrong with him. Could you call on Mam this afternoon?'

Faith would listen patiently and tell me it was probably nothing. I knew well enough that it was; I'd made it up myself. But she consented to believe me, and I succeeded in convincing them to stay, at least for a while.

That first summer, you came home for the whole three-month break. I was pleased to have you back, pleased by your endless complaints about college life.

'They don't drink, they don't even laugh, and God, if I get back five minutes after ten they cough and moan in their beds, to make the point that I've woken them up and disturbed their precious sleep!'

What kept you out until after ten, I dared not ask.

'So what's going on with Ted?' you asked. 'You've been engaged for a while now.' We were lying in the long grass near our old meeting tree, picking fallen gumnuts off the ground and leaning our heads together gently, like two animals in a field.

'I'm waiting,' I said. 'I want to wait.'

'What for?'

You, of course, you idiot. 'I don't think I'm ready for marriage,' I said instead, because that was the line I had taken with him. It sounded prim and cool and false in my mouth.

'Have you had sex with him?' you asked me. You were direct, your mother's daughter.

I blushed. 'Of course not.' I felt in the grass for your hand. 'Why, have you?'

'No. But that's not to say I haven't had the chance. You know, there's a lot more to choose from in the city.'

I leaned over to pick a blossom from your hair and rolled against you like a seal. 'Grace,' I said, and put my head in the small of your back. That way, you couldn't touch me.

You were cruel sometimes, but not always. If you had been consistent I might have borne it. I might have been able to cut the ties cleanly. But there was always this uncertainty about you. I never knew what you were going to do next.

That summer I did not stay with you, but we were together every day, and when Ted came around he'd have to put up with both of us or neither. More often, the two of us would go for long walks on the escarpment, finding the old hiding places in the bush. We never climbed to the top. That dark, cut-out shape of a giant in the rock watched us creep along the edge of its domain with an ancient coldness.

Once we followed the creek bed up to the tangle of figs that you'd found, years before.

'It looks so small,' you said.

'You're bigger,' I pointed out. The plants were so overgrown that we had to crawl into the space between them on our hands and knees. Once inside, we hid in the damp cool and listened to the birds.

'You're still running away.'

'You're still waiting for me.'

'I'm not. I have a life here. I have a home.'

'You're lucky.'

'So do you, if you want one.' You reached up an arm and pulled a leaf from the branches, twisted it in your hand.

'Do you remember when you told me that pirate story?'

'And you sailed away,' I said sadly.

'In my imagination, you were there. On the ship beside me. I always planned it that way. You were always in the story as well as telling it.'

'And now?' I reached for your face, but you turned away from me.

'I don't know, May. We were just kids.'

'Don't,' I said. 'Don't say that.'

You pulled my hand into your lap and lay down, pulled me down beside you. Against your body I could feel the shape of my engagement ring, cutting into my skin.

Your second year, you left the college and took a room in a house in Newtown. You started working in a dress shop to pay your rent. Work kept you in town, stopped you from coming home on weekends and mid-semester breaks. When you asked me to visit on the phone, I agreed straight away, knowing I had little choice but to do as I was told. I had to take you on your terms or not at all.

On the train I held my purse in my lap, my knees covered in cream cotton. I wondered how best to look sophisticated, but soon lost myself in staring at the landscape rushing by. The engine rattled into Central. You met me under the big clock – you were a whole minute late – and in that same tiny-waisted yellow dress that made you look like a frangipani, eminently crushable. There I was thinking intellectual life was all suits and dust, but I guess it was a Sunday. We pressed cheeks in awkward public greeting. Your face was as cold as marble against my own flushed cheek, but your hand found mine.

We took the tram from Railway Square to your digs near the university. The faces of the city people were dead and clean, not a speck of coal dust. I struggled to maintain some dignity while swinging off the leather strap. My blouse felt too tight against my raised arm. The tram was thick with a smell of varnish and cigarettes, and humid with sweat. The smokestacks slid past us, the bright advertisements blurred, and we swapped smiles at each nervous tilt of the machine.

You gratefully accepted a seat from a man and offered it to me with a wave of your hand. I could only shake my head over the noise and clutch my purse to my body like a shield. It wasn't because the seats were dirty, though there had been words to that effect spoken at some point by my mam. It was just that I didn't trust myself to cross the tram without slipping and stumbling into someone.

The room you rented was in an old terrace house with oleander and roses in the tiny front yard and a little stone porch with concrete colonnades. I followed you up the path and you opened the door with your key.

'Your landlady?' I asked. I was aware of her; I had been told 'moustache', and 'strong as an ox', and that she adored your faltered greetings in her tongue, the ones you'd picked up from your year in Charlie's shop.

'She's visiting her daughter. She'll be out all day. You want a cuppa?'

'All right.'

You busied yourself with the kettle and cut tiny slices of lemon. You seemed comfortable, if not quite at home, in the cool linoleum world of your borrowed kitchen.

'Here,' you said, pushing the saucer at me. 'My room's upstairs. Come on.'

It was a small box added on to the brick house, a wooden cube that leant over the back. A dingy room with a bare bulb swinging from a ceiling rose, it smelled of lard and old blankets. The light in that room was drained of gold. A sash window looked out over the small square lawn. A honeysuckle, thick and sweet, reached across the wall beneath it; under that, more roses and a grapevine. I could see over the tops of the neighbouring houses to a rugged sky. Dark clouds brewed out there. Inside, we sat coolly. On the wooden chair I had turned away from your desk, I smoothed my skirt and resisted an impulse to bite my nails. You perched on the edge of the bed. Your body seemed to glow white against the grey blanket, like a photograph.

'You have a lot of books,' was all I could think to say.

'Mmm. We're supposed to be doing Virgil but my Latin is dismal.'

I suppose I should have looked sympathetic at this, but didn't really grasp its importance. 'How is it?' I asked, looking at the corner where your red vinyl suitcase lurked, spilling white lace out of its ulcerated bowel. A bed, a chair, a desk, a hook for your coat; your life looked small.

'I love it,' you said. You must have seen my face fall, because you added, glancing sideways, 'But I miss you.'

'Well, I'm here now,' I offered.

'Yes.' You straightened your bedclothes with one flat hand, crumpling your fingers against the quilt and blowing air out of your nose like an animal.

I went to the window and mumbled something about the roses. I watched your landlady's underwear balloon on the line as the wind came in. Only a part of the sky was visible between the houses, which were all joined together, leaning on one another to ward off some great sadness. The storm clouds pulled the sky closed; they made the city vanish in a grey approach of rain.

Your arm appeared around my waist. Your breath was hot against the back of my neck. You pressed yourself against me and I felt a shiver run through you into my spine. I let go of the windowsill and pulled you close, wanting to take you into my skin.

Later, as we lay in our warmth and listened to the rain, it was new again. It was good to lie there and not think that we had to hide ourselves.

You said my name, but your large eyes stared as at a stranger from your narrow face. We might have said other things then, had we known we could. We were still wrapped in each other's secrets. So I held you, your face pressed into my neck like a child, and told you that you were my best friend.

I wanted to tell you a story. I wanted you to ask. I waited, but the rain soon soothed me to sleep. I woke to see you reading, a pencil in your hand, a frown on your face, and a golden strand of hair hanging over the book. You put your arm out to touch me, but didn't raise your eyes from the page.

'Read to me,' I said.

'It's in Latin. You won't understand it.' You bit into your pencil. I curled away from you and pretended to sleep.

The invitations to visit were few, and I couldn't just show up on your doorstep. When winter came around I realised I hadn't seen you for three months or more. I wondered what you were doing there, who else you invited into your private room, who else's eyes drifted over your small collection of belongings.

I learned to miss you slowly. I told myself stories in which you died or left the country, comforting myself with fictional reasons for the empty space in my life. I did this at night. In the daytime, I kept myself busy with work. I put on what is called a brave face, though mine betrayed me.

Da saw through me. 'You're looking pale,' he said. 'Go on out in the sunshine, run around.'

'There's lunch to get,' I pointed out. 'I can't. Besides, young women aren't supposed to run around.'

Da grinned at this. 'You're right. You're supposed to be chased. Which reminds me, Ted's been around this morning with the firewood.'

'Da, please.'

'He asked after you, as usual. He's a good young man. You can trust him.'

'I know, Da.'

'So you still haven't come up with a date then?' He put his hand on my shoulderblade and I curled out from under it, making for the kitchen. He followed me, cornered me at the fridge.

'No.'

'I don't want to see you unhappy, is all,' he said.

'I'm not. I just want to wait.' I hauled the meat out of the freezer and thumped it on the bar in front of him. He looked at me from under his creased brow and helped me carry the hard red package across to the bistro.

'You wait as long as you like, May. But sometimes there isn't a right time. Sometimes you have to jump in. Take your mother and me.'

'I know, Da, I've heard it.'

'Ah, not all of it you haven't,' he said, scratching his brow. He turned his head to check no one was listening, and I saw the memory of a younger man in the movement.

'I had another girl before her. Told me she wanted to wait, then went and broke my heart. Ran off with some stockman.' His eyes went astray for a moment. He shrugged and took up a rag off the nail, began to wipe down the bar.

'Far be it from me to interfere,' he said, 'it's not like I want you to go anywhere. We'd be lost without you.' He tapped the top of my head with one finger.

I was pleased at this close thing to thanks. I looked at his fallen face, that moment's youth gone, showing signs of old age. How could I have missed this until now? I took stock of his shaggy greying curls, of the squint in his eye and the claw-shape his hands were making. I tried to think of the last time he'd played his fiddle.

'You're okay, though, aren't you, Da? I'd be lost without you too.'

'Ah, now that's another conversation entirely,' he muttered, and wandered away from it.

'Mam?' I called on her one night when Da was out on one of his jaunts. We had a car of our own by this time, a grey-green

Holden, and he'd take it off to wherever he went at night, rumbling down the hill.

'Come in, May. You can hold the wool.'

'What are you making?' I asked as I took the ball of white lambs' wool in my hands.

'Oh, I don't know,' she smiled. 'Babies' things. For the Barrett girl.' She sighed. 'It'll be your turn soon.'

I chose to ignore this. 'Mam, I'm worried about Da.'

She simply nodded, giving nothing away, and looked back at her knitting. I tried again.

'Do you know where he goes at night?'

'If I did, I'd track him down and kill him,' she said. She smiled one of her rare wry smiles and clicked the needles harder.

I had begun to suspect my father of having an affair, but the idea of it didn't seem to fit. I was relieved when Mam didn't seem too worried.

'Mam, I want to ask you something.' She nodded and tugged. I let out two feet of wool and watched her strong, nimble hands move. 'Did you love Da straight off?'

'Well, yes, I must have, or I would have picked a smarter man,' she said, barely a flicker of a smile on her lips. 'Oh, I loved him all right, from the first moment. But that kind of love doesn't last very long. A year or two at the most. After that, it's mostly hard work.'

A year or two, I thought. You and me, we'd been going on like this for several. But what kind of comparison was that? I knew that Ted would never make me feel the intense, physical passion that you made me feel, but I also knew he and I could grow to love each other. Hard work sounded like a breeze after what I'd already been through.

'Mam, if I haven't set a date with Ted it's not because I'm not sure. I know it's the right thing to do. But I was born here. I don't want to go and live somewhere else.'

She put her knitting down and patted my knee. 'May, I was going to ask you. I don't want you to go either. Ted's already spoken to me about it.'

'He has?'

'He loves this place. And Lord knows your brothers won't want it. They've got their own lives now. When your da and me go, I'll want you to have it. We're not so young any more.'

'Oh, you're young, Mam, you're still young.' I hugged her, spilling the wool and earning a frown. It was only afterwards, in my own room, that I found time to wonder at her quiet conspiracy, recruiting Ted and planning my future for me.

The letters kept coming, and I collected them in a bundle, bound them to each other with brown twine. I stored them under my bed, shoring up evidence of your affection against what I knew was coming.

In your letters, you told me about a visiting fellow who taught you, a mildly famous poet. At ten years your senior I supposed your teacher was an adolescent crush, but it continued. He was not quietly small-minded or ashamed of his class, like the other men you met there. He was an American; he was allowed to revel in success.

He taught you the Objectivists, and loaned you the Beats on the sly. You were attracted to their revolutionary style. With his smart clothes, rich language and passion for culture, I suppose he represented everything you felt you lacked. You refused to warn your parents about him, let alone introduce them. Instead, you told me at great length about his genius. I began to imagine his genius as another animal, a bronze fox draped over his shoulder like a ridiculous regal gown.

First he was your favourite professor, and you worried over your work. Then he was inviting you to literary readings, and then to coffee in his study. Soon you started calling him by his first name.

Eventually, after an entire semester of these gushing letters, Richard was no longer mentioned. When you visited in the mid-year break, there was colour in your cheeks, the kind I once put there. A healthy blush. Your smile was a closed door to a private room.

'You've been with him,' I said.

'Who?' You hid your face in your hair, but you couldn't hide from me so easily. You should have known that I could read you like a book. I'd written it myself.

A week before your graduation you came down to Coal carrying your red case. It was empty. You were more birdlike than ever, flicking your eyes at every sound. You came to see me on Saturday morning to ask me to lunch, to be the barricade between you and your parents. I still hadn't learned to say no to you.

Although it was easily thirty degrees, your mother baked shepherd's pie. Her and Jack gazed at you with a kind of fond shock. It was easier to talk about the weather, the political situation, the local gossip than your actual life. I conspired and filled you in: little Joe Cullen and Mercy Thorne were an item.

Your father said, 'The boss's daughter!' He cracked open his third bottle of beer. 'Still,' he continued, looking across at me from under his eyebrows, 'everyone seems to be getting engaged these days.'

'This is great, Faith,' I complimented your mother on the food, which was really too heavy for summer. Perhaps she was trying to weigh you down.

As I helped clear the plates, a flock of cockatoos screeched by outside. I saw Faith flinch and I felt myself do the same. The shadows of their flight passed across the kitchen window and she put a hand on my arm.

'I'll get this, May, you go and sit with her.'

I followed you dumbly into your room. The small rectangular space was still much the same as you had left it. You pulled a box from under your bed and started sorting through the possessions you had collected here.

'I don't know why I keep all this rubbish,' you said, piling a small heap of sea-polished glass on the rug.

'I like them,' I said. 'They're beautiful.' I had an equal pile at home. I picked one up and turned it in my hand. You tossed a lace garment onto your bed. The red mouth of your case was closed like a pippi shell.

'Oh, you can have this back,' you said offhandedly, pulling out a book and tossing it onto my lap. I looked down. It was my copy of Blake.

I didn't open it. I held the book against my lap as you rifled through everything. You packed with furious energy, like a nesting bird. Each thrown object hurled a tightness into my chest. I felt that if I offered to help, I would be drawn into that fury. If I put out a hand, it would be torn from me.

Finally you paused, glanced across to where I sat, and gave me a curious look. 'Gertrude Stein,' you began, then stopped.

I felt stupid, heavy, sitting clumsily with this old book in my hands, another hand-me-down. 'Who gives a shit about Gertrude Stein?' I wanted to shout. I don't think I knew who she was.

'You love him,' I said, low enough that it might not be heard.

'Who?' You said vaguely, but you saw that the game was up. 'Oh, all right, I can't lie to you.' You emphasised the last word as if this was somehow my fault, and got up to close your bedroom door.

'Yes, I really do,' you said. 'He's amazing.' You must have seen the pain in my face, because you added, 'Us, that's different. We're – we'll always be a part of each other. But it's too close. It's too close and it's not . . . you know it's not right.'

'No.' My fingernails dug into the spine of the book. 'It was right,' I said. I sounded defeated, but I meant what I said. It had been right, until recently.

'May, if I tell you a secret, will you promise to keep it?'

I shook my head. I didn't want the responsibility. Suddenly, all I wanted was to be free of you. But the glow in your face was infectious and my curiosity got the better of me, turning the shake into a nod.

'We're getting hitched,' you said. 'Soon.'

'I thought he was already married.'

'They don't even live together.'

'That doesn't make it right.'

'Oh, what do you know about right and wrong,' you spluttered, 'you've no idea what it's like in the real world.'

I put my hand on your knee. 'This isn't real?' I said. 'This isn't real?' I kissed you against your will, fighting your neck with my hand.

You pushed me roughly away and shook your head. 'You think I'm going to sit around here and keep doing this while you have a life?'

'I'll call it off then. I'll tell him —'

'What, and wreck your only chance of happiness? I'm going

away. You deserve better than this. You should have a life, and kids, you always wanted kids.'

I didn't argue any further. You were right, it was time for me to face the real world. We had belonged together only in my imagination, if at all.

You were never going to spend the rest of your life here, but I thought perhaps another year, another month. Another week, another night with you.

Your parents were invited to your graduation. Your mother, at the last minute, had an important meeting, and your father claimed illness. You were angry, but I knew that they were doing you a favour. They didn't want to embarrass you.

I went alone. I no longer cared if I embarrassed you, or so I told myself. I caught the train up, feeling awkward in a borrowed tweed skirt I knew to be shamefully old fashioned.

I would like to blame circumstances. These days, we would be more free. But the truth is it wasn't shame that drove us apart, but a lack of courage. You moved in literary circles by then, you knew it was possible for two women to be in love. Gertrude Stein and all, though it took me years to figure that one out.

I arrived late and was too shy to ask directions from the idle, lolling figures on the lawns. I walked in circles until I found the hall. The alien world of yours loomed with its tall, British architecture. The solemn, gothic stone seemed silly under such a bright summer sky. I sneaked in the back like a sinner.

The ceremony bored me. An elderly man made a speech I could barely hear from the back of the hall. After the speeches, the names were called in alphabetical order. You looked just like everyone else in your black robes, a genderless shape in a stupid hat. Perhaps you were always meant to be this way, I thought. Just like everyone else.

Afterwards I found you on the lawn. You and your cohorts were laughing at some private joke. I waved you over. You stepped towards me, your face broke into a big warm smile, but your eyes didn't meet mine. Someone else had caught them. I went to get myself a sandwich and watch him. I wouldn't make a nuisance of myself. I loitered at the sandwich stand and sweated, wishing I hadn't worn the tweed.

'May, you came!' You grabbed my shoulder, kissed my cheek which blushed in spite of me, and thrust a glass of champagne into my hand.

'She said it was unbecoming,' you gasped, 'for young ladies without the orange juice,' and made a face. We giggled, and for a moment it felt like old times. But something about your energy was too bright.

'I've got half an hour,' you said, 'come and help me take this monkey fur back to the office.' You were the scholarship girl in a borrowed gown. I had almost forgotten.

We walked down some steps and you disappeared into an underground room. You emerged after a moment in a knee-length blue dress. 'Do you like it?' You span. The drink had moistened your eyes. I couldn't help thinking of the villainous pixies in my da's stories.

'He said it makes me look like an actress,' you said in a whisper, and checked your watch. 'I've just got time to walk you to Central, if you like.'

I had of course thought we'd spend the afternoon together. I said yes, because this was all I was going to get, though I would really have preferred to be alone.

We passed alongside the high, stone walls and out into the

park. You went quiet and I chattered about the trees and the weather and the ducks just to fill the space between us. Halfway down the hill, where the road dipped, I grabbed your hand.

'Grace.'

You wouldn't look at me. You fished in your purse and pulled out a handkerchief, a lipstick, a piece of paper folded into a triangle.

'I'm sorry,' you said, 'but will you promise not to read this until you're home?'

You looked at me with sharpened eyes. I suppose you were trying to memorise me. I could say I knew that this moment was our last meeting face to face; I could say I divined the instant of our separation, the instant you made that last transition into memory. I didn't. I thought you were being melodramatic, that the champagne had gone to your head. I took you by the shoulders, kissed your fine skin and hair, your wet cheeks, and let go.

'You had better get back, they'll miss you.' You were crying, but my eyes were dry as two stones.

'I'll see you soon,' I said, and walked away, careful not to look back over my shoulder.

On the train, I fingered the triangle for fifteen minutes before curiosity won out. I read that letter over and over, until I had it memorised. When the train emerged from the tunnel and I could see the broad, bright ocean all around, I folded it into a small brick and threw it out the window. Your voice echoed in my head, 'What, and wreck your only chance of happiness?' I let it drown in the sound of the rattling train.

You were gone. A disappearing act, brought to its finale at last. I should have been relieved of the tension of wondering, but I wasn't. I still had to worry about the consequences. I still had to live here, in this little town by the sea, and see the same people I had seen every day; and because you were my best friend, my inseparable twin, my honorary sister, I had to explain you.

For two days, I kept your secret. I assumed you would write yourself to Jack and Faith, which you did, but you mailed your letter to them. I had to pretend I knew nothing, which was unfair. Maybe you thought I would be grateful that you'd told me first, but it felt like a punishment.

Your father came into the bar and ordered a whiskey. He had a few extra years on his face, and it was only the afternoon. I knew what was coming, so I poured him a double.

'Grace is gone,' he said, draining the brown liquid in one gulp.

'Gone?' I pretended to be shocked. I was glad that I'd been lying about you for years. It came in handy.

'She's gone off with that American.'

I grabbed the bottle and topped up his glass. 'Where?'

'New York,' he said, drawing the two syllables out mournfully. 'It's my fault, I should never have left her.'

'It's not your fault,' I said, wishing someone could tell me the same.

'I'm sorry to be the one to tell ya. I know she was special to you.'

It was the past tense that hit me. Only later, replaying the conversation to myself, did I catch something in his tone. A suspicion of mockery, a hint of something like relief.

Mam shook her head and said she gave you a year. That became a personal deadline. I waited for news that never came, because why would you write to me when you wanted to cut off all connections with your past?

I waited that year out. I waited every day for a sign or a letter, something more than the marks we had left on the landscape, the map you had left on my body. I avoided the escarpment. I spent hours on the beach. I hid myself in my work.

To make matters worse, Da grew ill. He coughed, spluttered and mumbled his way through the days. It was years since he'd worked in the mine, but the black lung got him anyway. Miner's complaint, they used to call it, and he complained constantly. His illness made it hard for him to keep the bar in shape. We spent more time cleaning up after him than the customers.

When the year was out, I took the bundle of letters from under my bed and walked to the tip of the headland at dusk on the night of the full moon. I watched it rise from the sea. Its yellow body separated from the water, as if the ocean was transforming a part of itself into rock. I untied the knot that bound the pages. It was a simple double overhand, and should have been easy to release.

But this type of knot is also called a bloodknot. With the placement of an object, the bloodknot can be worked up into a stranglehold. When my fingers failed to undo my work, I tried to pull the folded pages from the sheaf. I wanted to throw them off the headland, one by one. There was no wind. They would have floated down like feathers. I imagined the ink dissolving in the sea, like the panic of little paper squid. But they would not let me let go.

I could still see the words in the other letter, the tiny brick I threw from the train window. 'I wish you and Ted all the happiness that you deserve,' you had written in that letter. It sounded like a backhanded insult. Without that I might have turned around, might have jumped off the train and gone back to the city and stopped you. Instead I chose to be satisfied with what I deserved.

By the end of that year, Da was seriously ill. His breathing was laboured, his eyes were failing, and he was losing control of the bar he'd run for twenty-five years. His mind couldn't cope with his weakness. Everywhere he went, he left a trace of chaos. Spilled ashtrays and broken glass, the trail frustrated him more than it did us.

Mam and I were closer by then. I guess she'd softened, or I'd grown to appreciate her practicality. Faced with Da's illness, she took charge of him. From medicine to scolding, she was always one step ahead of Da, who insisted on working through the coughs. Where I tried to comfort him, to soothe him into taking it easy, she would smack him over the head with a rolled up newspaper and tell him to lie back down or she'd kill him herself.

Unsentimentally, she made me work and clean up after my father and kept me busy. I tried to console myself with the art of being necessary.

Ted and I still took the vegetables in from the shop together, and on Fridays he waded in from his fishing spot out on the rocks with a bucket full of snapper or prawns. He was always around; I can't remember us ever going on a date, but I find it just as hard to recall a time after you were gone when he wasn't by my side.

'You know what,' I said one morning as he handed me a bucket of prawns, 'we should do a raffle. Raise some extra money.' I'd become used to telling him my plans for the Danker like he was a part of the place. 'They can cook them on the barbecue.'

We'd recently installed a little brick barbie on the headland for people to cook their own meals; Mam and I had downscaled the bistro now that Da wasn't working the full complement of hours, and we were struggling to make our bills.

'Why don't you get some of those pokies in, like they have at the RSL?'

'Oh, those things!' I shook my shoulders. His red hair glowed in the sun. 'Come up for a bit?'

He smiled and followed me up the track. When we got to the top I saw the Danker there, shadowed by the escarpment, holding itself up despite its obvious state of disrepair. I ran through my mental list of things that needed fixing, a habit I have to this day. Then I took a breath and turned to him.

'Hey, Ted?'

'Yeah?' I could see the sand in his hair. It matched his freckles.

'I guess I'm ready. I guess we can get married now.'

'You guess?' He laughed and picked me up by the waist. 'Oh, you guess, do you?' He spun me around.

'Stop it! I'll drop the prawns.'

'Bugger them,' he said, playfully twisting me under his arm. 'How about tomorrow?'

I didn't want a church wedding or anything fine, but I convinced Ted that if he'd waited so long already he could wait another month or so. We got married right here on the headland. It was a perfect day, weather-wise. I was breathless with joy, of a final, comforting kind. We spent our honeymoon in the hotel upstairs; neither of us had any money to go away, but we were happy. We promised each other that we could be. I loved him just as he was, and he was constant, Grace, constant. Uncon-ditional. I've never regretted it.

That same month, I buried my father. He should have keeled over behind the bar, passed out on the floor, he should have gone out singing, but he went gently instead, in his sleep.

'It's a mercy,' Mam said. 'It's a mercy he went quick in the end. I don't know how much longer I'd have put up with his moaning.'

She and I washed him ourselves, after the priest came to say the rites. The washing was a soothing ritual for just the two of us. We laid him out in the bistro, where the meetings had gone on all night when he was king of this place, and Mam placed his fiddle in his arms like a dead child. The bistro wasn't exactly sombre with its lino tables, plastic chairs and smell of old grease, but we couldn't very well have left him in the bar.

I couldn't let her bury the instrument. I took it out before we closed the coffin lid. It's still here somewhere, gathering dust in the attic.

He never looked like he was sleeping, because he never kept still in his sleep. Snored enough to wake the dead, but there was no waking him any more. My brothers, Ted, and Joe and Alfie Cullen carried him down to the churchyard.

The whole town was at the wake. I was kept busy behind the bar with Mam. The boys, like Da, were better at socialising, making everyone feel at home. Mam and I were in our own worlds, each trying not to let ourselves cry for the other's sake. She cracked the whiskey open but didn't touch a drop herself.

Long after eleven, we closed up and looked around us at the empty bar. It was dead quiet. Not a single melody had ended my father's send-off, he who'd sung tunes for every death, birth and marriage in Coal for so many years. Without him around, we'd simply forgotten.

It was music and it was you I missed that made the tears come. Ted sat with me while I cried, not saying a word. I kept my head in my hands. I couldn't look at him, let alone tell him that what I really needed was you: a laugh, distraction, a story that would take me out of myself.

In the night I woke suddenly to a cacophonous crash. My first thought was that we'd been hit by lightning; it was cold and still and silent though, no trace of a storm. I could only hear a low, strangled drone, barely discernable under the constant gentle roar of the ocean. I got up and went to my window but could see nothing, only the moon hanging there, a mocking lantern. Then I heard another bizarre sound: my mother was cackling.

I hurried to her room. She was standing in the doorway to the balcony, laughing like a madwoman. Her hair was down and the sea winds blew it around wildly.

'Mam, are you all right?'

'It's that bloody piano,' she said, stifling laughter against the back of her hand. Beyond her, the balcony doors were open to the night. There was a space visible where the instrument should have been. I brushed past her to look down through the gaping hole in the slats. The balcony had finally been defeated by weather and gravity. Our house had broken in protest at its loss, spilling one of Da's great follies from its side. We stared down at the instrument lying in the moonlight. Its guts had burst open, leaving a splintering pile of teeth and string. I could still hear that fading, strangled chord.

'That bugger,' she said quietly. She smiled. 'Thought I'd get a decent night's sleep for once.' Then finally, after a long holding back, a dam burst in her, and she began to cry.

I took her hand and lead her back to bed.

'There,' I said, soothing her forehead as she once did mine. I talked her to sleep. The sight of my mother's tears frightened me. I couldn't remember her ever crying in my presence before. She gazed into space, a long-held distance in her eyes.

'My girls have sailor's eyes,' Da used to say when he caught me or Mam or sometimes both of us looking out to sea with an unspeakable longing. That was a long time ago. I recognised them in my son when he was born and knew he'd be troubled. Dreamers. It's hardly a distinguishing mark; more of a family curse.

The light of that longing left no mark on me. If I'm occasionally absentminded and find things I thought destroyed, it's not the distance of looking out to sea that makes me so; just the effort of maintaining the weight of a whole life, and the lives of others, and keeping on.

I don't look back. Even if I wanted to I couldn't return to who I used to be. If circumstances hadn't separated us, we'd have grown apart instead. You write now because you need something from me. Affirmation, confirmation, absolution. But what I feel is triumph. After all this time it is your restlessness that needs me, your dark place that wants a light. I'm still breathing. I can still see.

After Da passed away, Brendan and Callum stayed around for a short time to help sort things out. Me, I knew I had to stay. The Danker didn't deserve to be abandoned, and nor did my mam. I had no other place in the world, nowhere I would rather be, or could imagine. I had Ted and I had my plans. I was trying hard to believe only in what I could hold in my hands.

Brendan, who always had a good head for figures, pulled out all the old ledgers and he and Mam began to disentangle the chaos of Da's accounts, which Mam couldn't bear to repair alone. At first, she would lift both her hands up in the air in despair.

'I don't know about all these numbers,' she would say.

After a few days, she was cursing her dead husband as if he were still alive.

'You're a bloody fool and a useless idiot, Sean, and if I ever catch you in hell I'll wring your neck.'

'Mam, don't be angry. I'm sure it's just a bit out of order. We can fix it up. Sit down, have a cup of tea, I can get you a Bex if you want.' I would try and reassure her; I worried about her anxiety. She threw herself into work around the place so violently that it put me to shame. It was the cure for her sorrow, but it exhausted her. Sometimes I found her staring into space above the accounts in a kind of fug. But when I tried to take the books away to see for myself, she held onto them stubbornly. I was becoming more concerned about her health than the numbers.

In the end it was Brendan who revealed to me the full scale of the crisis we were in. He took me aside one afternoon when Mam was out of earshot. The Danker was borrowed and pawned to the hilt. Da's little jaunts had gambled away the very foundations of our life. We were so far into the red, he explained, that we might have to close up and sell the land. He suggested we move up to Queensland with him, where land was still cheap. I shook my head.

'We'll make it,' I said.

'I know you're both pretty tough,' he said, 'and Ted's here, but this is too much for the three of you. If you don't make the repayments you'll be giving this place to the bank.'

But my book-smart brother had underestimated this town.

Coal got behind the Danker in unexpected ways. Early one morning I woke to the sound of hammering and reached for Ted to find a cold, empty space beside me. By the time I was up and showered he had fixed the hole in the balcony and was halfway through repainting the railings.

'Where did you get the paint?' I asked. 'We can't afford it.'

'Oh, fell off the back of a truck near Cullen's place,' he said.

'What's that noise?' I asked. A loud, electric buzzing was shaking the Danker to its foundations.

'That'll be Joe,' he said. 'Putting the pokies in.'

'Ted! I won't have those machines in my bar! Do you want them all to end like Da, dying up to their elbows in debt?'

'Better them than you,' he said. He took my hand. 'Look, May, it's just for a little while. Think of the tourists as well. Joe's got a mate who's got a mate who works for the company and they've given us a really good deal.'

A truck rumbled into the driveway and halted with a squeal of brakes.

'Now what?'

'Oh, that'll be the stage,' he said.

'Stage?'

'For the band.'

I looked down to see a group of blokes pulling wood out of the truck and calling to each other.

'Fundraiser,' Ted explained. 'Just a little party to make the most urgent bills, and then we'll see.'

'Ted,' I said, trying to be calm, 'I mean, thank you, but this is too much. I don't want you to do all of this, certainly not without consulting me.' I didn't want the kind of husband who would make decisions for me. I was ready to fight for that, but my clenched fists relaxed when I heard what he had to say next.

'It's not me,' he said. 'I've hardly done a thing. One minute your mother's talking about the books with a few of the blokes, and the next minute – all this.'

Mam stuck her head out the balcony door, a sheepish smile on her face. 'All right there?'

'I want a word with you,' I said.

'It had better be thank you,' she smiled, and skipped back into her room.

But busy as we were, I had not forgotten you, Grace.

After several years of silence, you sent me a letter from New York with your address printed neatly on the back of the envelope. It was a single page, and it said little, but the very simplicity of your language spoke of boredom.

Picture me, if you can. I was just shy of thirty, still so young, in a loose white dress with green flowers. I was sitting at this same table, pen in hand. My skin was glowing, my eyes bright, thinking about you.

I was pouring my heart out, apologising, reliving the wrench I felt when you left. Reliving my coldness to you in the last months, and trying desperately to atone. Your letter, which I considered regretful and homesick, was tucked in my purse. White leather, a wedding gift from Ted's family that came stuffed with bills that I tried and failed to return. Mam was running the bar, Ted was out fishing. The little half house seemed empty.

I wanted you back so badly now that it was impossible.

I bolted down to the shop to post my letter before Ted came in. How exciting it seemed, even the words New York printed on the front made my own handwriting look faintly mythical. All I had to do was buy stamps and drop it in the red box and you would know exactly what you meant to me. You would know that I needed you. And if you didn't come home, I'd know too.

And if you did? From the beach I could see Ted's figure out on the rocks, his legs comically shortened to stumps by the waves, pulling something in. I paused, letter in hand, to watch him.

I made a deal with myself. If this is a fish, I decided, I will take this letter home with me. I stood there for the longest moment, watching him reel in and let out, reel in and let out, giving it chase. His body leaned gently into the rhythm of it, his skin shone in the afternoon sun. He leaned back, his arms taut, and I saw the golden flash of a wriggling body on the end of his line. I put the letter back in my purse and walked home.

The next day I went to the doctor, as I'd been feeling unusual. The emotional, out-of-charge feelings I'd been having were starting to manifest as physical illness.

There was a good explanation, and it wasn't grief. I was pregnant with Lisa.

I never did post that letter. It's still in the box with the rest of them, where this one might end up. You never sent me your address again. You stopped writing letters, and so did I. Except that I never did stop, not in my head. I've been writing this for years, even if it's only the last few months I've put pen to paper. I must be mad to do it, telling tales to a ghost.

For a long time I believed I would write when the time was right. Having kids changes that. There's never a right time to risk your children. Your security seems so much more flimsy. And they were a delight and a distraction. My life was no longer a priority; theirs were.

How different things would have been if Ted's line had been empty. I wonder I left it all to hinge on a single fish. Perhaps I always did have a little of Da's gambling blood.

So now you know, except you don't, and you won't unless I send you this. It's true this story is getting longer. I thought I threw all those other letters away a long time ago. I thought I had stopped torturing myself. But then I found them, still in their bundle in the shoebox. I haven't read them again, but I know they're there, lurking in the kitchen drawer, tucked under the teatowels.

My pregnancy changed other things too. For one, Mercy Thorne became a kind and generous neighbour. She lived with Joe and his parents and the occasional brother in their crowded house, despite the fact there would have been more room at hers. She would often come up with eggs and milk to save me the trip to the shop. Cullen's cow had died by then and they didn't replace her, but Sylvia still made better bread and cakes than any shop could provide. Once we were both married, Mercy and I forgot our childhood differences and became friends.

She tried to live simply, but class is a powerful force. Mercy was restless. She'd grown from a frail child into a beautiful woman, and Joe wasn't the only man who admired her. As her father grew old, Mercy began to take over the business side of the mine, and surprised everyone with her efficiency. After her father passed away comfortably from old age, Mercy had full control of the enterprise. She sold the mine for a packet and filed for divorce in the same week.

I sort of adopted Joe after that as an honorary brother. Mine were gone and with his family all boys he didn't get much female company. He and Ted were officially friends, but it was me he would come to with his troubles, or a remark about the colour of the sky that day.

I made Joe godparent to Lisa. Ted was a good, reliable father, but it was Joe you would find crawling around on the floor in some convoluted game of pretend. Making a face or a selection of silly noises when she pulled his ear. He'd let the kids crawl all over him like a tree. It's sad Joe never had any of his own.

He started painting after his wife left him: the same things over and over, the landscape viewed from anywhere in walking distance. He was shy about it at first, but before long he was bringing his easel and oils up here and making camp on the porch.

After you left your father's temper worsened. Without my da's gentle whiskey arguments, his power to calm the man down and end the night in a laugh and a song, Jack grew bitter. Faith threw herself into committees even more. As May Day lost its charm amid the Cold War climate, she got more involved in the school; the women's auxiliary went underground, hiding its radical reasons behind practical, acceptably feminine pursuits. They set up a small local library, raised the money with lamington drives and favours. Mam would never join in the meetings, though she always baked for the fairs and put a little aside for charity, a habit I've kept on with.

Eventually Faith and Jack moved to be closer to the steelworks and the factory. There was nothing left for them in Coal but reminders of what they had lost. Faith still came up for a beer every now and then, and we would talk, but mostly about you; and as I never had any news, the visits eventually petered out.

I can still see Ted on the back step mending his net like some ageless peasant. He only used the net when he took the boat out, or on weekend trips down to the lake with Tick and Fish. The rest of the time, it hung from the wall in the laundry. It's in the attic now, with his rod and reels, and a box of his clothes I always meant to give to the Salvos.

It was Ted who taught me about knots. He was a collector. His hands would twist things automatically, binding two lines for strength or beauty, for movement or slip. At times I would find the curtain strings knotted into bowlines, the strap of a handbag hitched neatly to a kitchen chair.

The anchor bend is tight, like a braid, but many sailor's knots come apart with a tug. 'Not a very good knot then, is it,' I joked once.

He tugged the string open. 'If you're on a boat you need the rope more than the mooring,' he said. 'Ropes were hard to come by once.'

'Show me another,' I said, to avoid the discourse on sixteenth-century rope manufacture. He twisted two strings together, looping each one around the other.

'Lovers' knot,' he said. 'See? It allows a certain amount of give and take.' He pulled the two ends apart and back together to show me. When I looked at his face, I saw that he was blushing.

Our love was as real as the floor beneath our feet and just as rarely mentioned. Both of us were afraid of making too much of a marriage we suspected of a degree of convenience. It's because

I took so long to let him into my life, but one of the things I loved most about him was that he always knew where he belonged, even more than I did. It was Ted who taught me how to take my time.

He handed me the knot gently, as if it was alive. It contained an echo of the sideways figure-eight that signifies infinity. I held it in the palm of my hand.

Eternity in this small life. I committed to it, not because it was inevitable but because I wanted to. I love this place. I love my children, and I loved Ted. I turned this pub around and raised a family. I got us out of debt and I held this town together during the closures, the crises, the births and deaths and terrors, I made this life, and I'm happy here. Do you really expect me to let you back in after all that you did? Look at what I have to lose.

And still you don't know me. By writing this maybe I've allowed you to see a little too closely the way I saw things, but it's only to prove to myself that I deserve everything I have, every happiness, yes, and even the bruises. Say what you like about regret. All anyone ever does is their best in the circumstances. Even you.

But I am not being completely honest with you. I'm afraid to trust you. I am still in negotiations with your ghost. I have to hold some of my cards close to my chest, if only because I know what you are capable of.

eighteen

Blake's heavy scripture still springs to mind unbidden. I remember tearing the pages from that book you gave me, stole back, and returned. Ripping the paper from the old blue spine, tearing poems I had memorised anyway, and the way the rips went diagonal in my shaking hands. That was a long time ago, when I still couldn't see the lights of a ship on the horizon or hear a plane cut across the sky without thinking of you.

I found that book in the attic this week. Its pages were intact, the inscription still there: *To the ends of the earth, love Grace*, a dedication not to me but to your own future. Perhaps it was a different book I remember destroying.

It lay in a box of old papers, mostly defunct catalogues and invoices, nothing important. I don't remember putting it there. I don't really know why I was going through that box, what I was looking for. I have been trying to tidy up the mess upstairs without examining it too closely, but I am beginning to think that the attic has it in for me. Another post had fallen, and I was nailing it back into place, cursing the Danker through a mouthful of nails.

'You keep this up and I'll sell you,' I said.

I have laid the book on the kitchen table, next to the fruit bowl. It sits there and hums. I open it at a random page and find harlots howling in the streets of London. I wonder what we ever found in it.

As I was climbing down the ladder through the trapdoor, I noticed Da's dusty fiddle case and decided to take a look. I opened it nervously, as afraid of decay as if I was digging up a body. The strings have shucked their pegs and hang loose from the tailpiece, the bridge has fallen, but the old thing must still work. It smells the same: of rosin and varnish and the musty felt that lines the inside of the case. It has hardly decayed at all. I might see if my grandson wants to learn one day. It's not doing any good cluttering the attic, after all.

It is still quiet, but the sharpest part of winter has come and gone, and the locals have crept back to the Danker. It seems too soon, but I'm glad. Sometimes we all need to distract each other.

'I'm bored,' Clare says. 'I can't paint, I'm going mental in that little shed.'

'Can I've another?' says Louie from down the bar. I count in my head.

'Keys,' I reply. He slides them to me along the bar, the Holden insignia familiar in my hand. I put them in a glass beside the register, where they sit growing cold away from his body, like false teeth.

'Drink?' I ask Clare while I'm pouring Louie's beer. She nods and I move another glass under the tap, but she wrinkles her nose.

'Not beer,' she says. 'I need something different. Make me something interesting.'

'Cocktails aren't really in my line,' I say. 'How about whiskey?'

'Sure,' she says, and I get the good bottle down from the shelf.

'Ice?'

She shakes her head. 'How about a story?'

Joe comes in before I can dodge the request, and I'm grateful for the interruption. He passes me his wallet and says, 'Beer until that's empty, May love. I've had a bastard of a day.'

I pull a schooner and raise an eyebrow. I don't need to ask what's wrong. The council has his block slated for redevelopment, and they've been leaning on him heavily. The Cullen place is the last bit of untamed green on the coast, defying the apartment blocks and weekender townhouses that encroach on us like an army of rectangles. They're calling it an eyesore.

An eyesore, that old house that's stood for as long as Coal's been here. Should be heritage listed, not demolished. But they're offering him a price that could keep him going for twenty years.

'Them people have been around again,' he says, licking the foam off his top lip. 'I swear to God they're waiting for me to die.'

'They'll be waiting a while,' I say. Joe's only five foot six but he's as fit and strong-hearted as you'd expect from all his swimming.

'I've a mind to build on the place myself now,' he says, 'if there's so much money in it. You know what they asked me? After they gave me the latest offer?' He leans back on his stool, tired-eyed, and mimics the voice of the company rep.

'You got no children, Mr Cullen? Who's going to look after you? I says I can bloody well look after myself. They got no business.' He downs half a glass. 'No business coming here and casting nasturtiums.'

Clare smiles into her drink and I give her a wink. I lean on the bar and listen to Joe's lament.

'We're in the same boat, anyway,' I say. 'If either of us relents, it will be the end for both of us. At least it's not family putting the hard word on you.'

Louie leans over and involves himself.

'It was in the paper already,' he says. 'About how they're a local company that'll do good things for the town. Local my arse. 'Scuse me,' he mutters this last to Clare.

'Seems to me,' he says, holding his glass up to the light like he's looking for an answer in the cloudy brew. 'Seems to me if it was the old days they'd have a fight on their hands.'

'He's right, Joe. We could do something.'

'Oh, don't go chaining yourself to any bulldozers on my account,' Joe says. 'They can wait til I die. Cullens live a long time. Dad was ninety. Would've stayed with us too if it wasn't for the dust.'

'Dust?' Clare asks. 'What dust?'

'Who's this bloody blow-in,' Joe says, and knocks his beer against hers. 'What dust indeed.'

The drink, the laughter flow, and I'm in their warm embrace. But I'm not of it.

I take in travellers sometimes. I don't get many people staying in the rooms upstairs – we only have the one cardboard sign. 'Rooms: Enquire at Bar', it says, like it always has. Paying guests are so rare that when I get them they have to wait in the bar while I do their rooms. Sometimes I'll get one that wants to work instead of pay, and they end up feeding the chooks, running errands, staying a week or two until they get bored and move on.

There's not much to do, so I end up telling them to go out and enjoy the water, go for a bushwalk. We both feel like I'm doing them a favour, but it's not out of charity. I am thinking of all the people that must have helped you, all over the world.

I never want them to stay long. If I'm honest I'll admit that I like having the place to myself. The bar's wooden line demarcates my unassailable territory. I couldn't do without that silence after closing. However efficient the visiting kids are, I'm always glad when they move on.

I've spent so long forming relationships that begin and end at that wooden line, friendships that close at eleven. Even when I've known someone all my life I don't let them jump the bar. I like to keep the world at that precise distance.

There are two bike-touring boys in the corner who might stay the night. I should ask them before it gets what passes for busy so I have time to make the room. Their bicycles, chained to the front fence, look fancy, strapped with gadgets, but they're mimicking a ghost. It's where Da's rusty one-speed used to lean when I was a child.

Runner wheels in, checking out the cyclists in the corner of his eye. That's my cue to approach them before he has a chance. 'Don't steal anything,' I tell him as I flip my trapdoor and let myself out of the bar. The boys don't look up when I approach. I am invisible when I clear glasses. I am a presence that wipes the tables, a piece of roaming furniture.

'If you're after a place to stay tonight, we've got rooms,' I say, swapping clean ashtrays. They look interested, and I negotiate a price with them.

'You can always camp up at the caravan park if you want,' I add charitably, 'but it looks like rain to me. Up to you.'

I walk back to the bar and give Runner the look which says 'they're all yours'. He hustles them and I'm glad that in an hour or so they won't want to be bothered with pitching a tent. Every bit helps at the moment. The licence is due again and it's always a rough time scraping the excess off every expenditure to pay the fees. Last time I renewed we almost ran out of beer. If I hadn't known the deliveryman's mother I think he'd have withheld credit. I'm not struggling, not as much as Lisa likes to think. It's just tight.

At least I finally own the place outright and not the bank. I took great pleasure, after I finally got the place back from the brink, in wrenching the old poker machines out of the wall. Would've thrown them off the headland if Lisa hadn't pointed out they were rented.

They're back now, of course. Newer models, same deal. I still hate the bloody things but I don't have much choice. I need the percentage.

I sneak upstairs to make up the room. It's a humble twin share, and not too dusty. I spread sheets out on the beds and check the heater's working. I brush a little dirt under the rug. I have to stop myself from going through the drawers, but I steal a look under the beds in case there's anything I've forgotten. There's nothing there. As I stand, the wind snaps the balcony doors open.

'Now what?' I mutter at my home. 'What are you trying to tell me?'

I go to shut them, allowing myself a glance outside at the dark ocean. It has begun to rain, and the water sheets down so heavily that the lights of Coal are blurred.

Down on the beach, a young woman is walking. I can't make out who she is. Probably a tourist caught in the downpour. She steps carelessly along the sand, her hands against her sides. Something in the way she moves prompts a memory.

I swallow. There is something caught in my throat. I close the doors and bolt them, turn and head down to the bar. I walk over to the table to tell the cyclists their room is ready, and glance out the window. The figure on the beach has gone.

nineteen

It was when Lisa was three that I got your first postcard. I remember her weight was almost too much for me when I carried her back from the letterbox. I put her on a barstool while I sifted through the bills and junk mail. When I saw your handwriting, so familiar, I could almost see your face. I had to blink a few times to focus enough to read the words.

'Starting again,' the card said. 'I've left R. Had enough.'

My heart leapt with joy when I read those words. I knew it! I knew you'd be back. The note continued, 'Will send my address when I'm settled.'

When I flipped the card over, there was a picture of Big Ben, a red double-decker bus driving past it, a chilly grey sky hovering too close to the buildings. You had escaped to a different island, across a different ocean, but surely it meant that return was possible. I taped the card to a wall behind the bar. I kept it close so that I could look at it in secret when my hands were free, which was rare enough in those days.

I stood back, leaning on my broom, and looked at the photo

on the wall. I whistled while I worked to keep my pace up. I winked at my young daughter sitting on a barstool with a serious look in her eye.

'Mum, I want a story,' she said.

'Go and ask your nan,' I replied. She grumbled and swung herself down off the stool. She strode clean under the bar's hinged trapdoor and headed into the kitchen.

Mam tried her best, through dish suds, half-feigned forgetfulness, and impatience, to retell the tales my da had told us all those years ago. She and my little daughter would both lose patience with the whole thing pretty quickly. When I finished my sweeping, I went into the kitchen to check on them. I found my mother with an account book open on the table in front of her and a fascinated child on her lap, explaining the processes of addition and subtraction.

'See, this is where you put the income,' she said, ruling a thick red line with her biro, 'and this is where you put the expenditure.'

'Spenditcha,' Lisa burbled.

'Mam, don't bore her with that stuff, she's just a kid,' I said. 'Lisa, don't you want to play something else?'

'She likes this,' Mam replied, stern but proud, and my child nodded at me slowly with her solemn eyes.

'And this,' her grandmother explained, 'is all the bad debt your grandfather got us into, and this is how far out of it we're crawling. See?'

'Mam!' Four clear eyes turned to stare at the strange, exasperated creature I was becoming, and I could do nothing but leave them to it. They were two peas in a pod from day one. I shook my head at them and went about my work.

★ ★ ★

266

Sometimes at the tail end of an evening, when the fire was dying down, I would invent things to do after closing up to get a moment to myself. After the children were asleep and Ted had given up on the cleaning, I would stand in the bar alone and inhale. I'd feel my body ache with tiredness from hard work. Busy days cleared my head, and by their end I'd be standing alone in a spotless bar, trying to remember why I had wanted this moment's solitude. And then I'd realise I'd forgotten you.

I waited for the address in London, but it never came. I had a young child, a business, and a lot of debt to deal with. For all that, I was free. All I had asked was to be able to hold in my hand something real, something solid. It was all I wanted to believe in. And now my hands were full.

I figured you had just forgotten about me, or moved on to some greater adventure. When I found I was pregnant again, I was even happier than the first time. My life was less complicated, I suppose. Nothing hung in the balance any more; there was no need to bet my future on a fish.

'A little boy we'll have, to play with Lisa,' I told Ted.

'Oh, you've decided, have you?'

I nodded. 'A son.'

My husband stood up to embrace me. I held onto him, to his silence. He leaned back to look at me, wonder in his eyes.

'I'm going to see if anything's biting,' he said. 'I'll be back in a minute.'

I heard him trying to sing as he walked down the hill.

When my son was born I recognised something in him, but at first I couldn't put my finger on it. When he opened his eyes I saw what it was. I wondered how Mam was going to react. She hadn't mentioned Patrick once since the telegram. I agonised over this for an entire afternoon as I lay in hospital, waiting for her to arrive.

When she did, her face was softened by joy. She took one look at the child in my arms and smiled cheekily at me.

'He looks just like Patrick,' she said, letting the tiny fingers clasp one of hers. I stared at her, alarmed. Perhaps her forgetfulness had its advantages.

When I brought him home, she pulled the family album out to show me. The resemblance to my brother as a baby was uncanny.

Ted's sister Bernie already had three more, all girls, and when Pat arrived he found himself in a world of women. He followed the gang of girls around, desperately trying to be accepted by his sister and his cousins. Lisa dressed him up like a doll and the girls took turns to carry him. He reminded me of myself, following my brothers around. Our nephew Greg, Bernie's eldest, was by now old enough to follow Ted out to sea and help him fish in the mornings, and disdained the company of women and babies.

Bernie and her husband moved away when Pat was seven, as her husband found a better job in Sydney. Pat took to the water with Ted, getting up at dawn to take the boat out before school. He delighted in the water, but he would still cling to me when he got home in the afternoons. He followed me around the bar like a small shadow, picking up objects and asking for stories about them.

My children were and are a wonder to me. Lisa's headstrong practicality made her and Mam fierce allies, so I was secretly glad when Pat grew dark and brooding. He still resembled the brother he was named for. He was gifted, anyone could see that, but he hid behind his hair and his father's legs and absorbed Ted's quiet ways.

As he grew up Pat became secretive, which was a little more worrying. He hid things, even from himself. Sometimes I still find them: marbles lurking in a drawer like lost jewels, a coloured ring pull from a drink can, a dusty bird's nest pressed into the space between the wardrobe and the wall.

A bowerbird, I used to think, but then it was cigarettes and other things he was hiding and I had to worry. I didn't like confronting him with his secret world. It's the worst part of parenting, this policing: the kitchen table war plan, working out how to break someone's defences and get them to surrender. Lisa was really no trouble; she never set a foot wrong. She told me off more than I her. But Pat would hide worlds in his dark eyes.

I knew this because I was hiding worlds of my own. I still wrote to you, thinking that you'd send me your address one day. I wrote you long true stories about my life, my children, the banal happenings of Coal. I put the letters away against the time when you would tell me where to send them.

You sent me no address, but the postcards kept arriving. Photographs of Lisbon, Oslo, Krakow, Beirut, with a few teasing lines on the back. Sometimes you simply wrote my address and left the card blank. The gaping space was a kind of message. I taped them to the wall, making a map of the world in the wrong shape, in the shape of your life.

In my imagination, that shape was true. It was a sphere, like the globe; to follow any direction on its surface would take you back to where you started. I wove the cards into a tidy narrative. I built your story up from these sporadic clues. I invented you again.

From behind my bar, I'd tell these stories as if I knew you. Strangers would often ask about my collection of postcards from around the world.

'That's my friend Grace,' I'd say. Even without a letter in years I still called you *friend*. I still do. I suppose there is something wrong with me. I don't let go easy.

Sometimes, I'd imagine you eavesdropping from behind the kitchen door as we used to and I'd wonder if you'd recognise yourself in these stories. My Grace, the extraordinary one, the one destined for great things. The adventurer, the success, she of the glamorous life. And your young self behind the kitchen door would roll her eyes at me for claiming I had a stake in a life I knew nothing about.

As I watched my children grow up, I saw Mam go slowly downhill. I had been trying for years to wrest the bar work away from her entirely, but she was always a stubborn woman. When she began to forget things she would hide this cleverly, claiming that Pat had run off with her good scissors or Lisa rearranged the kitchen utensils. I tied a chain to her glasses because she was constantly losing them. Eventually she began to accuse the Danker of moving things around behind her back. It was the Alzheimer's, of course, but now I can't help but agree.

One day she was trying to help me restock the fridge when she turned to me with a strange look in her eye.

'Where's Grace?' she said. I shook my head.

'Pakistan, Mam,' I said. 'Her last postcard was from Pakistan, anyway. She could be anywhere by now.'

'Oh,' she said, looking crestfallen. 'I like her. Such a pity.'

I regarded my mother with a look I hoped would prompt her

to explain herself, but she simply gazed through me. I gave up and continued my work.

She placed one frail hand on my arm and smiled. 'When's she coming to tea?'

I swallowed and filled a shelf with stubbies, pushing them back hard against the back of the fridge.

'She's not, Mam,' I said. 'She's gone.'

'Oh, she'll be back,' she replied. 'She loves you. I can see it in her eyes. Such a pretty girl. You're only young once, it would be a pity.'

'Mam, I'm forty years old,' I said, jamming a row of cans in beside the bottles.

'A pity,' she said again, and stood up. Her eyes were at sea. I watched her staring and felt the floor tremble beneath my feet.

'Where did I put my glasses?'

I stood and lifted them from around her neck and placed them on her nose.

'There,' I said. 'Maybe you should go and lie down now, okay?'

'Yes,' she said. 'Perhaps that would be the best thing.'

I sat on the floor behind the bar and wept. I didn't know if it was for my mother's obvious confusion or for your loss, still stinging after so many years. For the fact that you are only young once. When Pat found me there, he sat on the floor beside me and put his arm around my shoulder. My son gazed at me with his big, dark eyes, saying nothing.

As my finances improved, I was able to provide my children with everything they needed, and even a few luxuries. The mines were booming in the Seventies, and the population of Coal was growing again. The Danker derived extra income from temporary workers who filled the rooms upstairs, and the debts slowly shrank away.

It was easy to provide Pat and Lisa with a broader life. The local school was solid brick by then, thanks to the women's committee's campaigns, and restricted to primary, but I was able to send them to a proper high school down south. Exposed to diversity, they developed strong characters. By the time they were teenagers, Lisa was a model student, Pat a regular surfer. He took to the sea like he was a part of it, and would tease his big sister about missing out on the waves.

'Killer surf, Lise. You should go down for a swim at least,' he said, laughing.

'You'll be laughing when you miss out on a career,' she said. 'I'm going into business administration.'

'Not this one, you're not,' I interjected, taking my account book from the table and secreting it on a high shelf between some cookbooks where I hoped it would be out of her reach.

'I was just looking, Mum. I think you need to cut your expenses.'

'School lunches,' I began to count on my fingers, 'teenage wardrobes, textbooks, bicycles, driving lessons . . .'

'Seriously, if you carry on with these levels of expenditure, you'll get back into debt.'

I remembered her at three, sitting on Mam's lap, and laughed. 'Spenditcha,' I teased. 'You're a born accountant.'

'I'm just concerned, is all. I want to help out more. On the weekends and that.'

I regarded her with new interest. 'Really?'

'For a small fee,' Pat interrupted. 'A teensy little wage.'

'Might be good,' I said.

I didn't have a great deal of help around the place. Ted worked hard but spent so much of his time on the boat that I often felt like Mam and I ran the place alone. With her so frail, it was more often just me. I told Lisa I would think about it.

As for my brothers, though they were destined for third shares in the business they were not involved in running it. Callum and Brendan were long gone their own ways, and hadn't been to visit for years. I got letters from Brendan in Queensland, married with his own kids and the owner of a successful retail franchise in farm supplies and equipment. His letters were often brief, but had a humour in them and an attention to the details of his life that made it easy to picture. I got phone calls from Callum, who never was much of a writer. He'd call me late at night, just on closing, from his work at the port, as he often worked till dawn loading freighters. He never made it out to sea and he never married. I often wondered about him and all that male company. I wondered if the conversation we had shared on Christmas night so long ago had been more personal than I'd thought. I'm glad my children were spared that particular trait.

For all that she had shocked me by remembering you, I didn't realise how confused Mam was. I wouldn't put it past her to play tricks on me, and she still managed quite well, although she was terribly forgetful. It was months before I realised she was losing more than her glasses.

'Patrick's a good boy, isn't he?' Mam remarked one night while sampling his cooking.

'Yes, I'm very proud of him.' I smiled at my son across the table, and he continued to carve the pie as if he hadn't heard me.

'I don't want him to go away,' she said, which made him look up, startled.

'He's not going anywhere, Nan,' Lisa said. 'Are you Pat?'

Pat shook his head.

'He's gone to sea,' Mam continued, 'my little boy.' She started to cry. 'I always loved my boys,' she said.

'I know, Mam.' I took her hand. 'But I'm still here, aren't I? I'm not going to leave you.'

'You're not my son,' she said. When she looked at me, her eyes were frightened. 'I don't know who you are.'

We couldn't have borne to put her in a home, though we could have afforded it. Brendan had offered to send some money down for the purpose.

'I'd rather you came yourself,' I wrote back, but didn't get a response to that. It was only after she had a stroke and couldn't feed herself that I sent for my brothers with proper urgency.

When they came, I was surprised to discover they had aged. I realised I hadn't seen them for a long time. Callum had weathered from years of heavy, outdoor work. Brendan was losing his hair. I'd been playing along with Mam so long I'd forgotten that her little boys were middle aged. They followed me up to her bedroom in reverent silence.

'Oh, hello Callum. Your father's not here. He's out gambling our life away, the bloody drunkard.'

He hugged her, looking at me over her shoulder. I shrugged.

Later, when she'd gone to sleep, my brothers and I had a conference in the bar over a few beers.

'Has she been like this for long?' Callum asked.

I tried to remember. 'A few years, I guess, but not this bad.'

'You should have told me it was this bad,' Brendan said. 'I could have done something.'

I did, I thought, but I bit my tongue and shrugged. 'We manage,' I said.

'Manage? Place looks amazing,' Callum commented. 'Business must be good.'

'I keep busy,' I answered. 'Still a lot of work to do.'

We talked about the repairs, which led to the third shares they were promised in my mother's will, and what they wanted to do with them. Brendan was happy to remain a silent partner, to help out now and then and take his cut of any money made.

'I don't want it,' Callum said. 'You can have my bit. I'm happy enough.'

'You should keep your share, though. It's only fair.'

'You've done all this work,' he said, feeling the fresh paint with his heavy hand. 'Doesn't seem right.'

'But if we ever sell it,' Brendan said, 'you —'

I held up a hand. 'Never,' I said. 'Over my dead body.' I turned to Callum. 'But look, you can't just give it up. I'll have to check the books, but I should have enough to buy you out. Then you can pay off your place with that.' I knew my brother had a mortgage he was struggling with.

'I feel awful talking about this,' said Callum. 'She's not even dead.'

But the next morning when I went upstairs with her cup of tea, my Mam's body was cold. I held her cooling tea in one hand and her lifeless fingers in the other, and sat looking out to sea until the sun was high over the water.

You say that loss is a constant to the traveller, Grace. But loss is a constant to everyone. Even as an adult, it is an awful thing to be liberated of your parents, suddenly set adrift.

The shape of your absence was right there; that old hollow was my consolation. I sought out the anchor of a more familiar grief.

Mam's funeral passed in a blur of visitors. My brothers stayed on long enough to help me in their quiet ways by repairing a few things, Callum with his hands and Brendan with his credit card.

The kids were a great help, but they both grieved for their Nan. Ted's parents had long ago retired and moved down to Wagga, and while we visited them as often as we could it was hard with a business to run. I was never very close to his family; I was a bit fearful of Ted's mother's steely faith in her church, and always felt a little clumsy around her. Pat and Lisa had more of a relationship with my mother. I suppose the place wasn't the same without her, or maybe they were just growing up, because they started talking about moving out shortly after she passed away. I fell back on Mam's old trick and tried to make them too busy to leave.

I gave both my kids their first jobs. Lisa started behind the bar after school, and eventually I even let her have a go at my accounts. She did all right. Even I had to admit that it was a help. Pat took charge of the bistro and cooked up gourmet tucker for the tourists, earning this place a reputation it has since failed to live up to. I paid them decent wages, but after I'd bought out Callum's share, times became tight again. Coal's economy was starting to slide.

After a hundred years of mining, the seam finally dried up. Everyone seemed surprised by this, as if the coal was merely hiding, but it was true. The rock's bounty had been eaten away, and the holes left behind were no longer sources of wealth. I thought about how long that coal must have sat there before humans got to it, and how long it took to form. Millions of years, eaten up in a single century.

When the mine closed, many of the workers left. The extra source of money in the form of rent ceased, and the town began to shrink again. It has always had this ebb and flow, like the tides, but the early Eighties were a depressing time. There were huge job cuts at the steelworks, too, and many of my regulars either vanished up to Sydney or came in with stories of mates who had killed themselves. The remaining Cullen boys moved away, all except for Joe who stayed to care for his own ailing mother. I watched my customers change from weekend drinkers to drowners of sorrow. Some, like Louie, simply cashed their redundancies and drank them.

I reluctantly agreed with Lisa that moving out might be a good idea. I could handle an empty nest with Ted, I thought, assuming he would remain as robust as I imagined him to be. This world seems determined to punish me for my imagination.

My daughter passed high school with ease and got into university, leaving home to live with a few friends in a shared house in the city. I missed her, but part of me was glad to have control of my accounting back.

At seventeen, Pat left after her, but he skipped out of his last year of school, claiming that it bored him. He moved into a house by the beach in Maroubra with a few mates. He surfed every day and took to experimenting with drugs and generally wasting his life. By this time, Lisa was filing her nails as an advertising receptionist, working her way through a masters in business and economics.

I enjoyed visiting my children on the rare days I had off. Ted and I would go separately because we were reluctant to hire anyone to run the place without us. It was strange to go up to the city on my own, a middle-aged woman still frightened of the busy streets. Lisa's tasteful apartment made me self-conscious, and her relationship with an older man made me nervous.

I admired the view and marvelled at their good fortune in finding an affordable flat in the area.

'He's in real estate,' she explained.

I'd never heard her use that phrase before. I thought about it. I'm in a pub, I thought. I'm in paying attention.

Pat's house was a different matter. A mess of magazines and boy-paraphernalia, surfboards and pushbikes clogging up the hallway and the smell of incense failing to disguise the smell of pot. He always gave me cakes and biscuits to take home and I joked about his being a better mother than I was. I tried to convince him to get into chef school, but he preferred to work café jobs that didn't tax him with too much responsibility.

Lisa got married a few years ago, and even though it was to the Rat I was happy for her. She wouldn't have the ceremony here, though. It was up in the city, in the Botanical Gardens, with the reception afterwards in a posh hotel.

'It's all a bit traditional,' I said to Ted.

'It's all a bit expensive,' he replied.

'Oh, it's what she wanted. She saved up for it for months,' I said, turning to him. He coughed and plucked at the white napkin on his lap.

'What?'

'I sort of offered to help. C'mon, May, my only daughter gets married how often?'

'In that case, I better cash in on the food and grog,' I grinned, getting up.

Me and Pat met at the bar.

'Look at that,' I whispered, pointing at the unevenly poured row of wine glasses, some brimming over, some half-full. 'Can't even pour an even measure.'

He picked up a cracker with a lump of salmon wobbling over the edge of it, topped by a smudge of cream. 'And the presentation,' he whispered.

'Maybe you should go into catering,' I suggested. 'Make a fortune.'

'Mum,' he said, 'leave it.' He swallowed the cracker whole and put his hand on my shoulder. 'Some other time, okay?'

His hand had the weight of a man's. Strange how that happens all of a sudden.

I don't want to tell you about the years I had alone here with my husband, and not just because the wound is too fresh. I was happy; my happiness is sacred to me. I have to keep some of it for myself. If I can walk around the dark cleft in the rock of this story, I can skirt brighter places.

I miss my children, but it is a proud sort of grief; they have their own lives now, and I'm glad for them. When I became a grandmother, I was so happy that I shouted everyone a couple of rounds. Ernie doesn't come down as often as I'd like. Lisa says the smoky bar's not good for him, and I remind her of the ocean breeze which is fresher than anything you'd get in the city, even with a flat on the harbour.

Pat bought us a pup that year, with his usual sentimentality and lack of foresight. He was a little black runt with an ugly face. We named him Mallee for his habit of building piles of earth in the yard and going to sleep on them. Ted took to the pup right away and trained him well. But Ted wasn't around to see Mallee grow into the fine, loyal dog he is now.

As far as I knew, Ted was never sick a day of his life. When he became ill he was secretive about it. It wasn't out of character for him – he was always quiet – so I didn't worry until it was too late. He went to the doctor's on the sly, making other excuses to go to town. Once he got his diagnosis, he refused treatment. He might even have been embarrassed about his plumbing, he was that quiet about anything physical.

The only clue he gave me was so sudden, and so comforting, that I didn't catch it.

'I've never minded,' he said.

'Minded what?' I was tipping chairs upside-down on tables with automatic precision. I was tired from a busy night and in no mood to make the work last longer than it had to, so I kept stacking chairs with one eye on him. Ted was sitting at the bar, facing the back shelves. His body seemed heavy. We're getting on, I remember thinking.

'You know,' he said, and gestured to the postcards that papered an entire section of the wall. 'All that.'

I watched him climb down off the stool, his body moving with a kind of interior pain as he stepped towards me.

'Oh, Ted, I'm sorry,' I said. 'I'm selfish. I just . . .'

'Shhh,' he said, 'no need.' He took the chair from my hands and held me. It was the only time since you left that he had ever mentioned you.

There is too much shame hidden in our not talking. There was too much in my husband's silences, his pride shielding a hurt I didn't know was there. Here I am, wanting to keep some things to myself, but they insist on seeping out of me like tears. Maybe we don't say enough to each other because we are frightened of being left. And then we are left because we haven't spoken.

Silence is the gift he left me with, and a curse I've placed on myself.

Ted was out fishing the morning he died. I never would have guessed anything was wrong. I should have seen the pain in his face, should have asked him what the trouble was, but we weren't always close enough to touch.

'May, I'm going,' he said as we got ready for bed.

'Going where, Ted? There's restocking to do and I need you to fix the awning tomorrow, there's a heavy rain coming.'

'Everything's in order,' he said. 'Don't worry.'

He fell asleep with his head in my elbow and in the morning he was gone. Just a body I once knew.

We buried him in the churchyard along with the war heroes and the lost miners and my parents, half the people that I've ever known. His grave is right on the edge where he can see the ocean. I guess I know he can't see a thing now, but it comforts me that he still has that connection.

I still miss him. I wish I could have given him more of me. He deserved it. He was here and that's more than I ever asked of him.

While I buried my husband, I thought of you. That felt awful, the worst kind of betrayal.

If you had been here all this time, you'd never have let me get away with it. Living under the shade of a co-operative lie. You'd have dragged me kicking and screaming into the bright glare of the truth.

You were never the coward I was and am and maybe it would have been good for me, maybe it would have been right, but I'm glad you left before you had the chance. I've settled myself with the opinion that life is hard enough, and a few comfortable delusions make it easier to build memories that cannot be violated.

After the burial we all came back here for the wake. It was eleven in the morning. I pulled the flap up that separated me from the rest of Coal and went behind my bar, mine alone now. The space seemed vast and empty.

Ted's mates came in, and our families, and they all sat around talking. I stood behind the bar, sipping a light beer. I didn't feel like drinking, or being around people. Everyone must have sensed this, because they talked in low tones around tables away from the bar and left me alone.

Tick and Fish approached me with sly looks on their faces. Tick ordered a couple of beers, then pulled a bundle of newspaper from behind his back. 'Got something for you,' he said. 'Almost got away from me.' He glanced at his mate.

I unwrapped the parcel, and inside was the biggest fish I'd ever seen.

'He must have been out with us this morning,' Tick said. 'He'd have wanted you to have it.' He looked uncomfortable, but I suppose it's no easy feat to make a solemn gesture with a huge, dead snapper.

I looked down at the creature's dead eye. 'Thanks,' I said, swallowing. I called Pat over to me. 'Hey, can you do something with this?' I had to talk to Ted's two best friends.

'Sure can,' Pat replied. 'Lime and ginger and a little sea

salt – leave it to me.' He disappeared into the kitchen and I leaned on the bar.

'Did he tell you he was sick?' I challenged them. The two men shook their solid heads slowly, then looked at each other, and the shakes turned into nods.

'Sort of,' Tick began.

'Few months ago,' Fish admitted. 'We tried to get him to tell you but ...'

'He didn't want you to go through it with him. It's my pain, is what he said.'

I looked at them, shocked and disappointed. There was so much I could have done for him, but he chose to confide in his mates. We had our secrets and our separate inner lives, to the end.

'Bastard,' I said.

Tick and Fish nodded again, grinning. 'Yup, complete bastard. Always.'

I started to smile for the first time that day. I thought to myself, well, it wasn't so bad, and if these two had helped him, there was one thing I could do. The least I could do. I leaned between their thick, sunburnt ears.

'Open bar,' I said.

'You serious?'

'Just till sunset.'

'Well,' Tick said. 'Better make it two each then.'

By the time Pat came out with the magnificent feast, we were a little merrier. The fish seemed to go on forever, and it was good to eat and drink and feel for a moment that I had not failed him, that it was his choice to go quietly. That I had not lost it all by keeping a part of myself in reserve.

Even then, that part of me was asking for you, Grace. It might have been comfort I sought, if in the asking there had not been a shadow of anger that bristled in my neck. A shadow in a wall of rock.

Pat fell asleep in the afternoon, cigarette still burning away in his hand. I stubbed it out, woke him, and made him go up to one of the hotel beds and sleep it off. By early evening people were talking about going out on the water. I tried to dissuade them, as they were all pretty drunk. I gave up arguing and continued tidying as they discussed whose boat to take. When I stepped into the kitchen with a few dirty plates I caught Lisa going through my accounts.

'At a time like this!' I pulled the ledger out of her hands.

'Mum, I'm just looking. I'm just trying to help.'

'If you want to help you can bloody clear tables,' I said. My daughter glared at me but did as she was told.

Alan came in then, still in his uniform. He looked around at the revelry and someone, I think it was Louie, let on that the drinks were free.

'I could take your licence for this, May.'

'You wouldn't dare. Anyway, I was just about to start charging.'

'Course you were,' he chuckled, and handed me a fifty. 'Crack the whiskey would you?'

'I thought you were on duty.'

'I am. It's my duty to see Ted off. And make sure none of these bastards endanger themselves.'

There was no taking the boat out after that. We talked of wakes past and eulogised. It felt like we were eulogising Coal, marking the end of an era. I'm still here, I wanted to say. I'm not going anywhere.

When everyone finally cleared out, Pat came down from his

nap and made the three of us an omelette for dinner. The kids helped me clean the place up, but it's pretty much the last time they did. I've been on my own since.

Now, when they visit, I insist they relax. I don't want to need their help. I guess I have inherited my mam's stubbornness.

Later that year, the Danker and I turned seventy together. I hadn't had a party other than a wake for so long, I had almost forgotten how. In fact, it wasn't up to me: Coal insisted on it. I guess everyone thought I needed cheering up.

Tick and Fish were in early, scrubbing the place up and stocking the fridges. I tried to refuse them, but they were insistent; if I had fought, they would have carried me out of here.

The kids gave me the best present. When they handed over the envelope I thought I would just get a card, but there was a promise in it.

'Breakfast every Sunday for the next year!' I read. 'That's a big commitment.'

'Now you're on your own,' Pat said, 'I mean.' He ran his hand through his hair, embarrassed.

'You sure you'll remember?' I teased.

'It was his idea,' Lisa said, outraged for the both of them.

Joe shyly presented me with a painting of his, a landscape in oils of the point before it was developed. It's still hanging on the bistro wall, in pride of place.

The best part for me was the band they found, made up of a few of the local artists. It's one thing I love about the way Coal has changed. For years now, it's attracted creative types. It also has a long tradition of hermits. My friends had to work hard to pick the musicians out of the woodwork, and when they were all together on my little stage they looked spooked by the gaze of a dozen audience members.

This spontaneous collection of instruments somehow made one fantastic noise. The old place seemed to lift out of the air with the tunes. When I went to bed, I could still hear a fiddle, though there hadn't been one amongst the players that night. Maybe it was just the Danker creaking.

Seventy years in the same old house. I'm a grandmother. I must be mad, after all this time, to try and begin again. You can't. Beginning has lost its meaning. You can't just push what your life has meant out of the way.

It's eighteen months since my husband's death. I have learned to accept that he's gone. I no longer expect him to come in off the water with a fresh catch, singing atonally. It's funny, you'd think if there were ghosts here, they'd be his.

Instead I have you, running into my life like spilt ink into the cracks in old wood. I have a pen in my hand, a wall of disparate images, a sense of expectation. A pile of paper fit to start a thousand fires.

But this is not simple. I have an anger inside me that I cannot dislodge. It lies curled beneath too many layers, like a diamond deep in the rock. It is a single, hard brightness, wasted in the dark. I don't understand it, though I must have put it there myself.

twenty

I see you before you see me. You're running through the bar, marking a purposeful diagonal between the tables, headed for the bistro. You're just a kid of seven or eight, but I can see the grown woman in you.

No two children carry themselves the same. You tended to face forwards, to look where you were going instead of where you were putting your feet. Running ahead of something, or away, not a glance backwards. Your movements are unmistakable. I move out of your way and step back to watch you. For a fleeting moment I am able to smile fondly at your constant haste before the fondness catches in my throat. You run into the bistro and disappear.

These manifestations are occurring with higher frequency, but I don't mind so much any more. I feel like I'm getting used to them.

The act of remembering is cumulative. The more I think about you, the more I write; the more I write, the more you appear. I try not to think too much about why. I would like your ghost to be your real age. I no longer know what you look like, or how you move. What you wear. If your golden hair has turned white.

I look out at the escarpment for signs of cloud, but the sky is ruthlessly blue. Sometimes the rain begins there, mist forming in great billows from the top. You can watch whole clouds grow out of the rock like wild mushrooms. I can sense rain coming, a heavy downpour. I've been feeling the pressure of it for days, the slight swelling in my knuckles. Strange. It's not the season.

There are a lot of things to do today, but I'm ignoring them. I should have put the washing out on the line before now, because it's threatening to rain. This afternoon, if that southerly is anything to go by. I should be repairing the leak in the roof above the bedroom where the cyclists stayed, a leak their tenancy seemed to spring. There's a bucket under it. It can wait. I should put batteries in the clock, which has stopped. I would like to speak to my son, but I get no answer when I call. I remember it's Sunday, and he'll be at work on the boat.

How many Sundays is it since I've seen my kids? Lisa has come a few times, with the Rat or on her own, since Pat got that job, but the promise of last year seems to have faded from their minds. I wonder if I'm pushing them away somehow, but they are probably just busy.

I glance at the horizon, hoping for a storm, but see no great threat in the clouds, just a heaviness. It will be a long, solid rain, when it comes.

There's a dripping noise upstairs. I can't hear it, but I know it's there. I have put the Danker aside for you, and now the place is falling apart. I can hear mice in the cupboards, rot in the wood, the moaning of neglect. But I can do nothing about it until I finish this thing.

What would I do if I did? I can hardly send it to you as a letter. It's grown parcel-sized. It barely fits in the cutlery drawer. It keeps on going, growing tighter loops around me. The more I worry at these knots the harder it gets to break them open. I feel like I'm wound into a carrick bend that circles into itself.

I try to make myself busy, my mother's ancient cure. I go upstairs and climb on a chair to find the leak. The flaw in the plaster grows wider before my eyes. I can hear the rain thundering down outside. There's that much water coming in, the Danker must have thrown a tile. I can't fix that until the rain stops. I empty the bucket over the balcony and replace it under the leak.

'I'm only trying to help,' I tell the Danker.

'You're talking to your house now?' It's my da's voice, dry, musical, whiskey-worn. I shake my head and it clears. I can still hear him in my memory, explaining his fantastic logic to me between wheezes as we work side by side behind the bar.

'This place has a personality,' he says, 'and it has an opinion. You'll learn to listen to it.'

When I do, I hear it cracking. The wind in the eaves is an accusation. Do you know what you are doing? Go back, it says, go back to the break.

I know exactly what I'm doing. What I'm doing is avoiding the heart of the story, writing around it, but soon I will cut off the flow of its blood.

This is not simple. What I have told is not true. You see, Grace, there is a reason I cannot shift the weight of my life. It protects me from the things I have forgotten, have made myself for-get, have erased from the record to keep it clean. But what use is it any more, keeping secrets from myself? I must make my reckoning.

twenty-one

From down below, the cliff is hidden behind trees. It's hard to make out the shape of it unless the light is right. Shadows pretend too well.

But from the top of the escarpment you can see the whole world. The world as I choose to shrink it, at any rate: the entirety of Coal, south to the next town, and beyond to the haze of smokestacks that fade into the southern horizon. You can see north as far as the national park that separates us from Sydney. From up there, the horizon is a blur, and Coal resembles a gentle village. Looking down on the tree canopy gives you a strange perspective of the place. It looks as innocent as an architect's model.

When we were young, there weren't any steel ladders up the rock. If you wanted to, you had to climb up with your claws in the soft sandstone. I didn't dare. I preferred to stop in the lee of the rock and gaze down from a ledge, relatively safe. Anyway, at the top it was just another flat piece of bush; there weren't even safety rails in front of the cliff. There were plaques which some old Christian sect had put there to remind you to admire the view as God's. There's a servo up there now, and a small public garden for the tourists to have their barbecues on Sundays, and a car park for the day trippers down from Sydney. The plaques are still there, espousing bible verses at the wind.

I rarely walk up that track any more, preferring to stick to my lengths of the beach, but I was restless this morning. I suppose I wanted perspective. I put these pages away in the kitchen drawer, took some water in a soft drink bottle, and locked the doors. Mallee wanted to follow me, but I stayed him.

'You're too old,' I said, and he stuck his nose under a paw to dream out the morning.

It had been a while. The bush had changed, and I needed to pay attention to find the stable landmarks of rock and hefty trunk under the changeable, confusing signs of undergrowth and colour. The blackbutts were interspersed with high, frightening Gymea lilies, striking their red fists against the patches of sky. I was surprised they were flowering already. Up there, seasons seem to change out of time.

As I came to the end of the paved road, a chorus of lorikeets circled up in front of me, a tornado of colour and noise. I jumped, my heart quickened. When I saw the parrots I felt sheepish, mocked like a little old lady, and was tempted to shake my fist at them. I laughed at myself and struck on up the track.

It was harder going than I remembered. The neglect of various caretakers, I suppose, as it's stuck half-way between government departments who don't know if it's a resource or a park. Maybe it's just been a while between hikes and I had forgotten how far it was. I was trying to clear my head. I was hoping that, as it often does, a walk would let my thoughts fall gently into their proper shape. It is one thing, since you left at least, that I have always done alone.

Except that I was not quite alone.

In the bush there is no time, or if there is, it runs in wide circles to meet itself. As I felt my blood warm, my lungs work, and the earth rise beneath me, I felt time slipping.

I reached the top and caught my breath on the platform. Instead of climbing the steel ladder, I walked along the ledge beneath the sandstone wall as we used to do. A narrow crack in the rock just large enough to accommodate a person beckoned me to sit and cool down and watch the view through the trees. But as I approached the dark space, a shadow crossed my heart, and I collapsed more than sat there, breathing hard.

A butcherbird landed in front of me. It tapped a trunk with its beak and gazed at me with cool black eyes.

'It's not my heart,' I told it, though my chest was tight. Something seeped out of the rock at me, that ancient menace. I shut my eyes and saw you move in the undergrowth.

You are a blue shape between the trees. You are behind me when I look for you. We have walked this far together, but now it feels like a game of chase. I laugh when I make it to the top before you. I uncatch my dress from a clawing tree and move.

You follow me along the track that cuts across the rim of the escarpment, forming a cold ledge under the sheer rock. Between the trees, if we dare a glance down the sharp slope, we can see the white cuticles of beaches, the jutting headland and the point, the roads and homes – tiny satellites of human endeavour that barely make a dent in the green. Beyond this, all is ocean, stretching over the curve of the world. The horizon is only marked by the dark shapes of ships that wait to dock at the port.

We no longer look for pictures in the rock. Too many years have gone past us. I don't tell those old ghost stories any more, but I still examine the shadows as I press along the ledge, keeping several steps ahead. I know when I have found the human shape.

There's a crack in the rock. Inside there's evidence of a long abandoned campfire. The stones have spread out from their circle of ash, as though they've wandered off of their own accord. The crack stretches up into a sandstone tent. It is a narrow space. I crouch into it, ready to spring at you. This is a game.

I scan the rock for signs of history, for a carving from the old time. As my eyes adjust, I see a shape on the wall. I move closer. It is a crude drawing of a female form, grotesque and exaggerated. The cartoon breasts, charcoal circles, push out at me. The V is open like a wound. The figure has no head.

A sound behind me makes me gasp and turn. You are crouched and still like an animal in the dirt. I have forgotten to trick you.

You turn your head at a bird landing in the trees level with our faces. It's a butcherbird. It holds a lizard in its beak. After a glance at us, it begins to kill the thing against the branch with metronomic thwacks. I can tell the bird is not enjoying itself.

'I've passed,' you tell it. The bird snaps its prey with mechanical patience. You turn to face me. 'I've been accepted, I'm going to the university.'

'Congratulations,' I say, my voice a strangely amplified whisper in the cave. I wonder if the lizard feels pain. I remember it is cold blooded, but I can't remember what that means.

'What will happen to us?' you ask.

I am puzzled. It isn't up to me, it never has been. I say nothing.

There, the bird has killed it. He swallows and sings a little song of triumph. I look down to the speck of the Danker, to the roofs of the town nestled bright and patient in the trees. I extend my arm and enclose Coal in the circle of my thumb and forefinger.

'I'll only be in Sydney, you can get the train. It's not that far,' you say.

'Congratulations,' I say again. My lips are dry, and I can feel them form a thin, cruel line.

'May.' Your voice is cast out on the breeze like a kite.

'I don't want to stop,' you say, and I could reply 'don't go then', but I know you. Hell, I've been inventing your escape for years. Might as well try telling you not to jump off the pier or swim out to the rock or break up a bar fight. So I don't tell you to stay. I don't say 'take me with you'.

'Will you visit me?' you ask.

I examine your face. The eyes are testing mine but I can't meet them. The nose is straight, a smirk ever ready to break out of the downturned corners of your sharp mouth. I see the image carved into the rock. I want you. The bird sings triumph, flies to a near branch, swallows its kill.

I could say, 'Do what you want, but don't expect me to follow you.' I could say, 'I don't care any more.'

I remain silent.

My head knocks with a resounding crack against the sandstone wall behind me. There is not enough space on the ledge of rock for my prone body. I fall out of the hole, my arm flails over the precipice, and you have knelt astride me, are kissing me, your hands pressing my shoulders into the earth. The southerly comes up out of nowhere and breaks my skin into a tense shield of goosebumps. My arms go numb as our teeth are knocked together and I feel my lip burst with bright blood. I try to push you away, but you are locked onto me. Even as I struggle, I am inflamed with the familiarity of your body. That specific weight against my hips. My push is half-hearted, my efforts weak.

You wrestle my hands to the rock above my head, and the scrape sends shooting pain up my arms. In the act of restraining me you lift your body and I try to roll out from under you or kick out at you. Attempting both at once, I achieve neither. Your hands are everywhere, on my hands, my shoulders, my neck. Your eyes stare blankly into my face. I raise my knees to lift you off and your weight snaps them back down.

I give up. I go limp. I let you bring me to climax even as we lock eyes in intimate rage.

As I cry out in a private hell of pleasure, the bird sings its triumph again. You sigh and release your hold on me. It's not unusual for orgasm to bring tears to my eyes, but this time I am helpless against them.

'Grace.'

I pull at my dirty clothes, try to arrange myself. I don't know when it started raining, but my clothes are wet. You can't meet my eye. Your face is full of disgust. You turn on your heel and disappear into the forest.

'Grace!'

It echoes down the cliff. Against the wall of rock my voice stays close. I know you can hear me as if I am speaking in your ear, but you have gone. Your name is suspended, swinging in the wet air like a twisted knot, a hanging vine.

I am alone. I am half a mile high above the canopy of trees. White cockatoos circle slowly down below, calling their kin out of the weather. I sit up and move myself into the cave like a worm.

I stay there for a long time, staring out at the rain, numb and shivering. Eventually it gets dark. The rain eases off, but I am still.

I don't know how long I have been still. I look at the backs of my hands. The scratches are there, but they look ordinary; the sort you would get from bushwalking or gardening. I hold them out in the rain and let the blood and water mix. It isn't raining hard enough to wash them clean.

I climb down the track on shaking legs and the mud on my back slides off in a mixture of sweat and water. I brush past tree limbs laden with the afternoon's rain and the water falls on me heavily. The animals are in hiding, but there are frogs crossing my path. The water has collected in the folds of flesh at the feet of trees where it makes a soapy foam. The bodies of earthworms surface, pink and swollen in the flood.

I watched from the cave. Watched myself scramble down through the bush. As my young self disappeared, I looked at the walls for signs of the image, but it had long since faded. In its place, young people have carved their initials into the rock. I know the will to own something in this way, to mark it, is a violation. But I felt an urge to carve my own.

I make it home. I'm soaked through. In the bathroom I strip carelessly and look at myself in the oval mirror like I did the first night, after we had made what I thought was love. Apart from a couple of faint red marks on my neck, I can't see any evidence of your body on mine. What do I expect, stains? I feel no anger, only a bleak surprise, as when one wakes from a bad dream. My muscles ache, my breasts are sore. I'm premenstrual, about to spring a bloody leak. I climb into the bath to get the mud off my skin.

Mam bangs on the door.

'I'm sick,' I tell her. 'Got caught in the rain.'

I fake a sneeze and pull my knees up to my chest.

'I can't work tonight,' I say.

'Get some sleep,' she says through the door. 'Drink plenty of liquids.'

'Yes, Mam.' My voice sounds forlorn like a child's, and it comforts me.

When I crawl into my bed, I find I can't sleep, so I get up, dress hurriedly, and leave the Danker's warm society behind. I walk to your house. In the middle of the night the air is still warm. The earth glistens with water, muting and scattering the familiar sounds of trees and creatures. I am a criminal, a spy. I stand at your window and watch you sleep for a minute, an hour, who knows. You don't look gentle in your sleep like other people. You look young and also dead. I want to crawl in beside you and breathe your stale second-hand breath. I want to wake pressed between your body and the cold wall.

Your fist stretches itself from the sheets and curls against your face. Any hurt in it has gone. I turn in the dark and head for home.

I sat up on the cliff for a long time, long enough to watch the shadows change direction. A dry wind grew, spreading gusts of sound through the trees. They whispered to each other, telling secrets I can never know.

It's not that I had forgotten. It's that I failed to remember. In any story, the parts you leave out are just as important as what you tell. Not having told this for so long I have let it fade into shadow. Memory is a muscle and must be exercised.

What use is it to pull up these ghosts like so many weeds? They grow back too fast. I don't have a choice. My house is filled with ghosts, and my country sings their tune. They are right here. I have to deal with them, one way or another.

They say you should forgive and forget, but that's not right. If we forget we have achieved nothing. We go on causing the same kinds of pain, re-opening each other's scars, endlessly.

When the sun passed behind the rock at my back I stood and stretched my aching body. My knees cracked in protest, but I know my legs are strong. I ducked under the low branches and headed down the track. My feet moved through the scrub with the shaken confidence of old, remembered knowledge.

twenty-two

There are other stories.

You see, Grace, I may have fallen for the real world. Hard not to, with the ocean close beside me, the endless patterns of life right here in my pocket. But I never gave up telling stories. They were my revenge.

In my stories, Grace travelled with Bedouin tribes in Egypt; she worked on ships in Alexandria, danced with dervishes in Turkey, camped under the stars in the Sahara. My Grace climbed the Pyrenees with Basque rebels, the Alps with a Swiss millionaire, the Tatras with a Polish communist. She has skated across the frozen lakes and rivers of Europe. She saw the Berlin Wall come down, the northern lights come up, the sun rise over the Himalayas. Pyramids, palaces, lost cities of gold.

I have travelled the world with you. I have given the world to you.

When the flux of international visitors that mark the seasons ask me about the postcards, I tell them about you. I borrow an adventure here, a disaster there, and I reinvent you. I thought you were gone forever. It was a harmless pastime. As harmless as the stories I invented for you before you were gone.

I simply filled in the blanks, much as I have done with your real memory. The parts I know are a path through the under-growth, a series of landmarks. I find my way through the scrub and back to the real Grace, now. I hunt through the tangle of vines and stones, looking for your body. I follow the sound of your name.

The Catholics say grace is what God has given us to let us live. I think grace is a kind of merciful blindness. The blessing of being able to forget. What power God ever had to absolve us from our shameful past, to erase our mistakes, lies in our minds, in our ability to retell memories and shape our lives into stories. It is like the biochemistry in a woman's body that allows her to forget the pain of childbirth and remember only the joy. The tranquillising effect of tears. The loss of memory as we age. And above all, the fact that no love is ever as brutal, as cruelly whole, as overwhelming nor as unsatisfying as the first.

So here I am still pleading with your ghost, this endless bloody unfinished argument, and it feels for the first time in a long time that I am in a state of prayer. I am trying to find forgiveness in a web of half-truths and forgotten memories, in a collection of images, pages torn from a book. Begging for meaning to be caught somehow in this net of narratives. Searching for a way to bury the rage and recriminations. I'm drowning in it.

Now I have a pile of papers in front of me. A bundle of words. I'm no closer to you than I was. You can't regain intimacy in this way, with a stroke of the pen. You can only reinvent things as you would like them to be. There are no true stories. All I do is add the weight of more words to the burden of our history, shared and lost.

Here is an ending for you. My version of your handwriting has always been convincing. What if the whole elopement was an elaborate ruse? What if, instead of that letter, it was you I pushed out the window of the train that afternoon? Perhaps you were on your way back with me. Perhaps we went for a walk up the escarpment and found the place again where we had fought under the shapes we made in shadows. Perhaps I pushed you off the cliff. Perhaps I hated you. I could have made the rest up. And all this time my smiling hospitality disguised a psychopath.

It's tempting. It would explain the falling apart I'm feeling now, the sense that all this time I've been bailing water, afraid to leave the boat. But you won't let me. You come charging back in, expecting me to take up where I left off. You are stupidly, infuriatingly alive.

I came down the escarpment feeling shaken and uncertain. The Danker welcomed me with a shanty of shudders. In my absence, the wind had come up and shaken the guttering down, so it swung and sang on its rivets. I looked at the place and sighed.

'I wouldn't leave you,' I told it. 'Don't you worry.'

I climbed up on the fold-out ladder and knocked the gutter back into place, trying to ignore the sight of rust and rotting leaves that I should clear out. I looked down into the bar from my perch, and the yellow afternoon light tricked me; I could see a glint of fire, hear a few voices raised in song, see myself hiding behind the kitchen door on my knees, sneaking in.

'You keep playing tricks on me and I'll hammer you closed,' I muttered with a mouthful of nails. The wind died down, and the pub stood still for a moment.

★ ★ ★

The Danker will not sit still for long. First that leak and now the boards are starting to break beneath me. Rotten with the damp, I suppose. I should ask for help, but instead I find that I'm closed.

I'm sitting in the bar with this thing and the place is falling apart around me. I'll be washed out to sea when it does; swept out like a shipwreck, carrying my message amidst a thousand sinking bottles.

'This is nothing to do with you,' I tell the Danker, but of course it won't listen.

'You're too old,' it says. 'You're falling apart at the seams.'

'Speak for yourself, you bastard.'

There is an actual, literal crack in the wall, between the bistro and the kitchen, that wall at the centre of the building, and I swear I can hear it widening.

Am I losing it? Is this what happens? I have neglected this old place, and for what? I feel as though I am unravelling. Sailor's knots, monkey's fists, sea-ropes that are tied and grown together from years of salt and wet and wearing. I am exhausted and haven't yet begun. Nothing will come of this. But I am trying. I will keep trying.

It is dark. I can't see my words. But if I turn the lights on, people will think I am open. I kneel to light the fire, stuffing twisted newspaper in the angled gaps between kindling.

Before I can get it going I'm interrupted by a knock at the door.

'I'm closed,' I say, but not loud enough for whoever it is to hear. I get up to open the door, expecting a thirsty Louie, or maybe Clare after a story. I don't have the energy tonight, I think, I'll turn them away. But it's a different face at the door.

'Aunt Betty? What are you doing here?'

'I just thought I'd drop in for a cuppa on my way home,' she says. She looks around, appraising the space with her shrewd gaze. She steps on a board and it cracks beneath her feet.

'Giving this place to the bulldozers are you?'

'No,' I smile. 'I'm just tired.'

'Not too tired to make a cup of tea I hope. Mine's milk and two sugars, and leave the teabag in.'

I go obediently to the kitchen. I make us both cups of tea and bring them to the fireplace, where Betty has made herself comfortable.

'You know,' she says, stoking the fire up, 'I get tired sometimes too. But it doesn't mean I can stop working.' She glances at me, checks my face for signs of shame.

'Been down in Canberra,' she mentions, once she is satisfied.

'How's the claim?' I ask. I feel guilty that I have not been following it, but once the protest tent was forced off the point the contest moved into courtrooms and politicians' offices, spaces I know nothing about. I wouldn't be much use.

Betty shakes her head slowly. 'We got enough lawyers for a footy team, but they just keep stalling.'

'Well they should listen to you,' I say, 'you can yell loud enough: Take me in! Take me in!'

Betty laughs at the memory, but my throat is dry. We fall silent. The unsweetened tea leaves a bitter taste in my mouth.

'What's the matter with you, woman? Somebody die around here?'

I glance up at her, alarmed, but she is joking with me. I feel that tightness across my chest again, an urge to confess. 'It's this place,' I begin, but I can't articulate my fears. I swallow and ask her how the Tent Embassy is going.

As I listen to Betty speak I feel myself grow still, soothed almost to sleep by a voice as I haven't been since my da was alive. Even the Danker has slowed its croaking to a muffled percussion. The wind has stopped in its tracks.

Finally, she looks at her watch. 'I better get that next train, or I'll be stuck here for another hour with you and your ghosts,' she says.

'Oh, they're not so bad. You get used to them,' I make a maudlin attempt at a joke.

'Well, don't get too used to them. They'll end up running the place.' She examines my face. 'You want to talk about it?'

I feel her eyes on me, and I am heavy as a stone.

'You'll miss your train.'

I take the empty mugs over to the bar and Betty lets herself out. When she has left, I flip the sign on the door to Open. No one comes in, but it makes me feel less wretched. I make more tea and take up this letter. I sit by the fire with these pages in my lap.

Paper enough to burn the whole night. I watch the coals die down, eating time. Tonight, I see no ghosts.

twenty-three

Clare comes in, carrying a big, square burden. She slips in backwards to make room for the unwieldy frame, her legs apart like a mother to save any part of her child from knocking on the wall. Sometimes Clare moves like a woman twice her age. When I see her face, though, it's as excited as a little kid's. She steps up to the bar holding the painting against her body, facing it away from me. It's Monday and the place is dead except for Louie who's been propping up his end of the bar all afternoon. I have no reason to feel like I'm being watched. I wait, but Clare says nothing until I relent.

'Okay, what have you got there,' I ask her. A sliver of cheeky activity flies across her face. I have a sudden memory of walking past the door that separates the kitchen from the bar when I was a child, coming down at night to sneak the cream from the milk bottles and seeing the slip of a warm, bright life buzzing through the gap.

She takes a couple of steps backward and spins the canvas.

It's you, Grace. Your seven-year-old ghost at centre stage,

surrounded by a blur of red and violet shadows. There's me off to the side, wearing the white dress. We've both been blended into the abstract noise that encircles us in a rageful silence, like an angry womb. Rendered in oils, you have a sheen like a wet animal. Your wide blue eyes are gazing out to sea, a sea hinted at only by their reflected distance. A suggestion of your hand is pressed against my chest.

It's an impossible painting. She has stuck her hand down my throat and given the story chase, dredged you into being. How does she know? I turn away and pour myself a glass of water, gulp it down. This is worse than ghosts; I can't pretend it's only me.

'It's not right,' I say, and I bite my tongue, because I know I sound ungrateful.

'Is it the light?' she asks, disappointed. 'I had trouble with the light.'

I collect myself and look at the image again. I try to see it as a painting, not a memory. It is beautiful, at that.

'No, no,' I reassure her. 'It's perfect.'

'I thought . . .' She holds the painting up towards the place above the swing doors where everyone will see it as they walk out, but takes it down again before I can comment. She can read my face, of course. It's an open book.

'It's too much, isn't it.'

I flick an eye at Louie, but he's reliably absorbed in his glass.

'No, it's perfect. It's just a shock.' I hide my hands under the bar, playing with the bottle opener, feeling the surface sprinkled with a thin layer of dust I should be getting around to cleaning.

'I'll put it in the house,' I say. 'Come around.' I wave her around the side. 'Louie, I'll be five minutes.' I pour him another schooner and put it in front of him in case he gets any ideas.

'Rightyo,' he nods.

I duck through to the kitchen on quick feet. I pick my pile of paper up off the table, hold it to my chest. I look around for a hiding place. It's far too much to stuff in my shirt. Eventually I jam it in the cutlery drawer, close it, and look around the room for other evidence, breathing too quickly.

I let Clare in at the screen door. She leans the painting against my kitchen table and I get my purse off the bench behind me. I try to press fifties into her hand, but she snaps it to her side.

'Go on, they won't bite.'

'I can't take your money May, it's a gift. And anyway, it's not quite finished. Not properly.' She is looking at the painting with a love refracted through resentment, and I realise that it must be the kind of look I give this letter.

'I don't have time to argue with you,' I say, 'take it. We all have to eat.' She relents and pockets the money without counting it.

'Thank you,' she says. 'I hope I haven't been too personal. I could see something in the story, that's all. Love. Probably just projecting, thinking about my ex.' She dismisses the canvas with a sideways look. I almost reach a hand out to touch her weary shoulder. But I see that she has spotted the pen on the table, the blank paper I left there in my haste.

'What are you writing?'

'Nothing. A letter.' I shoo her out of my kitchen, cursing myself for letting her in in the first place.

When I close the bar, I sit in the kitchen, examining her work. It feels strange, looking at the back of my own seven-year-old head. I am trying to remember what that day was really like. I can revisit the moment but it's me as I am now that I think of there in the cold church, hidden in the dark with you and unsure what we have stumbled upon, whose gods we have disturbed.

Now that I can see the image in detail, it's not quite you. The nose is wrong, and the shape of your face too thick. I don't think she's really read my mind. There is something in it though, too close for comfort. It's there in the shadows that surround us: something dark and wet that pushes us close. The violet in the corners darkens to the colour of a storm. I notice that your eyes have flecks of that same violet in them.

I see that my painted body is blurred, and I recall the shape of the woman I saw on the beach, abstracted by the rain. Now that I remember, I recognise myself. This story has been returned to me, bringing with it a kind of heat.

Clare said it wasn't finished, but the painting is perfect. It's the moment that is unfinished.

I know why you're here, Grace.

twenty-four

It's Sunday. No kids again. This morning I walk Mallee out along the beach. It's a clear, bright morning and the tide is so far out that the stretch of rock at the far end shines, exposed to the sun. The sea tells the story of change, but it's the same story, over and over.

I meet a stranger out there. She's picking around in the rocks, looking for something. I assume she's a tourist; she looks the part, though the warmer weather is still a couple of weeks away. She's about my age, perhaps a little older. She has dyed red hair and a red tracksuit, which show up the powdered white of her face. Typical Sydney, I think, wearing makeup on the beach, but there's no need to be unfriendly around here.

'What've you lost?' I ask her as I pass.

'Nothing.' She smiles into the sun. 'I collect seahorses,' she explains.

I have seen their frail bodies washed up along the reef. They are nothing like horses. They are strange, limbless, geometric creatures. To look at them you'd think they might never have lived.

'Interesting,' I remark. 'What do you do with them?'

'Nothing,' she says. 'I just collect them. It passes the time.'

I nod in a way I hope is sympathetic but unpitying. Mallee sits and knocks his head against my legs patiently. A gull swoops nearby, but he makes no effort to chase it.

The woman shrugs. 'I'm retired. You?'

'Not a chance,' I say. 'I run the pub up there.'

I nod my head to where the Danker perches on the headland, crumbling and square like a big, uneaten cake. The woman turns and cranes her neck to look at it. When she turns back, there is something like distaste on her lips.

'I suppose we all have to keep busy,' she says. She moves off to stare into another rock pool, and I push at my old dog with one foot.

'Get up, Mal. C'mon.'

I circle back here, feeling defeated. All this looking back has made me tired. Am I just keeping busy? I walk into the kitchen, make myself a cup of tea, look at the pile of paper onto which I've scrawled my life. I've gone through fourteen pads of paper and who knows how many pens. The girl at the newsagent's must think I have a lot of correspondents. I lift the pile, feel its thickness. If I put it in a bottle and threw it in the sea, it would probably sink.

I am not just passing time. I am telling a story, and it can't end the way it began, with nothing but regret. There are too many unfinished stories in this letter and too many questions to count. After all this, it's not enough. I can't go on addressing this to the sea. I need you where I can talk to you, so we can spread the stories out into a conversation. Our conversations always had more truth in them than words could.

As I write this, the kitchen door swings open. The Danker is awake, groaning, feeling its joints. I get up and close the kitchen door, and as it clicks shut I hear a knocking in the bar. When I go in to see what it is, I find that the front door has burst its catch as well. I cross the room to shut it and the windows leap open, letting in the light and the chill sea air. I rush back to the kitchen, and the door is open again. I turn to my table, but these pages are still despite the wind. Light fills the room. The fresh breeze rushing through this place makes a whistling song. I can't help laughing; I have so much work to do.

I leave the windows open, and I hold this letter down with a convenient rock. You can see the layers in it, slices of ancient sediment, the years of settling sands that make a pattern. Time has set them.

I go down to the garden to get some lettuce for the lunches, and as I squat in the dirt I renew my anxiety about the soil. But the earth hasn't flown away yet. We got plenty of rain this year, just a little late.

'Better late than never,' I mutter. Red crows mightily.

'What is it, Red?' I ask him. He blinks at me, and I remember.

As I snap leaves, I think about your letter, and I think about my future. I make a decision, squatting in the dirt. When I have made it I smile; there can't have been any other choice. There never was, with you.

'I took my time,' I tell Red, and I shake my head. 'I took my bloody time.'

I make a few burgers and chips for the lunchtime tourists. When they've gone I scrub the tables down. I sweep out the ashes from last night's fire and pile the wood up neat and tidy. I clean the windows of their crust of salt and polish them. I vacuum the carpet and the chairs. I ring the flooring place for a quote. I get up on a stool and wipe the dust from the bottles. I even put fresh batteries in the stopped clock. I work hard and the afternoon goes quickly. By dusk, the Danker shines.

The bar fills up with the usual crowd and I greet each one of them like a long-lost friend. I whistle one of Da's old songs, a song I thought I had forgotten. I'm so chirpy that Louie leans over the bar at me and asks me what's the matter.

'What do you mean?' I ask him.

'Place is so clean. Looks like you got a feller,' he says.

I wink at him. 'Just you wait, Louie,' I say, 'You'll see.'

Clare raises an eyebrow at me. 'You do look happy,' she says.

'Prob'ly sold the headland out from under us,' Joe jokes. 'Prob'ly got a million bucks in the till tonight.'

'Never,' I say, and raise a fist. 'I'm staying right here. They'll have to cut me up in little pieces to get me out the door.'

Louie leans over and puts one hand on mine. 'Oh c'mon, May,' he urges, 'you can tell me. Who is he?'

'If I tell you, you have to promise to keep a secret,' I say. He leans in close. I put my lips to his ear. 'Your wife's on the phone,' I whisper, and laugh as he sinks back into his stool. I laugh so hard that tears come to my eyes.

'You're not funny,' he mutters into his glass. 'I've met funny and you're not him.'

This sets Joe off, and he starts to hoot like an owl. Clare's nursing her schooner, trying to keep her cool, but soon she's off as well.

Before long the whole lot of us, Runner and Alan and Tick and Fish and the tourists and all my memories are here, laughing, and the Danker shakes with us. The building lets out a grand old self-satisfied squeak and settles into a low chuckle. We're all here, Grace. We're waiting for you, ghosts and all.

I admit I am nervous. What if you say no? What if you don't come? I am too excited to sleep, but sleep I must. Tomorrow morning I will post my letter, and I won't bet my future on a bloody fish ever again.

I laugh now at the way I thought you were one of the sea people, at first. I was small and full of fairytales. You're not from the sea. You're from this country just as much as I am. You're a story, Grace, and stories belong to places, stories live in the earth. You have to come from somewhere. You have to return there, if you want to know anything at all.